A Fatal Yarn

Books by Peggy Ehrhart

MURDER, SHE KNIT

DIED IN THE WOOL

KNIT ONE, DIE TWO

SILENT KNIT, DEADLY KNIT

A FATAL YARN

Published by Kensington Publishing Corporation

A Fatal Yarn

Peggy Ehrhart

KENSINGTON BOOKS
www.kensingtonbooks.com

KENSINGTON BOOKS are published by

Kensington Publishing Corp.
119 West 40th Street
New York, NY 10018

All Kensington titles, imprints, and distributed lines are available at special quantity discounts for bulk purchases for sales promotion, premiums, fund-raising, educational, or institutional use.

Special book excerpts or customized printings can also be created to fit specific needs. For details, write or phone the office of the Kensington Sales Manager: Attn.: Sales Department. Kensington Publishing Corp., 119 West 40th Street, New York, NY 10018. Phone: 1-800-221-2647.

Kensington and the K logo Reg. U.S. Pat. & TM Off.

First Printing: April 2020
ISBN-13: 978-1-4967-2364-2
ISBN-10: 1-4967-2364-3

ISBN-13: 978-1-4967-2367-3 (ebook)
ISBN-10: 1-4967-2367-8 (ebook)

10 9 8 7 6 5 4 3 2 1

Printed in the United States of America

For my aunt, Rosemary Pellegrini-Quarantotti

Acknowledgments

Abundant thanks, again, to my agent
Evan Marshall, and to my editor at
Kensington Books, John Scognamiglio.

Chapter 1

If you were going to give a tree a sweater, wouldn't you do it in the fall—not in the spring when days were warming and nature was coming back to life? Yet the first thing Pamela Paterson had noticed when she stepped outside to collect the newspaper that morning was the swath of knitting wrapped around the trunk of the tree occupying the strip of land between the sidewalk and the street. It was fashioned from yarn in an eye-catching assortment of textures and colors—red, orange, green, purple, and more—and even featured buttons and buttonholes.

Now she paused to study it again in the twilight. Her day had been busy, so busy that she'd missed her usual walk. As associate editor of *Fiber Craft* magazine, Pamela enjoyed the fact that she could work from home most days. But some days that work—evaluating articles for publication and then editing the ones chosen—kept her at her computer from after breakfast to dinner time and beyond. And only the occasional email from her daughter, who was away at college, provided a break.

Today she'd dispatched the edited version of "Depression-Era Style: Frugal Fashion for the Home Knitter" off to her boss at *Fiber Craft* just in time to warm up a quick dinner of leftover stew and set off for that evening's meeting of the Arborville knitting club, nicknamed Knit and Nibble. This evening Pamela's neighbor and best friend, Bettina Fraser, was hosting the group, so Pamela had only to cross the street.

So immersed had Pamela been in her editorial duties that she was initially nonplussed by Bettina's greeting. She'd no sooner stepped into the Frasers' welcoming living room than Bettina announced, "I'm sorry he's dead, of course, but the timing couldn't be better for this week's issue of the *Advocate*. Clayborn is squeezing me in for a meeting tomorrow morning." Clayborn was Arborville's lone police detective and Bettina was the chief reporter for the town's weekly newspaper.

"What? Who?" Pamela stared at her friend, who was in bright pink tonight—a jersey wrap dress that accented her ample curves. She'd accessorized it with matching kitten heels and her favorite coral and gold earrings. The effect was striking with her scarlet hair.

"Mayor Diefenbach, of course," Bettina said. "Haven't you seen any news today?"

"Nose to the grindstone." Pamela shrugged. "I had a mountain of work for the magazine." Bettina's words sank in and Pamela felt herself frown. "What on earth happened to him?" she asked

Bettina started to answer but was distracted by the doorbell. As she headed for the door, Pamela settled onto Bettina's comfy sage-green sofa. Punkin the cat, who was stretched languidly along the back of the sofa, raised her head briefly then resumed her nap. Woofus the shelter dog peered nervously from the edge of the dining room.

Bettina pulled back the door and Holly Perkins stepped in, followed by Karen Dowling. They were the two youngest members of the group and fast friends, despite their considerable differences. "That's quite a dramatic story for you, Bettina," Holly said by way of greeting. "A murder, right here in little Arborville." Her dark eyes widened dramatically, but given the topic she suppressed her usual smile, with its dimple and flash of perfect teeth.

"Murder?" Pamela half-rose from the sofa. "You didn't say he was murdered!"

"Clunked right on the head—" Holly began.

Bettina finished the thought: "—in his own kitchen."

Karen, a delicate blonde with a diffident manner, shuddered.

The evening was warm for the end of March, and the door still stood open as this conversation took place. So there was no need for Nell Bascomb to ring. She simply stepped into the doorway with a cheerful greeting, her white hair floating in a cloud around her face. But her cheer faded as Bettina continued speaking. "Then he fell, hit his head on the edge of his counter, and again on his tile floor. One or both of those bumps are probably what killed him, Clayborn said, though there's been no autopsy yet."

"This is sad news for our little town," Nell said. "Harold came home from the Co-Op Grocery today and reported that everyone he ran into was buzzing about it, wondering what will become of Diefenbach's ambitious plans for the town." She put a comforting arm around Karen. "Shall we sit down and get to work? There's nothing like knitting to soothe the spirits."

Their jackets stowed in the closet, she and Karen made their way to the sofa, where they settled in beside Pamela, who had already extracted her project from her knitting bag. It was to be a gift for her daughter Penny, a lacy tunic in a delicate shade of lilac. Penny had picked out the pattern and the yarn—a silk and merino wool blend—at Christmas, and the tunic had been Pamela's Knit and Nibble project ever since. Bettina and Holly lingered at the door looking out toward the yard, and a moment later Roland DeCamp stepped over the threshold.

"I believe I'm the last one," he said, scanning the room, and he pulled the door closed behind him.

"Take an armchair, Roland, please." Bettina gestured toward the armchairs that faced the sofa across a long coffee table. "And you too, Holly."

"No, no, no." Roland waved his free hand in a dismissive gesture. In his other he carried the impressive leather briefcase in which he stored his knitting. "You ladies, please have the armchairs. I'll be fine with one of these cushions on the hearth." A row of bright cushions lined up on Bettina's hearth complemented the sage-green and tan color scheme of her living room.

He strode toward the fireplace and perched on a cushion, looking somewhat incongruous in the flawlessly tailored pinstripe suit and aggressively starched shirt that marked him as a high-powered corporate lawyer.

Holly had pulled out her knitting needles and was casting on with fuzzy yarn in a vibrant shade of green, but once everyone was settled, she broke the silence. "What were Bill Diefenbach's plans for the town?" she asked. "Desmond and I spend so much time at work in Meadowside, we know more about town politics there than right here in Arborville where we live."

Roland and Nell spoke at once. Their voices overlapped, with Roland observing, "Excellent ideas. Just the leader Arborville needed," while Nell commented, "Horribly distressing. No sense of what makes Arborville Arborville."

"Well!" Holly laughed and the dimple appeared. "You first, Nell."

Nell surveyed the group with her faded blue eyes. The hands holding her knitting needles trembled slightly. "I'll grant he gave a lot of his time to the town, heading up the Arborists and serving on the town council for years and years, and then taking on the job of mayor. But he wanted to sell the community gardens to a developer. The community gardens serve a valuable purpose, especially for people who live in apartments. And Arborville doesn't need more development."

Roland was leaning forward, his lean face intense and his knitting forgotten for the moment. "Of course it does," he said. "My property taxes go up every year, and everybody likes the things their taxes pay for, like the schools and the police and road repair—though I'm still waiting for the broken curb in front of my house to be fixed. More development means more people to share the tax burden."

"The developer wanted to get that land rezoned for a high rise!" Nell was leaning forward too, her expression more sad than intense. "Can you imagine a high rise, looming over a residential neighborhood? And with commercial space at street level? Arborville doesn't have adequate parking for its existing shops."

"That could be easily remedied." Roland's tone suggested the parking problem simply hadn't been addressed by anyone with common sense. "A multilevel garage would solve the problem."

Nell's face tightened and her voice took on a scolding edge. "A multilevel garage would completely destroy the small-town feel of Arborville's shopping district—and it would encourage people to use their cars when they could just as easily walk."

"It's the twenty-first century now," Roland said with a laugh. "Arborville needs to keep up with the times."

"That was Bill Diefenbach's view." Nell shook her head sadly. "And apparently a majority of voters agreed with him, a *narrow* majority."

"Enough of a majority for him to win"—Roland was scowling now—"and a good thing. How many people does that land serve as community gardens? Twenty or thirty?" He laughed again. "Taxes on a high rise with commercial space would lighten the tax burden for everybody who lives in this town."

Nell's faded blue eyes brightened. "The community gardens serve a valuable purpose for people who don't have yards of their own. Home-grown food is healthy and economical and—"

Roland half rose and his knitting slipped from his lap. "They don't have yards of their own because they made poor choices in life. If they wanted to own their own land, they should have worked harder. It's not my responsibility to subsidize—"

Nell cut him off, her voice rising to a pitch Pamela had seldom heard from her gentle friend. "We are all each other's responsibility," Nell said as she tossed her knitting aside and pulled herself up from the sofa. Karen, sitting next to her, stared in alarm and Punkin the cat leapt from the sofa's back to its arm, from there to the floor, and scurried toward the dining room.

Suddenly Bettina was on her feet too, gazing back and forth from Nell to Roland with her eyes wide and her lips, bright pink to match her dress, stretched into a grimace. She was about to speak when from the dining room came a hearty "Is everyone present and accounted for?" Wilfred Fraser appeared in the arch that separated the dining room from the living room, an apron tied over the bib overalls that had been his customary garb since his retirement.

"Dear wife!" he exclaimed, his ruddy face beaming. "Why didn't you let me know?" He surveyed the group, as if unaware that anything was amiss, but Pamela caught a subtle wink as he glanced in her direction. "Tea, as usual, Nell? And Karen?" Looking somewhat chastened, Nell sank back onto the sofa with a nod. "And coffee for everyone else? Roland?" Roland nodded too, cleared his throat, and lowered himself onto his cushion. He retrieved his knitting from the floor and began to examine it more intently than perhaps strictly necessary.

"I'll get things started then," Wilfred said, and headed back toward the kitchen with a cheerful wave.

Looking relieved, Bettina sat back down. "He was baking all afternoon," she said. "He does so look forward to having an audience for his pies."

"Ohh, I can hardly wait! What kind is it?" Holly exclaimed, even more animated than usual, as if to do her part in restoring cheer to the group.

"Shoo fly," Bettina said. "Perhaps it will sweeten us all up a bit." Roland, totally absorbed in his knitting, didn't notice the glance she aimed in his direction.

But Pamela did. A fresh topic was definitely in order—and in fact the interesting development she'd come prepared to discuss had been driven completely from her mind by the revelation of Bill Diefenbach's murder. Now she summoned it back.

"My tree has a sweater," she said.

"So does mine," Holly chimed in. "And one of Karen's trees has one too." From across the room, Karen met her friend's gaze and nodded. "What on earth can be going on?"

"It's a group," Bettina said. "The Yarnvaders. I was working on the story for the *Advocate* before this Diefenbach thing happened. A few people had already posted about it on AccessArborville. They wake up in the morning and discover their trees have sweaters. It's knitters that are doing it, obviously, and they're doing strange things like that everywhere—even in Russia. In Los Angeles they covered an entire building with a giant sweater. I found some things on the internet."

Roland looked up with a frown, started to speak but then evidently thought better of it and returned to his knitting.

"It seems wasteful," Nell observed. "When there are *people* who could use sweaters. Who are these knitters, anyway?" Nell herself devoted her knitting to worthy causes—currently knitted caps to donate to hospitals for newborns.

"No one knows," Bettina said. "The members are all sworn to secrecy. Some of us could be Yarnvaders for all the rest of us know."

The teasing aroma of freshly brewed coffee had been growing stronger and stronger as they spoke, along with the aroma of something richly sugary baking. Pamela worked steadily on her knitting, enjoying the way the lacy pattern with its filigreed shells took shape as row followed row. Tucked between her and Nell on the sofa, Karen was engrossed in a lacy pattern of her own, in pink. The Dowlings' first child, Lily, had been born at Christmas. Many tiny knitted garments had been prepared for her arrival and Pamela was sure Lily would be supplied for years to come with the fruits of her mother's artistry. Across from Pamela, Bettina had relaxed back into her project, a Nordic-style sweater for Wilfred—which Bettina, not the fastest knitter, had said just might be finished in time for next Christmas.

The sugary aroma had become almost unbearably tempting—sweet to be sure, but with an interesting darker undertone—when Roland spoke up from his perch on the hearth. Consulting the impressive watch that had been revealed when he pushed back his aggressively starched shirt cuff, he intoned, "Exactly eight p.m. and I believe it's time—"

"For refreshments." Wilfred stepped into the arch that separated the dining room from the living room and completed the thought.

"I can help," Holly said. "I've never seen shoo fly pie before. Or tasted it." She rested knitting needles with an inch-long swath of vibrant green suspended from them on the arm of her chair and jumped to her feet. Bettina started to rise too, but Holly urged her to stay put and hurried out looking as excited as if experiencing shoo fly pie had been a life-long dream.

"I haven't either," Pamela said, and followed Holly toward the dining room and thence into the Frasers' spacious kitchen.

Woofus was sprawled in his favorite corner when they entered. He raised his head in alarm and trotted to Wilfred's side. The shaggy beast reached Wilfred's thigh, but he cowered against his master, trembling visibly.

"The poor fellow," Wilfred sighed. "He's gotten so much better than when we first brought him home from the shelter, but I guess he'll always be nervous."

"Some people just are." Sympathy replaced excitement on Holly's expressive face. "And dogs," she added. Then excitement returned. "Oh! Is this it?" She stepped toward the high counter that separated the cooking area of the Frasers' kitchen from the eating area, with its well-scrubbed antique pine table and four chairs.

The pie—which had been the source of the tantalizing aroma—was a magnificent creation. An elegantly fluted crust, flaky and golden brown, framed a filling that was lustrous in spots and so dark it was nearly black, while other spots resembled the granulated topping of crumb cake.

"Molasses," Wilfred supplied. "That's the main ingredient, and brown sugar. But it's sometimes called shoo fly cake, because the brown sugar is mixed with flour and shortening and layered in." He gazed at his creation fondly. "It's still warm. That's the best way to serve it, with whipped cream."

Next to it on the counter sat a pottery bowl cradling a gleaming drift of whipped cream, and seven of Bettina's sage-green plates, dessert-size, were stacked nearby. Near the stove, a carafe with a plastic cone balanced on top held freshly made coffee, and on the stove was a steaming tea kettle. Mugs for coffee and tea had been staged on the pine table. A rustic wooden tray held colorful cloth napkins, forks and spoons, and a sugar bowl and cream pitcher.

"I'll watch you cut the first slice," Pamela said. "Then I'll take the tray to the coffee table and come back to pour coffee and do tea."

Wilfred picked up a large knife and aimed it right at the center of the pie. With two long strokes he carved out a wedge and used a pie server to transfer it to a plate. The dark syrupy filling oozed onto the sage-green plate, blurring the wedge's neat geometry.

Holly was gazing back and forth from Wilfred's face to the pie. "That is just too amazing," she cooed. "You are an awesome cook."

Wilfred laughed. "You can catch more flies with a spoonful of sugar than with a barrel of vinegar—but we'll see. The proof of the pudding—or pie, in this case—is in the eating." He prepared to cut another slice, then paused. "It's an Amish recipe," he said. "Bettina and I first tasted it on a trip to Pennsylvania. I think the Amish invented it long ago for times of the year when no fresh fruit was in season for pies."

Holly picked up the large spoon that had been staged next to the bowl of whipped cream.

"Go ahead." Wilfred smiled. "And I'll keep slicing."

Pamela returned to find an assembly line in progress. Four plates containing pie wedges topped with drifts of whipped cream were lined up along the counter, and Holly was waiting with her spoon poised over the whipped cream bowl as Wilfred slipped a fifth slice onto a plate.

"Tiny ones for Nell and Roland," Pamela said. "Nell said she can tell just by the aroma that it's loaded with sugar. And neither one wants anything on top."

"I'll cut this one in half for them then." Wilfred plied his knife on the slice he had just served and transferred a sliver to a fresh plate. "None of the slices are very big though—with one pie for seven people. And I only put in a tiny bit of sugar when I whipped the cream. But to each his own."

Pamela slipped behind the counter, removed the plastic drip cone from the top of the carafe, and bore the carafe to the pine table. Tea bags waited in two of the sage-green mugs. Before she poured the coffee, she returned to the stove to fetch the kettle. Wilfred had turned off the burner under the kettle while Pamela was delivering the tray to the coffee table, but the wisps of steam drifting up from its spout showed that the water was just right to set tea steeping. Once the tea was in progress, she filled the remaining mugs with coffee.

Pamela and Holly set out for the living room together, Pamela bearing the mugs of tea for Nell and Karen, and Holly with two slices of shoo fly pie—a little one bare of whipped cream for Nell and the other for Karen.

Nell leaned forward to receive her tea with one hand and her pie with the other. "This looks just right," she said, "though really people don't need to eat any sugar at all." She lowered mug and plate to the coffee table.

Across from her Bettina laughed. "Don't *need*, perhaps. But what's the harm in a special treat now and then? And Wilfred so enjoys his baking."

Karen studied her own piece of pie as if wondering whether she'd be able to manage such a hearty serving.

"Go ahead," Bettina urged as Karen blushed. "You're a nursing mother—eating for two."

After a few more trips, everyone had pie, coffee had been delivered to the coffee-drinkers, Pamela and Holly had resumed their seats, and Wilfred had joined Roland on the hearth.

"Perfectly amazing," Holly pronounced as she lowered her fork to her plate after her first bite. She closed her eyes and curved her pretty lips into a blissful smile.

Pamela had to agree. The whipped cream, smooth and cool and barely sugared at all, was the perfect complement for the pie filling, dense and warm and achingly sweet, but with an elusive slightly metallic flavor. And the flaky crust set off the contrast to perfection.

Even Roland was impressed. "Excellent work," he commented, turning to Wilfred. "Very skillfully done."

For a few minutes, there was no sound but the click of forks against plates and the occasional moan of pleasure, even from Nell. Then Bettina asked Karen how she and Dave were adjusting to parenthood, and soon separate conversations had popped up here and there. Pamela and her neighbors on the sofa, Karen and Nell, were chatting about the early signs of spring appearing in their yards—daffodils!—while Holly enthused to Bettina about the latter's good fortune in having a husband who was such an amazing cook, and Wilfred and Roland talked about cars.

Suddenly, however, all conversation came to a halt when the doorbell rang.

"Who on earth could that be at this time of night?" Bettina said, pulling herself out of her armchair. Wilfred rose too, and stood poised near the fireplace as Bettina stepped toward the door.

She reached for the knob, pulled the door open, and took a few steps back. From where Pamela sat on the sofa, she could see Bettina's face only in profile. But even in profile it was clear her eyes were wide and her mouth agape.

"Of . . . of course," Bettina said in a voice that barely resembled her own. "Yes, he's here . . . but what . . . ?"

Chapter 2

Wilfred by this time had reached his wife's side and slipped a comforting hand around her waist. From the porch came indistinct voices that nonetheless sounded authoritative. Then Wilfred turned back toward the living room. "Roland?" he said. "You're wanted outside."

Looking more irritated than curious, Roland bounded up from the hearth and strode toward the door. More voices, still indistinct, and Roland stepped through the door.

Wilfred and Bettina stood in the open doorway watching for a minute. Then Bettina turned away.

"That was the police," she said in a small, puzzled voice. "They've arrested Roland."

Karen grabbed Nell's hand.

"Arrested?" Nell's cheery expression usually softened the lines engraved by her eighty-plus years, but at this moment she looked her age. "Are you sure?" she asked.

Bettina nodded. "Just the way they do it on TV."

Holly stirred in her armchair.

"What could he have done to get arrested?" she murmured. "Roland, of all people!"

Wilfred closed the door, slipped his arm around Bettina's waist again, and led her back to her chair. He continued on toward the hearth, where he sat and picked up Roland's briefcase. He opened it and carefully arranged Roland's yarn, needles, and partly completed project inside.

As if taking the cue that useful action was the best response to shocking news, Holly rose and began collecting pie plates, forks, spoons, and napkins. Bettina picked up Holly's mug and her own, and Pamela joined in the cleanup.

A few minutes later the five remaining Knit and Nibblers sat staring at one another across the coffee table, now cleared, as the sound of running water from the kitchen suggested that Wilfred had found another useful activity. Pamela turned her attention to her knitting needles and lilac yarn, trying to reconstruct where in the complicated pattern she had left off. The arrival of the police to arrest Roland had driven from her mind all that had transpired earlier that evening.

Holly, too, had been studying her project, an inch-wide strip of vibrant green worked in the garter stitch. She thrust her right needle through the loop of yarn at the end of her left needle and hooked her index finger to catch up the long strand that fed from the skein at her side. But suddenly she stopped. "I've never seen anyone get arrested before," she blurted. "I just don't think I can concentrate on this." Her serious expression was at odds with her whimsical toilette—Holly and her husband owned a hair salon, and Holly enjoyed experimenting with different colored streaks in her luxuriant raven hair. Tonight bright orange streaks were echoed by matching nail enamel, and for earrings one ear sported a bright golden sun and the other a silver crescent moon.

"Me neither," Karen piped up at Pamela's side, her voice even tinier than usual.

"Busy hands ease troubled minds," Nell said. A partly finished infant cap in a soft shade of yellow rested on her thigh. She picked up the needles from which the cap dangled and launched a new row.

But it was no use. Holly tugged her knitting bag onto her lap and began to tuck her work away. "I'm sorry," she said, "but I really can't focus. Poor Roland. He wasn't at his best tonight, but he's an okay guy. And what will his wife do? I can't imagine how I'd feel if Desmond got arrested." Karen began to pack her work up too.

Holding her knitting bag, Holly rose from her chair. "Did you walk, Nell?" she asked. Nell's energy and lithe physique were a testament to her habit of never driving to a destination she could reach on foot.

"I did," Nell said. "And I'll be fine getting home on my own"—her eyes strayed to Bettina, whose knitting lay untouched in her lap—"unless . . . of course, if no one feels like carrying on with the knitting . . . I don't want to be in your way."

"You'd never be in our way, Nell." Bettina leaned forward with a comforting smile. "But I don't like the idea of you walking around Arborville at night with a killer on the loose."

"I don't either," Holly said. "And I'd have picked you up at your house if I'd known you were going to set out on foot."

Nell sighed. "Busy hands *do* ease troubled minds," she said. "And so do busy feet. But I know when I'm outnumbered." She lifted her knitting bag from the floor and slipped her project, abandoned in mid-row, inside.

"Dear Nell." Karen stood too and offered Nell a hand as she began to rise. The two of them, followed by Holly, made their way toward Bettina's door.

"I'm meeting with Clayborn tomorrow morning," Bettina told them as she fetched their jackets from the closet. "To get the Diefenbach story for the *Advocate.* But I'll see what I can find out about Roland." She twisted the doorknob and swung the door back.

Pamela was on her feet too, edging away from the sofa with knitting bag in hand, but Bettina motioned her to stay. Nell, Karen, and Holly stepped over the threshold and a chorus of somewhat despondent goodnights echoed from the porch. Bettina waved and replied, then she closed the door.

"It never rains but it pours, as Wilfred would say," she commented, shaking her head and setting the bright tendrils of her hair to vibrating.

Sensing that only familiar humans remained in

the house, Woofus ventured cautiously through the arch that separated the Frasers' dining room from their living room. He made his way to Bettina's side and snuggled up against the pink jersey of her dress. She rested a hand on his shaggy back. Punkin returned also, and resumed her languorous pose along the back of the sofa.

The animals were followed by Wilfred, who had removed his apron, a signal that his cleanup work was done. "Dear, dear wife," he sighed. "What a day this has been. I'm going to retreat to my den with a book." With a courtly bow to Pamela, he was on his way up the stairs, accompanied by Woofus.

"I think there's some pie left," Bettina said, suddenly cheering. "And more whipped cream. Shall we?" She set off for the kitchen. Pamela followed, dropping her knitting bag in an armchair as she passed.

"Two pieces left," Bettina announced from the counter as Pamela entered. "Just as I suspected."

"I honestly couldn't." Pamela patted her stomach. "The one slice with the whipped cream was just enough. I'll have a little coffee though, if there's any to reheat."

"That's why you're thin and I'm not." Pamela was not only thinner than her friend, she was also a head taller. And Pamela's disinterest in fashion, despite having the figure to display stylish clothes to advantage, was a constant source of amazement to Bettina, who dressed for her life in Arborville with the flair and enthusiasm of a confirmed fashionista.

Bettina surveyed the stove and its neighboring

counter, then shook her head. "Wilfred cleaned everything up. But I'll make more. I'd like a cup too."

So ten minutes later the two friends were sitting at Bettina's well-scrubbed pine table with two cups of coffee and one slice of pie, liberally topped with whipped cream.

"The news didn't say anything about what the murder weapon actually was," Bettina said as she used her fork to tease away a bite of the flaky crust with its dense syrupy topping. "But Clayborn should have more details tomorrow. The residents of Arborville certainly deserve to know all the facts. I didn't care for Diefenbach myself, but enough people liked him to elect him mayor."

Pamela set her coffee mug down after an exploratory sip of the bitter brew, still too hot to drink. "He wasn't supposed to win," she observed. "The Wendelstaff College poll had Brandon MacDonald leading by a good margin."

Bettina shrugged. "MacDonald had been the mayor forever. Diefenbach proposed to really shake up the town government—Arborville was stuck in the past, he said, and his ideas would propel it into the future. Maybe people were embarrassed to admit to the pollsters that he had a point. Everybody likes MacDonald but he never really got much done."

"I think MacDonald and Diefenbach lived right next door to each other," Pamela said. "Wasn't that in one of the articles you wrote about the election for the *Advocate*?"

Bettina nodded. " 'Competition for Top Spot Pits Neighbor Against Neighbor.' That was the headline. I interviewed them both. As different as night and day—MacDonald so easy going and Diefenbach wound as tight as . . . well, as tight as Roland. No wonder Roland liked him." She scooped up a bigger forkful of pie, making sure to include a daub of whipped cream.

"Roland." Pamela shook her head. "What on earth could that all be about?"

Bettina mirrored the head-shake, setting her coral and gold earrings to swaying. "Like Holly said, he certainly wasn't at his best tonight. But Poor Melanie!" Melanie was Roland's wife. "What must she be thinking?"

"Maybe it's just some kind of mistake." Pamela sampled her coffee again and found that the temperature was just right for drinking.

"Maybe it was," Bettina agreed. "I'll know more after my meeting with Clayborn."

Chapter 3

The next day, Pamela was hard at work in her office when the doorbell chimed at a little after ten a.m. She transferred Ginger the cat from her lap to the floor and hurried toward the stairs. On the landing she paused and glanced toward her front door. Through the lace that curtained the door's oval window, she could make out a blur of bright yellow accented by a touch of vivid scarlet above.

When she reached the entry, she was greeted first by her other cat, Catrina, who was lounging in the spot of sunlight that reliably set the colors in the worn Persian rug aglow every morning. Pamela opened the door to discover Bettina. The blur of bright yellow resolved into a stylish trench coat in a glazed fabric that looked almost like patent leather, and the vivid accent was Bettina's scarlet hair, which she herself described as a color not found in nature.

But Bettina's expression was far from cheery, and her message so dire that she began speaking before she even stepped over the threshold.

"They think Roland killed Diefenbach," she wailed.

"How could they?" Pamela felt her heart thump heavily. She reached out and drew her friend inside.

"Ohhh . . . they've got it all figured out, or think they do." Bettina handed Pamela a white bakery box secured with a double twist of string. Then she unbelted and unbuttoned her coat, shrugged it off, and dropped it on the chair that, with a small table, made up the entry's furniture. Catrina raised her head briefly then returned to her nap. "Is there coffee?" Bettina asked. "I only had time for one cup before I had to run out for my meeting with Clayborn."

"There certainly can be," Pamela said, slipping one arm around Bettina's shoulders and cradling the bakery box in the other. "Come on out to the kitchen."

"Roland had an argument with Diefenbach early Monday evening," Bettina said as she filled Pamela's cut-glass cream pitcher with heavy cream. She set it next to its companion sugar bowl on Pamela's kitchen table and settled into her accustomed chair. Pamela stood at the counter measuring coffee beans into her coffee grinder. She'd already started water boiling on the stove.

Bettina went on. "It was a very public argument, out on Roland's front lawn, and several of his neighbors witnessed it."

When Bettina finished speaking, Pamela pressed

down on the grinder's cover, and for a moment the whir and clatter of coffee beans being ground took the place of conversation.

"Two thoughts," Pamela replied when a low snarl and then silence marked the grinding's completion. "First of all, people have arguments—even public ones—all the time without deciding to kill each other. And second, why would Roland argue with Diefenbach? From what he said last night, he sounded like a big fan."

She placed a paper filter in the plastic cone balanced on top of her carafe and carefully poured in the ground beans. The kettle hadn't yet begun to hoot, so she opened the cupboard where she kept her wedding china and took out two cups and two saucers.

"We'll need plates too," Bettina said. Bettina had untied the string on the bakery box and folded back the top flap to reveal two large pieces of Co-Op crumb cake.

Pamela arranged the saucers, with the cups nestled atop them, on the table and returned to the cupboard to reach down two of the dessert plates that were part of her set. She had decided long ago that there was no point in having nice things that only came out a few times a year—though, except for the wedding china, most of her treasures were thrift-store and tag-sale finds.

"Roland didn't say he liked Diefenbach," Bettina said. "He only said he liked his ideas."

"So what were they—?" Pamela began, but the question was interrupted by the shrill hoot of the kettle.

Bettina answered anyway, as Pamela tilted the

kettle over the carafe's plastic cone and the boiling water began to drip through the ground beans, infusing the small kitchen with the rich and bitter aroma of brewing coffee. "Diefenbach is still on that tree committee," she explained. "The Arborists. This is the time of year they come around and check for trees that are likely to interfere with the power lines when their growing season starts."

"And they'd targeted one of Roland's trees?" Pamela transferred the plastic cone to the sink and stepped toward the table with the steaming carafe.

Bettina nodded. "They spray red Xs on them. Then the DPW comes around and cuts them down. Mostly they're trees on that strip of land between the sidewalk and the street."

Pamela looked up from pouring coffee, dark against the pale porcelain, into the wedding china cups. "But people plant those trees themselves," she said. "The town doesn't plant them."

Bettina nodded again and her coral and gold earrings, a repeat from the previous day and a favorite pair, swayed. "It's true the trees are planted by homeowners, but the town has authority to remove them. Tree branches and power wires aren't a good combination." She jumped up, fetched a spatula and two forks from Pamela's silverware drawer, and slid pieces of crumb cake onto the dessert plates. Each piece was a square of golden sponge topped with a thick layer of buttery crumble the color of a camel-hair coat.

"But Bill Diefenbach wasn't killed in the early evening in Roland's front yard," Pamela said, feeling a puzzled wrinkle form between her brows.

"He was killed in his own kitchen slightly after nine p.m." That morning's edition of the county's daily paper, the *Register*, had added more details to the report of the crime than the Knit and Nibblers had supplied.

But Bettina, fresh from her meeting with Detective Clayborn, knew even more. "There was another argument," she said, "and Diefenbach's neighbors heard it. It was unusually warm Monday night, and last night too—remember?—so Diefenbach had his kitchen windows open. And neighbors were taking out their garbage and walking their dogs and what-not. So when the police came around asking if anyone had seen or heard anything unusual . . ."

The lure of the crumb cake caused Bettina to break off and pick up her fork. She had already added sugar to her coffee, and stirred in cream until the liquid in her cup reached the precise light mocha shade that she preferred.

Pamela sampled her own square of crumb cake, enjoying the slight hint of lemon in the sponge and the slight hint of cinnamon in the rich, buttery crumble of the topping. She followed her first bite with a sip of coffee. She preferred her coffee black, especially with the goodies that always accompanied her chats with Bettina.

Restored by a few bites of crumb cake and a few sips of coffee, Bettina went on. "It must have been quite an argument. Clayborn said the heavy object Diefenbach was hit with wasn't located at the scene, but somehow a jar of jam fell or was thrown to the floor and broke. Diefenbach's kitchen floor is tile like yours." Bettina glanced at Pamela's floor, alternating squares of black and white ceramic tile.

Pamela's fork, bearing another bite of crumb cake, paused halfway to her mouth. "I can't imagine that Diefenbach's neighbors identified the voice of the person he was arguing with as specifically Roland DeCamp," she observed. She noted that her voice had taken on the mocking tone she'd tried to avoid in raising her daughter, preferring to let her words rather than her manner make her point.

Bettina looked startled. "*I* don't think Roland did it," she exclaimed. "And nobody said it was Roland's voice. In fact, they said the only voice they could really make out was Diefenbach's. But Diefenbach was known to have a real temper, and it was clear he was arguing with someone."

Pamela rested her fork, still bearing the morsel of crumb cake, back on her plate. "But why assume that that someone was *Roland?* Just because Diefenbach and Roland had argued hours earlier?"

"Somebody saw Roland's *car*"—Bettina's brightly lipsticked lips tightened into a mournful twist—"at just about nine p.m., in front of Diefenbach's house. That white Porsche of Roland's is pretty distinctive."

Pamela sighed. "Well . . . I can see why Detective Clayborn thinks he's figured out what happened. But I just don't think Roland would do a thing like that—hit someone with a . . . whatever . . . and then watch him fall and knock his head on the counter and land on the floor. And stand there while he died. And you said they haven't found the murder weapon—so no fingerprints to make it conclusive."

They both returned to their coffee and crumb cake, but the cheer that usually accompanied their cozy morning chats was absent. Easter was approaching and Pamela's daughter Penny would be home for spring break soon, but even that topic was raised and dispatched with nary a smile.

At last Bettina coaxed the last few crumbs of crumb cake onto her fork, transported them to her mouth, and tipped her cup to drain the last few sweet drops of coffee.

"I'll be off then," she said. "I know you've got work to do for the magazine."

Pamela nodded. Her work evaluating and editing manuscripts was demanding, but like knitting, it could also soothe. Losing herself in an article about the silk industry in eighteenth-century France or status markers in Viking women's wear could be just the antidote to the disturbing news of Diefenbach's murder and Roland's possible role.

In the entry, Bettina slipped back into her bright yellow trench coat. Pamela gave her a hug, reached for the doorknob, and pulled the door open. Just as Bettina was about to step over the threshold, she paused.

"I almost forgot," she exclaimed, clutching Pamela's arm. "Roland's back at home—out on bail. I called Melanie this morning."

"That's a relief," Pamela said. "At least he's not sitting in a jail cell over in Haversack." Haversack was the county seat.

"He *is* a lawyer, after all." Bettina raised her

carefully shaped brows. "Not a criminal lawyer, but I'm sure he knows his way around the legal process." She paused again on the porch to add, "He wants his knitting, so I'm going over there with it later."

"I'll come along," Pamela said. "He can be annoying at times, but he's a fellow knitter, and Knit and Nibble is like a family."

"We're driving though," Bettina said firmly, with the first hint of a smile she'd shown that day. "I know you like your exercise, and Arborville isn't all that big, but pretty shoes aren't made for hiking." She extended a foot to admire a fetching chartreuse pump adorned with a matching grosgrain bow.

"It *is* colorful," Bettina said. "Quite a cute idea—yarn in public places. The photo of the building those yarn people covered in Los Angeles is amazing."

It was a few hours later and Pamela and Bettina were standing in Bettina's driveway, just about to climb into Bettina's faithful Toyota. Bettina was gazing across Orchard Street at the sweater-wearing tree in Pamela's front yard. Then she turned her gaze to Pamela. "Has Richard Larkin said anything to you about it?" she asked.

Pamela knew what was coming, but she tried to summon up a neutral tone for her response. "No," she said. "Why would he?"

"This morning when Wilfred went out to get the newspaper he said Richard was admiring it. Richard crossed over for a little chat . . . wanted to know if making sweaters for trees was a new Knit and Nibble project."

"Well, we don't know, do we?" Pamela said. "One—or more—of those yarn people could be among us without us knowing it. But it's kind of him to be interested in our little group."

"You know who he's particularly interested in," Bettina said with a sly smile. She lifted a brow and regarded Pamela from beneath an eyelid accented with green eye shadow.

"I don't know at all," Pamela said with what she hoped was a pleasant, but dismissive, laugh. Richard Larkin was the eligible architect who had bought the house next to hers going on two years ago. Bettina had been playing matchmaker for nearly that long, insisting that seven years was a long enough time for Pamela to mourn Michael Paterson, who had also been an architect and who had been killed in a tragic accident on a construction site.

"For heaven's sake, Pamela!" Bettina put her hands on her hips and tilted her head to capture Pamela's gaze. "It's as plain as the nose on your face."

In fact, Pamela had to admit, his interest—though gentlemanly—was quite obvious. And he *was* attractive. It was just that . . . well, she wasn't sure what it was. Maybe she was just too old to start all over again. Not that forty-four was old, as Bettina kept reminding her, and not that she looked forty-four, with the tomboyish build that her simple wardrobe of jeans and sweaters suited quite well.

*   *   *

Roland lived at the north end of Arborville, in a neighborhood the Arborville old-timers still called "The Farm." For generations the land had been farmed by the Van Ripers, descendants of long-ago Dutch settlers—until an upstart Van Riper, tired of farming, sold the land to a developer. Split-level houses popped up, with more square footage than anyone could rationally need and too many bathrooms—though some people grudgingly agreed that owning a house built closer to the end of the twentieth century than the beginning would allow one to banish worries about quirky plumbing or eccentric wiring.

Bettina guided her Toyota up Orchard Street, crossed Arborville Avenue at the top of the block, and continued on Orchard as it climbed the hill created by the bluffs that overlooked the Hudson River on the New Jersey side. A few blocks above Arborville Avenue, she turned left. En route to The Farm, they cruised past pleasant houses, various in style but solid and old: two-story wood-frame houses with wide porches and clapboard siding and little dormer windows peering down from peaked roofed attics, or sturdy red brick houses with white pillars and symmetrical windows above and below, or even houses built of natural stone.

"My goodness, look at that," Bettina said suddenly, braking and veering toward the curb.

"What?" Pamela tipped her head toward the window on her side.

"It's . . . I've passed it now." Bettina opened her door and swung her feet onto the asphalt. She scurried around the back of the car and approached a large tree. Pamela, meanwhile, had climbed out too and was standing on the narrow strip of grass between the sidewalk and the curb. The tree was about five feet away, rooted in the same strip of grass—it had been in place so long that its roots had raised a substantial bump in the neighboring patch of sidewalk.

"You can't see it from there," Bettina said. "You have to come around to this side."

Pamela joined her to find Bettina pointing an accusing finger, tipped with a bright pink fingernail, at a large red X spray-painted on the trunk.

"It's doomed," Bettina said. "Poor thing."

Pamela tipped her head back. Indeed there were power wires up above, and from the look of the tree's branches previous attempts had been made to prevent it from damaging the power supply. The pattern of the branches was clear because spring hadn't yet advanced far enough to cloak the tree's crest in leaves. Only a haze of pale green suggested the foliage to come.

Two huge branches veered out over the street and three more loomed over the sidewalk, but others had been cut away, scooping out a path for the wires. Evidently, though, this stratagem had been judged ineffective and the tree was now marked for removal.

Pamela returned her gaze to the trunk, and the damning red X. It looked familiar—and it was. "My tree had one of those!" she exclaimed. "Of course. I noticed it when I brought the paper in on Monday. But then I forgot all about it because . . ."

"The sweater!" Bettina supplied, her eyes lively.

"The sweater is hiding the red X." Their voices overlapped.

"Someone is trying to protect the trees."

"Someone who's a knitter," Pamela concluded.

"A Yarnvader," Bettina added.

They returned to the car, settled into their seats, and continued on their way. Several of the houses they passed as they approached the edge of The Farm featured trees springing from the narrow strip of grass between the curb and the sidewalk and wearing sweaters.

Chapter 4

Melanie DeCamp answered the door, glanced at the briefcase in Bettina's hand, and mouthed "thank you." Melanie barely resembled her usual chic self. Her smooth blonde hair was twisted into a careless knot secured with a clip, and her face was bare of the makeup that could have softened the purple shadows beneath her eyes. She stepped back and ushered them into the stylish living room where the Knit and Nibblers had gathered on many happier occasions.

Roland was perched on the angular turquoise chair that matched the DeCamps' low-slung sofa. He wasn't wearing his usual pinstripe suit, but the shirt collar that the V of his dark blue sweater revealed was as aggressively starched as always and the crease in his smooth wool slacks just as sharp. His lean face was impassive but his right hand was in motion, nervous motion, as it stroked the lustrous fur of the cat stretched across his lap. From ears to tail the hand traced the same path, again and again.

"I don't know what kind of a state he'd be in without Cuddles," Melanie whispered. "What a blessing that cat has been." She squeezed Pamela's hand.

Pamela was indeed responsible for Cuddles—or actually Catrina was. The previous summer Catrina had borne an unplanned litter of six kittens, three inky black males and three ginger females. Faced with the dilemma of finding homes for such a large brood, Pamela had heeded Bettina's advice about the irresistible appeal of kittens when viewed in person. As the kittens neared a suitable age for adoption, she let them frolic into the midst of a Knit and Nibble meeting and two adoptions were arranged as a result. Amazingly the buttoned-up Roland succumbed to the charms of one of the males, the smallest and shyest kitten of the whole batch.

Almost fully mature now, Cuddles was still small, but sleek and self-confident. He raised his head lazily to regard the visitors then snuggled contentedly back into his master's lap. Bettina stepped closer to Roland and held out the briefcase.

"They've brought your knitting," Melanie explained. She took the briefcase and set it on the carpet near Roland's chair. And then, as if recalling the protocol of a social visit, she turned toward Pamela and Bettina, struggled to summon a smile, and gestured toward the sofa. "Please sit down," she said, "and let me make some coffee."

Bettina eyed the low-slung sofa warily. Melanie noticed the hesitation. "Do take the armchair if you prefer," she urged Bettina as Pamela sank down onto the sofa, wondering whether she herself would be able to regain her feet without help.

"We don't need coffee," Pamela said. "I know you have a lot on your mind and we won't stay. We just wanted to drop off the knitting."

"I didn't kill Diefenbach," Roland announced suddenly, his busy hand pausing in mid-stroke.

"We know that," Bettina said comfortingly from the depths of the comfy armchair. She leaned toward Roland, her face puckered with concern. "And I'm sure the police will realize that and figure out what really happened."

"I have my doubts," Roland muttered grimly. "For all the money we pay in taxes I've never been that impressed with the Arborville police force."

"Clayborn said one of Diefenbach's neighbors saw your car in front of his house at nine p.m. . . ." Bettina let the sentence trail off as if to invite a rebuttal.

Roland sighed. "It *was* in front of Diefenbach's house . . . for about thirty seconds—because Diefenbach's house is on a corner and there's a stop sign there and so I stopped."

Melanie had joined Pamela on the sofa. "He went out to buy cat food," she explained.

"If anyone can suggest a more direct way to get from here to the Co-Op Grocery without passing Diefenbach's house, I'd like to hear it." The hint of sarcasm in his voice, as if he was addressing a group of his corporate colleagues whose logic he found wanting, suggested that his spirit hadn't been completely beaten down by his current circumstances.

"Why so late?" Pamela asked. The DeCamps had always struck Pamela as too organized to find themselves in need of last-minute dashes to the market.

"We were trying a new brand." Melanie raised an elegant shoulder in a shrug. "And Cuddles absolutely would not touch it." She shaped her mouth, lovely even without its customary lipstick, into a sad smile. "So Roland went out to get more of the old kind, and his route took him past Diefenbach's house, and here we are now"—a wave of her well-manicured hands took in the room, her husband, herself, and the cat—"in this terrible mess." The last few words came out in a thin wail.

Bettina jumped up from the armchair and hurried across the carpet. She lowered herself onto the sofa and grabbed Melanie's nearest hand. "I know everything will get straightened out. Clayborn is a decent man, and a smart man." She wrapped an arm around Melanie's shoulders. "It will be fine. *Really*."

Melanie tried to smile, but from the other side of the room came a snort that Roland didn't try to disguise.

"We should get going," Bettina said, "but we'll be in touch." She took Melanie's hand again and gave it a squeeze. "If there's anything you need, just call me. Or Pamela."

Anticipating that her help might be needed when it was time for Bettina to rise from the sofa, Pamela climbed to her feet and offered her friend a hand. Melanie stood as well and the three proceeded toward the door. As they lingered for a moment in the hallway that led past the living room to the back of the house, there came the sound of toenails clicking on a wooden floor. In a moment they had been joined by the DeCamps' dachshund, Ramona, her elongated chestnut body twitching with each wave of her gyrating tail.

"Oh, dear," Melanie sighed. "We've been neglecting her terribly." She stooped toward the excited dog. "You want a walk, don't you?" she cooed. "The backyard is fenced, so she can go out, but she really enjoys her jaunts around the neighborhood."

"No problems with Cuddles then?" Pamela asked. Ramona had long been a fixture in the De-Camp household, and when Roland suggested adopting one of Catrina's kittens, Pamela had feared the dog would be an impediment.

"No problems," Melanie said. "They're as happy together as . . . Roland and I." She cast a fond glance toward her husband, who had resumed his nervous stroking.

"I'm not as confident of Clayborn's abilities as I made out to Melanie," Bettina said as she and Pamela settled themselves back into the Toyota. Melanie had emerged from the DeCamps' large split-level house with Ramona on a leash and was heading down the walk that bisected her carefully landscaped front yard. The large tree on the strip of grass between the sidewalk and the street was marked with a red X.

"I'm not too confident of them either," Pamela agreed. "Poor Melanie."

"And Roland," Bettina added.

For such a pleasant little town, Arborville had had a startling number of murders. They weren't the sorts of murders that arise from rampant crime or social ills. They were murders carried out by people who one would never imagine might do such a thing . . . but then they did. And Pamela had been surprised to discover that she—with the aid of Bettina—often made connections and saw patterns the police unaccountably overlooked. How she and Bettina could be smarter than the police, Pamela had no idea. Yet she and Bettina had solved a number of murders over the years.

Bettina steered the Toyota back in the direction they had come, leaving the curving streets and the cul de sacs of The Farm behind and proceeding along blocks of the older houses that character- ized most of Arborville's housing stock. As they drove, they passed the sweater-wearing trees they had noticed earlier.

Pamela realized she was frowning, hard, and staring at each of the colorful apparitions as Bet- tina cruised slowly by. Suddenly Bettina swerved to the curb and turned off the ignition. They were right across from the tree with the big red X that had made them suspect the sweaters were in- tended as more than decoration.

"Are you thinking what I'm thinking?" Bettina asked as Pamela turned, her forehead still marked by the ferocious frown.

"I imagine I am." Pamela nodded.

"This knitting person is so committed to protecting these trees —" Bettina began.

Pamela finished the thought, "—that she, or he, decided Diefenbach had to go."

"Diefenbach isn't the only Arborist." Bettina's frown matched Pamela's.

Pamela nodded. "Some of the other Arborists are probably going around with cans of red spray paint marking trees. They could be in danger."

Bettina nodded too, then her expression turned mournful. "I hate to think that a knitter would murder people, even to rescue trees. Knitting is such a constructive pursuit."

"Maybe the tree-protecting knitter didn't really intend to *kill* Diefenbach," Pamela suggested. She went on, slowly, as if working the idea out as she spoke. "Diefenbach and the killer had been arguing . . . so the killer could have shown up at Diefenbach's house merely to complain about the tree-removal plan. But then . . ."

"Diefenbach was a very hot-headed person." Excited by the idea Pamela was developing, Bettina spoke quickly.

"He starts yelling." Pamela frowned, as if imagining Diefenbach's anger.

"And the other person yells back," Bettina frowned, caught up in the scene. "And then it escalates—"

"And the other person picks up a heavy thing—" Pamela was speaking quickly now too.

"I think that's it." Bettina settled back in her seat with a pleased smile. She twisted her key in the ignition and the Toyota's engine grumbled back to life.

"Turn around though," Pamela said. "Let's make sure there are really red X's under those tree-sweaters."

Bettina glanced around and made a quick U-turn. Soon she and Pamela were standing next to a tree sporting a knitted sheath that covered its trunk from just about the height of a human's waist to the height of a human's shoulders. As Pamela had noticed when she paused to study the sweater that adorned her own tree, the knitter had used a wide variety of yarns—different colors, textures, and weights, as if drawing from a bin where odds and ends left from old projects had been stored.

This tree's sweater featured stripes of random widths, bright yellow neighboring deep violet, then very fuzzy chartreuse, then a smooth orange that looked like cashmere. The knitter had been skilled—no dropped stitches were evident—but also hurried. The yarn tails that remained where one color yielded to the next had been left to wave slightly in the spring breeze.

Pamela grabbed hold of the knitted sheath at its bottom and began to roll and push it gently upwards, exposing the rough brown trunk that it hid. After about a foot of the hidden trunk had been revealed, she noticed a smear of red smudged across one of the ridges that formed the tree's bark. She pushed the knitting farther up and the lower half of a red X came into view. Bettina leaned closer and traced the red smears with her fastidiously manicured fingernail.

"It's clear what these sweaters are intended to

do," Pamela said, easing the knitted sheath back into its original position as Bettina retracted her finger. "Now we just need a scissors."

Bettina jumped back, eyes and mouth wide open. "You're not going to cut the sweater off, are you?" she demanded. "I feel bad about these trees being cut down too."

Pamela smiled at her friend. "I'm just going to cut off the tails," she said soothingly, and reached for the few inches of violet yarn that dangled from the joint where a violet stripe gave way to fuzzy chartreuse. "We'll collect as many tails as we can find, wherever the sweater is hiding a red X—and I suspect that will be all of them."

After a quick trip back to Orchard Street to pick up scissors and a large zip-lock bag, and collect five yarn samples in assorted colors, textures, and weights from the sweater on the tree right in front of Pamela's house, Pamela and Bettina once again headed up the block toward Arborville Avenue. They paused to collect yarn samples from a tree in front of the stately brick apartment building at the corner, then turned left and began zigzagging down one cross street as far as County Road and up the next, across Arborville Avenue and up the hill. Every time they came to a tree wearing a sweater, Pamela jumped out of the Toyota and snipped off as many tails as she could find.

When they returned to Orchard Street and Bettina pulled up in front of Pamela's house, Pamela took charge of the zip-lock bag, now a puffy pillow stuffed with a kaleidoscope of yarn samples.

"The next step is to visit the yarn shop in Timberley," she said as she climbed out of the Toyota. "Tomorrow. Do you want to come?"

"Of course!" Bettina said. "I don't know what you're up to, but I wouldn't miss it for the world. I have to cover a luncheon program at the senior center though, so how does two p.m. sound?"

It was Thursday morning. Pamela sat at her kitchen table finishing up her morning coffee and paging one last time through the *Register*. No follow-up articles on the murder of Bill Diefenbach had appeared, suggesting the police were happy with their arrest of Roland, which had featured prominently in the previous day's edition.

Ginger was in a lively mood, batting a catnip mouse over the black and white tile floor. The catnip essence that had been its original attraction had faded long ago, but it had a long yarn tail that made a tantalizing target as the mouse skittered here and there. Catrina had eaten her breakfast and retreated to the entry in search of her favorite sunny spot.

After a few minutes, Pamela folded the newspaper into a compact bundle, drained the last drops of coffee from her wedding china cup, and stood up. She rinsed the cup at the sink, proceeded to the entry where she stepped past Catrina to deposit the newspaper in the recycling basket, and headed up the stairs to dress.

Unlike her fashionable friend, Pamela had little

interest in clothes. And with a job that let her work from home most days, she had little reason to pay attention to fashion. Her customary uniform was jeans—with a simple cotton blouse and sandals in the summer, and a handknit sweater and loafers in the winter.

She'd noticed when she went out to fetch the newspaper that the unseasonable warm spell of the past few days had been blown away in the night by an encroaching cold front, so she took her cozy Icelandic-style sweater down from her closet shelf. It had been a very satisfying knitting project, created from undyed wool in natural brown and white, with a snowflake pattern around the neck and shoulders. Bettina would be coming after lunch and they would drive to Timberley, but the errand for the morning was a visit to the Co-Op Grocery to replenish her bare larder.

The Co-Op errand would be carried out on foot. Arborville was small, and walkable. That had been part of its appeal long ago when Pamela and her husband were shopping for a house. With its old houses and sidewalks and big trees, Arborville had reminded them of the college town where they met and fell in love. They had bought an old house—a hundred-year-old house—and they had done their best to bring it back to its former glory, with its parquet floors and solid wood doors and elegant moldings. Pamela had raised her daughter Penny there after Michael Paterson was gone, wanting to preserve as many constants in Penny's life as possible. Now Penny was at college and

Pamela was alone in her big house, but she felt the presence of her beloved husband every day and was loathe to move.

Back downstairs, Pamela took a jacket from the closet in the entry, along with several canvas bags, a gift from Nell. Nell was a devoted conservationist and made sure that her friends were all supplied with alternatives to paper and plastic.

The day was indeed chilly, but Pamela's walk up Orchard Street took her past many reminders that spring was springing: snowdrops and crocus clustered in sunny spots along the sidewalk, forsythia blazed yellow in yards, and a few small trees even displayed blush-pink blossoms against spindly branches. When she reached the stately brick apartment building at the corner, she detoured into the parking lot at the back of the building, where a length of wooden fencing hid the trash cans from the street. One person's trash was truly another's treasure and over the years Pamela had rescued a number of treasures cast off by the building's residents. Nothing caught her eye on this particular day however.

The Co-Op Grocery was about five blocks from Orchard Street. It anchored Arborville's small commercial district at its southern end. Walking farther along Arborville Avenue, one came to such Arborville institutions as Hyler's Luncheonette, When in Rome Pizza, and the Chinese takeout place, as well as banks, a hair salon, and a liquor store—all in narrow storefronts, some dressed up with awnings and many with apartments or offices above. But Pamela's only business today was with the Co-Op, so she halted there.

Many features of the Co-Op harkened back to an earlier time, like its narrow aisles, creaky wooden floors, and the bulletin board affixed to its façade. Since before the days of the internet (and Arborville's own listserv: AccessArborville), the Co-Op bulletin board had kept the town up to date on the doings of the town council, the activities of the scouts, and programs at the Arborville Library. And anyone with an event to publicize was welcome to post a flyer.

A small group of women were clustered around the bulletin board now, among them Bettina's friend Marlene Pepper, a cheerful soul about Bettina's age.

"Such a shame," Marlene was saying, "but it was only a matter of time."

Pamela glanced at the bulletin board, but she could see nothing that would provoke the tut-tutting and head-shaking that had afflicted the group.

"She barely looked like herself toward the end there," another said. "So skinny."

One item on the bulletin board did catch Pamela's eye however. A flyer printed in a bold typeface on fuchsia paper announced:

HUGE TAG SALE
CONTENTS OF WHOLE HOUSE
SATURDAY & SUNDAY
APRIL 4 & 5—10 AM to 5 PM

And the flyer went on to give an address on a street that paralleled Arborville Avenue a few blocks up the hill.

Pamela leaned closer to make sure she'd seen the address correctly. Finding a treasure at a tag sale was nearly as exciting as finding a treasure abandoned behind the stately brick apartment building.

"Did you know her?" Marlene asked suddenly, grabbing Pamela by the arm.

"Who?" Pamela asked, puzzled.

"Why Cassie Griswold, of course." Marlene responded looking equally puzzled.

Pamela loved her little town, and she tried to be sociable, but she'd never been one for the kind of sociability that involved knowing more about one's neighbors than they sometimes knew about themselves.

"That's her house," Marlene went on. "Seems a little rushed—to be clearing everything out so soon after her death. But I guess her daughter's in a hurry to sell."

Once inside the Co-Op, Pamela took a cart and steered it in the direction of the produce section. There she selected two cucumbers and a pint of cherry tomatoes in a little plastic box. Pamela grew her own tomatoes in the summer and savored the aroma and flavor of sun-warmed tomatoes fresh from her back yard. Winter tomatoes from the market didn't taste like much of anything, but she'd discovered that the small ones weren't as disappointing as the large ones that looked so appealing but weren't. In the next aisle

over, where the fruit was, she added three apples
to her cart.

When she reached the meat counter at the back
of the store, she studied the offerings. A tempting
array of roasts, chops, steaks, and poultry was available, much of it from local farms. Even after her
husband was gone, Pamela had continued to cook
proper meals for herself and her daughter. With
Penny away at college, she still cooked real food
for herself, most of the time, though she ate her
solitary dinners at her kitchen table rather than in
her dining room, and a chicken might last an entire week.

A pot roast would be nice, she thought, especially
with the weather suddenly feeling wintry again. She
picked up a piece of chuck, three pounds, which
really would last a week, then backtracked to the
produce department for a few potatoes. In the
canned goods section, she added three cans of cat
food to the cart.

The next stop was the cheese counter, with a
tempting display that included huge golden rounds
of cheddar, pale wedges of Swiss filigreed with
holes, disk-like Goudas covered with red wax, little
white pillows of chevre. After a few minutes of de-
liberation, she requested a half pound of Swiss and
a half pound of the Co-Op's special Vermont cheddar.

Finally she maneuvered her way to the bakery
counter. Fresh loaves—round, oblong, angular, and
ranging in color from caramel to deepest ma-
hogany—waited behind slanted glass. She requested
her favorite whole-grain, waited for it to be sliced

and slipped into a plastic bag, and nestled the bag into her cart.

Soon she was on her way home, strolling south on Arborville Avenue, with a canvas grocery bag in each hand and her purse slung over her shoulder.

Chapter 5

At home, Pamela wrote the address of the tag sale down on a note pad that had recently arrived, unbidden, from a charitable group. Anticipating spring, the small sheets featured daffodils and bunnies. She fastened the note to her refrigerator with her mitten magnet and set about putting her groceries away. As if Catrina and Ginger knew her shopping trip had included food for them, the cats milled about her feet, black fur interweaving with butterscotch in a complicated pattern.

Bettina was coming at two for the visit to the Timberley yarn shop. It was barely eleven now, and not yet time for lunch. The morning's email had brought two articles to be edited for *Fiber Craft*, due back by five p.m. Friday, but Pamela thought she might as well get started. The afternoon's activities might extend beyond the yarn shop in Timberley, and she might find herself pressed for time.

Upstairs in her office, she pushed the button that brought her computer to chirping and whirring life and was soon immersed in "Weeping Willow and Yew: Botanical Themes in Nineteenth-Century Mourning Samplers." The article was captivating, dealing as it did with the notion that needlework was once a means of mourning the dead, and the illustrations of the samplers were charming. Designs featured graceful willows with branches drooping to the ground, stalwart yews, and sorrowful young woman draped over gravestones—all rendered in careful embroidery, once-bright colors muted by age. Pamela was so caught up in her work that only when her stomach informed her that it was past time to eat did she realize how late it had gotten. She commanded the computer to save her work, exited from Word, and clicked on "Shut down."

Grilled Vermont cheddar on fresh slices of whole-grain bread would be the perfect lunch, she decided on her way down the stairs, and ten minutes later she was sitting at her kitchen table teasing off the first bite of her grilled-cheese sandwich. The bread had been rendered just the right shade of toasty brown and it gleamed with a glaze of melted butter. The cheese had melted just enough to mark the seam between the top slice and the bottom slice of bread with a glossy golden stripe of oozing cheddar.

A quarter of a sandwich still remained when the doorbell chimed. Pamela glanced up at the clock.

It was nearly two. Hurrying to the entry, she opened the door to admit Bettina.

Bettina had traded the bright yellow trench coat of the previous day for a puffy down coat the color of a pumpkin. Now she shrugged the coat off to reveal an olive-green frock that hugged her torso then flared at the waist into a knee-length skirt. Her olive-green suede booties completed the look, along with a chunky gold necklace and earrings to match. She'd accented her hazel eyes with a touch of olive-green shadow.

"I am completely stuffed," she said, patting her stomach. "Those seniors really put on a nice lunch—pot luck but it wasn't just Jello salads. And the speaker was so interesting—a woman from the group that planted the butterfly garden at the edge of the nature preserve. She told all about the migration patterns of the Monarchs."

"I'm just finishing my lunch." Pamela gestured toward the door that led to the kitchen. "Come on out here. A few more bites and then we'll go."

Bettina tossed her coat on the chair by the mail table. Ginger, who had been lurking under the chair, darted out to sniff at one of the booties then sauntered toward the living room. Bettina followed Pamela into the kitchen and settled into her accustomed chair facing Pamela.

"I'd offer you something," Pamela said, "but you've just come from lunch." She teased off another bite of the grilled-cheese sandwich.

"What's that?" Bettina asked, gazing past Pamela to the sheet of note paper with the daffodils and bunnies fastened to the refrigerator door. "That address?"

Pamela responded without turning her head. "There's a tag sale, starting Saturday. I saw a flyer on the bulletin board at the Co-Op. Your friend Marlene Pepper said it's Cassie Griswold's house and the house is to be sold because she has died."

Bettina nodded. "I knew she wasn't doing well." She directed her gaze to the remains of the sandwich on Pamela's plate. "Her house is in the next block from Diefenbach's," she added. "Of course Cassie wasn't murdered, but it is a little creepy—two deaths on the same street, so close together."

"I'm sure it doesn't mean anything," Pamela said. "Coincidences like that happen all the time."

"Is that the Vermont cheddar?" Bettina asked, suddenly changing the subject. "From the Co-Op?"

Pamela was chewing so she simply tipped her head.

"I haven't bought any for a while." Bettina studied the remaining bite of sandwich. "Is it still as good as it used to be?"

"Better, I'd say." Pamela's lips turned up in a teasing smile. She paused for a full minute, then she added, "Would you like a little piece?"

"Yes!" Bettina exclaimed. "But tiny."

Pamela speared the last bite of her sandwich and transferred it to her mouth. Still chewing, she rose and fetched from the refrigerator the wedge of cheddar she'd brought home that morning. She extracted it from its plastic bag and placed it on her wooden cutting board.

"Here you are," she said as she placed the offering before Bettina. She added a napkin and a knife and sat back down.

Bettina shaved off a small slice and began to

nibble on it. "I should tell Clayborn what we fig- ured out," she said, pausing in her nibbling, "about the connection between the tree-sweaters and the red X's. That somebody who's trying to protect the trees by hiding the red X's might have decided to go one step farther and kill Diefen- bach. And might be planning to go after the rest of the Arborists too."

Pamela frowned. "I'm not sure we should give Detective Clayborn a further reason to think a knitter might be responsible. We want to prove that Roland *didn't* do it—not link him even more firmly with the murder."

Bettina nodded and shaved off another slice of cheese, larger this time.

Pamela went on. "If we could point to a specific knitter though, a specific knitter that isn't Roland, it might be worth passing the information along to Detective Clayborn."

Bettina's hand, bearing the slice of cheese, paused halfway to her mouth. "How will we do that?" she asked, raising her carefully shaped brows.

"We'll see what we can find out in Timberley," Pamela said. "Shall I wrap the cheese up again?"

"I'm babysitting for the Arborville grandchil- dren Saturday morning." In the entry, Bettina tugged her coat on. "Otherwise I'd come to that tag sale with you."

County Road, at the bottom of Orchard Street, had been a busy thoroughfare since Colonial times, before Arborville was Arborville, connect- ing the farms of northern New Jersey with markets for their produce. Now it connected populous towns that blended one into the other. Timberley was the next town north of Arborville. It was a bit larger and offered more elegant shopping and dining possibilities than were to be found in Arborville's commercial district—including a yarn shop to which local knitters resorted when they were looking to spend more on the yarn for a sweater than a ready-made sweater, even from a fancy store at the mall, would cost. It was from the Timberley yarn shop that Pamela had bought Icelandic yarn from Icelandic sheep for the very sweater she was wearing.

The east-west streets of Arborville all dead-ended into County Road. The land on the other side was the nature preserve, owned by the county.

"You can't see the butterfly garden from County Road," Bettina said as they cruised past stands of trees, still bare except for a hint of delicate green where new leaves were beginning to unfurl. "You have to turn off at that little road that leads back into it. The butterfly garden doesn't look like much at this time of year anyway, I'm sure."

"Forsythia's coming out though," Pamela commented. "It's pretty along here. I'm glad the county's keeping this stretch undeveloped."

"Those signs left over from last fall's election don't add much." Bettina tipped her head toward the shoulder between the curb and the trees, where a row of cardboard posters much bedraggled after several months of rain and snow drooped from wooden stakes.

"Mostly Diefenbach's," Pamela observed. "He

certainly went in for the patriotic imagery." The posters' color scheme was red, white, and blue, with a large American flag valiantly waving behind the bold letters that spelled out "Bill Diefenbach—The Future Is Now!"

"You'd think the election committee would come around and collect the signs after the election," Bettina said. "It's just like littering at this point."

Pamela nodded in agreement, and their conversation turned to spring yard cleanup. Already landscapers' trucks had been appearing on Arborville's streets, with crews of men swarming here and there with rakes and leaf-blowers.

The yarn shop was one storefront in a row of charming shops along a block in Timberley's commercial district. A florist's window offered tulips and daffodils, and a fanciful miniature tree fashioned from pussy willow boughs and decorated with elaborately painted Easter eggs. A bakery's tempting fare included cakes decorated in soft pastels with flowers cleverly shaped from buttercream frosting. And a candy shop displayed a whole family of chocolate rabbits, as well as baskets of foil-wrapped eggs on beds of Easter grass, finely shredded cellophane in bright green.

Once inside the yarn shop, yarn met their eyes no matter where they looked. Shelves on every wall reached nearly to the ceiling, piled with skeins of yarn in colors and textures ranging from a rustic ply in natural cream to a delicate filament in deepest black—and every shade of the rainbow as well.

The stylish blonde woman behind the counter greeted Pamela and Bettina cordially. As they approached the counter, her eyes fastened particularly on Pamela.

"The yarn in your sweater looks familiar," she said with an approving smile. "Did you buy it here?"

"I certainly did," Pamela said with a smile of her own. She lifted the zip-lock bag with its colorful assortment of yarn samples from her purse and added, "I hope you'll recognize some of your other yarns." She unzipped the bag, pulled out a clump of the yarn samples, and set them on the glass of the counter.

"We're looking for a person"—Bettina stepped forward—"a person who might have bought some of this yarn from your shop. Maybe a regular customer? Someone you know?"

The blonde woman's smile didn't disappear, but her expression froze for a moment as if she was processing this curious request.

"I'm a reporter," Bettina said, "for the *Arborville Advocate.*"

Pamela wasn't sure how Bettina was going to link the quest to track down the purchaser of the yarns in the zip-lock bag with the responsibility of the *Advocate* to keep the residents of Arborville informed, but fortunately the blonde woman seemed to accept Bettina's self-identification as reason enough to lend her expertise to the task at hand.

She fingered the clump of yarn on the counter,

teased the strands—red, yellow, blue, pink, and two shades of green—apart, and looked up. "These are all just acrylic," she said. "The yarn could have come from any hobby store, or even the dollar store. We don't carry anything like this." She picked up the bag and pulled out the entire contents, spreading a colorful carpet of yarn tails over the glass counter top.

Pamela studied the assortment and began to cull the tails that were obviously acrylic. At the same time, the blonde woman picked out a few that were clearly finer quality. She held up a three-inch-long piece of mohair yarn in a rich umber shade.

"We've carried yarn like this," she said, "but I don't recall this color."

She held up another, a rugged ply in pale gray.

"This is that Icelandic yarn like you bought," she explained, glancing toward Pamela. "Also undyed. The sheep can be cream-colored, brown, or gray."

"Do you recall someone buying that yarn?" Bettina asked, her eyes widening slightly.

The woman shrugged and tightened her lips into a puzzled knot. "We sell a lot of it. I couldn't really point to any one particular knitter." She resumed fingering the yarn tails spread out before her. She picked up a another strand, mustard-yellow and thicker than the others. "A woman from Arborville bought ten skeins of this around Christmastime. I remember it because mustard isn't a color that everyone can wear, and it's quite an expensive brand."

The blonde woman herself clearly understood

what flattered. She had set off her pale hair and eyes with a sweater the delicate pink of cherry blossoms.

"Arborville?" Bettina's voice rose in pitch and her eyes got wider.

"I don't know her name," the blonde woman said as if anticipating Bettina's next question. "I haven't seen her since then, but for a while she came into the shop quite often. She always paid cash, so there wouldn't be a credit card record or anything like that." She focused her gaze on Pamela. "Maybe if you told me what you're actually trying to do, I could be more helpful."

"There's a group," Pamela said. "They display knitting in public places—unexpected things, like sweaters for trees. They've put sweaters on a whole bunch of trees in Arborville." She gestured toward the yarn tails strewn along the counter. "They leave bits of yarn hanging sometimes . . ."

"And you're trying to identify these knitters?" The woman's expression suggested she was pleased with her deduction.

"Why, yes," Pamela said, suddenly inspired to add, "Bettina is doing an article on them for the *Advocate*."

"I know about the group," the woman said. "The Yarnvaders, but I believe the members prefer to remain anonymous." Was there a teasing edge to her voice? As if she herself was one of them? Pamela wasn't sure. The blonde woman went on. "So I couldn't tell you, could I? Even if I knew who they were."

"No." Pamela started to gather up the yarn tails and tuck them back into the zip-lock bag. "You couldn't tell us."

Back in the car, Pamela and Bettina looked at each other and sighed. "Well," Bettina said, "we did our best. And we found out *something*. I wonder who this Arborville knitter is."

"Have you noticed anyone in town wearing a hand-knit mustard sweater?" Pamela asked, her tone suggesting the question was quite futile.

"Not really." Bettina turned the key in the ignition and the Toyota grumbled briefly and came to life. "Home then?"

"We're not through." Pamela's voice was lively again. "There are other yarn shops. We just won't tell them that we're trying to identify members of the secret knitting group."

"Okay." Bettina's customary cheer reasserted itself and she smiled. "Where to first?"

But visits to yarn shops in Meadowside and Newfield and beyond yielded nothing useful.

It was getting dark by the time Pamela and Bettina returned to Arborville. Back in her own house, Pamela fed the cats, checked her email, and started the pot roast that was to be her dinner.

Chapter 6

The next morning Pamela was hard at work in her office, untangling the convoluted syntax with which the author of "Confederate Motifs in Civil-War Era Quilt Design" had set forth her discoveries. She was puzzling over a sentence that ran on for nearly three-quarters of a page when a notice popped up at the bottom of her screen to tell her that she had a new email. Often she tried to ignore such notices, forging on with her editing and catching up on email only when she took breaks. But this email was from Bettina, and since Bettina lived right across the street, an email message from her signaled that something interesting or untoward had happened.

The message itself was brief, only two words: "Check AccessArborville."

Curiosity, plus the promise of a respite from the brain-numbing task she'd been engaged in, led Pamela to save her Word document, minimize it, bring up the Google page, and key "Access Arborville" into the search box. When the town listserv came up, a glance at the post headings that filled the screen made it clear Arborville was abuzz with the topic of Bill Diefenbach's murder.

Skimming even a few posts made Pamela feel slightly queasy. How could a pleasant town like Arborville contain people with such vitriol in their veins? And people who posted on AccessArborville couldn't even do so anonymously. If they could, heaven only knew what they would spew forth.

It was widely believed, by Diefenbach's supporters, that MacDonald's supporters were rejoicing at the news of Diefenbach's death—even if, the Diefenbach supporters admitted, the actual deed had been done by Roland DeCamp, who was not a MacDonald supporter.

Moreover, MacDonald's supporters were derided as tree-hugging know-nothings, pot-smoking hippies (probably introducing Arborville's youth to drugs at this very moment), and shiftless layabouts who expected the town to provide them with land on which to grow the food that made up their effete vegetarian diets—as well as the marijuana that addled their brains. If they ate red meat like real men they'd understand the benefits of Diefenbach's wish to sell off the Arborville community garden land to a developer for a mixed-use structure with sixty apartments and street-level commercial space.

A timid rebuttal by a MacDonald supporter was greeted with the taunt "Old MacDonald had a farm, E-I-E-I-O." That poster went on to remind readers of the listserv that during his tenure as mayor (which went on for way too long), MacDonald had been deaf to the complaints of Arborville residents who objected to the fact that someone in Arborville was raising chickens in his back yard.

"Diefenbach swore he'd put an end to that," another poster contributed.

"Live and let live," a MacDonald supporter countered. "After all, most of Arborville used to be farmland."

"Not anymore—and good riddance, tree-hugger!" was the response. "The future is now!"

A number of posters chimed in to echo that theme, as well as to ask MacDonald supporters how they would like to be awakened by a crowing rooster at six a.m. every day, even on weekends, and earlier in the summer.

"They crow at the break of dawn," one Diefenbach supporter explained helpfully.

Pamela sighed and closed her eyes. After ten minutes of exposure to the questionable thought processes of the people who spent their time communicating via AccessArborville, a return to the article on Civil-War era quilts would be a relief. She opened her eyes again to click on the X that would eradicate AccessArborville from her computer screen, then she responded to Bettina's email: "At least they're so caught up in insulting each other that they're leaving poor Roland alone." Soon she was back at work untangling the endless sentence.

Bettina popped in briefly at lunchtime to chat about AccessArborville and remind Pamela that she wouldn't be able to go to the tag sale at Cassie Griswold's house the next day because she had to babysit the Arborville grandchildren. "Stop in for coffee and crumb cake first," Pamela suggested. "The sale doesn't start till ten."

The offer of crumb cake supplied the pretext for a walk uptown, and the knowledge that Saturday would be devoted not to household chores but to the manifold delights of a tag-sale browse made Pamela resolve that after the walk she would dedicate herself to housecleaning and laundry.

Accordingly, at six p.m. she was bustling about her house, enjoying the mingled aromas of Pine-Sol and lemon oil, and tending to the final touches that made a house-cleaning session complete. In the dining room she settled the chairs, displaced for vacuuming, back into place around the table. In the living room she fluffed and rearranged the row of needlepoint pillows that decorated the sofa, making sure the needlepoint cat wasn't standing on its head.

Catrina and Ginger had warily returned after being driven upstairs by the vacuum cleaner, and Pamela knew they were waiting in the corner of the kitchen where their dinner regularly appeared. She was hurriedly straightening out the stacks of magazines on the coffee table so she could tend to them when she was distracted by the doorbell's chime.

It was nearly dark outside, so she switched on the porch light before reaching for the doorknob. Through the lace that curtained the oval window she could see that her caller was clearly not Bettina. The person illuminated by the porch light was tall, very tall—but familiar.

Richard Larkin greeted her with a dip of his shaggy blond head as the door swung back. "I'm not . . . um . . . disturbing you, I hope," he said in the voice that had struck her the first time she heard it as . . . a very nice voice, somehow in keeping with his bony face and strong nose.

"No, I'm—" Pamela stepped back to let him in but he remained standing on the porch, studying her in an intent way. For some reason, she suddenly needed to remind herself to breathe.

His stern features relaxed, and she realized he was looking past her. She glanced over her shoulder. Ginger had wandered into the entry, curious about the visitor or perhaps just wondering where her dinner was.

"You're doing okay? With your cat?" Pamela asked, tilting her head to meet his eyes, which had shifted back to her. The previous fall he had adopted one of Catrina's kittens.

"Um?" His eyes widened in puzzlement as if he'd been lost in thought and the question had caught him off guard.

"Your cat," Pamela said.

"Oh, yes. My cat." He smiled and his features relaxed again, but he didn't elaborate. He was studying the doormat now and seemed happy to remain on the porch, so Pamela stepped closer to the threshold, scouring her mind for a new topic of conversation.

But before she could speak, he raised his head and said, all in a rush, "There's a banquet, architects, the Saturday after Easter, in the city. They want to give me an award, and I was wondering— that is, if you're free—if you'd like to come." As he spoke, his eyes seemed imported from some whole other face, so ill did their vulnerable expression assort with his rugged features.

"Oh, I—" Pamela broke off, distracted by the commotion in her chest. Like a speeded-up film, a whole scenario played itself out in her brain in less time than it took to draw a breath. "I—" Now the doormat claimed her interest too, and she pondered the complicated knots that had shaped jute into a waffle-like grid.

"Thank you, but I just can't," she said at last, without looking up.

"Yes, I see. Yes." He turned, and was off.

The freshly ground coffee beans were waiting in the paper filter nestled into the filter cone atop the carafe, and the kettle was aboil, a slight wisp of steam already rising from its spout. On Pamela's kitchen table, a wedding china platter held a generous portion of Co-Op crumb cake, carefully sliced into squares. Small wedding china plates, one on either side of the kitchen table, sat ready to receive them. Cups and saucers accompanied the plates, as well as forks, spoons, and napkins. The cut-glass sugar bowl had been topped up and the matching cream pitcher filled with the heavy cream that Bettina doted on.

But when Bettina stepped into the kitchen, she scarcely glanced at the preparations for the morning's coffee ritual.

"I cannot believe the outrageous things people post on that listserv," she announced, her fearsome scowl engraving a deep line between her brows. The scarlet tendrils of her hair quivered with irritation.

"I know," Pamela said. "I checked it after I got

your email yesterday. The comments from those Diefenbach supporters were so annoying—and stupid—that I logged off after a few minutes." She gave Bettina's shoulder a comforting pat. "It's best to just ignore it."

"I can't," Bettina sighed, still scowling. "I have to keep up with it for my job. It's a way to keep track of what's going on in town, what the *Advocate* should be looking into." She sank heavily into her customary chair, as if defeated by the knowledge that Arborville harbored people capable of such hostility. She was dressed today for her babysitting duties, in a turquoise leggings and tunic ensemble set off by her bright red sneakers. Earrings fashioned from large glass beads, in the same bright red, dangled from her ears.

Pamela's attention was drawn to the stove by the frantic hooting of the kettle. For a moment the only sound was a faint trickle as the boiling water seeped through the ground beans and dripped into the carafe beneath. The process released the rich coffee fragrance and at once the cozy kitchen became even cozier.

"I didn't know about that rooster though," Bettina said, sounding more like herself, perhaps calmed by the impending coffee and crumb cake. "I'm surprised people weren't writing letters to the editor about it if they've been so bothered."

Pamela joined her at the table with the carafe and carefully filled the waiting cups with the steaming brew. As Bettina measured sugar into her cup and then added cream until the pale liquid in her cup barely hinted at its origin, Pamela eased squares of crumb cake onto the plates.

"The person with the chickens must be at the other end of town, up by where Roland lives or near the community gardens," Pamela said. "I've certainly never heard a rooster here on Orchard Street."

Bettina had forked off a bite of crumb cake and was raising it to her mouth. "And that's another thing." The hand holding the fork paused. "The community gardens! What nonsense to say that the people who use community garden plots are vegetarian layabouts who grow marijuana on them! The Boston children are vegetarians and they're hardly layabouts, and Marlene Pepper has had a community garden plot forever. She's . . . well, she's . . ."

"A pillar of the community," Pamela supplied.

"Yes!" Bettina nodded, setting the tendrils of her scarlet hair in motion again. "A pillar of the community."

Pamela tried a sip of her coffee and decided it was still too hot to drink. She separated a bite of crumb cake from the substantial portion on her plate and conveyed it to her mouth. The cake was light and toothsome, and the crumb topping buttery and sugary with a hint of cinnamon.

Bettina had now sampled her first bite as well. She hummed her appreciation and followed the bite with a swallow of coffee. "I think this crumb cake is my favorite thing the Co-Op bakery makes," she said as she carved a second forkful from the square on her plate.

For several minutes the two friends alternated between eating, sipping coffee, and chatting— mostly about the other offerings available at the

Co-Op bakery counter. Ginger had ambled in from the entry. She was sniffing at Bettina's jaunty sneaker and batting at the tails of the shoelaces. Bettina gave the cat a fond smile, then checked her watch. "Nine-thirty," she commented. "I'm not due at Maxie and Wilfred Jr.'s yet, but you've got a tag sale to get to."

Pamela laughed. "I don't have to be there the moment it starts," she said—though it was true that sometimes the best treasures got snapped up by the early birds. "Please have another piece of crumb cake, and there's plenty of coffee. I can warm the carafe up a bit."

Bettina served herself another portion of crumb cake and Pamela rose, transferred the carafe to the stove, and lit the burner under it. As she waited for the tiny bubbles that would signal the coffee was hot again, she remarked in an offhand way, "Richard Larkin invited me to an architecture thing, a banquet in the city."

Bettina's fork clattered against her plate and she was on her feet in an instant. "We'll go to the mall, this very afternoon!" Her eyes were bright with purpose. "You'll need the perfect dress, something glamorous but elegant. Maybe blue. Deep blue, a kind of indigo. And shoes to go with, of course. And you can wear those sparkly dangly earrings I gave you for Christmas. And depending on the dress we pick out, we can go through my evening bags. I'm sure I have something that will be . . . just . . . ." Her voice trailed off.

Pamela was aware that a frown had invaded her forehead.

"I know you don't like to think about clothes"—

Bettina sounded somewhat chastened—"but for an occasion like this . . ."

"I told him no," Pamela said in a small voice.

"You *what!*" Bettina's voice soared to a pitch more suited to a startled animal. Ginger looked up in alarm and scurried from the room.

"I told him no," Pamela repeated.

"Why on earth?" For the second time that morning, Bettina sank down into her chair looking defeated.

Pamela used an oven mitt to carry the carafe back to the table. Temporarily ignoring Bettina's question, she refilled both cups. Only after she had returned the carafe to the stove and settled back into her chair did she speak.

"It sounded like an important event," she said. "He's being given an award."

"And so therefore you . . ." Bettina looked like she was about to cry.

"People would think we were a couple," Pamela said. "It sounded like the sort of thing you'd want your nearest and dearest to share with you."

"Maybe *you* are his nearest and dearest." Now Bettina was regarding her with the same sympathetic expression Nell's face sometimes wore—like a patient mother explaining something to a wayward daughter. "You know he's interested in you. And at this point he knows you well enough that it's not just a mindless crush. And you know him."

Pamela sighed. "I like him." In her mind a little voice said, people don't get breathless and tongue-tied the way you did when he came to the door because they merely *like* someone. "I'm just not ready to be part of a couple again. You give things up."

"But you gain so much . . ."

"I know," Pamela said. "I look at you and Wilfred, and Nell and Harold, and sometimes I wish . . ." She stared at her coffee cup, surprised to see that it was full once again, so distracted had she been by the thought of Richard Larkin's invitation. What did she wish?

She wished she could relive that morning when Michael Paterson left for work never suspecting he wasn't to return that night. She wished she could call him back, could say, "Don't go, just this one day. They'll do okay without you." She and Michael had been so close, so much a part of each other. How could that ever be replaced?

Pamela looked back up. "Penny's coming home this Friday," she said brightly. "For spring break."

Bettina was already halfway across the porch when she turned. "There's going to be a memorial reception billed as 'Remembering Bill Diefenbach' tomorrow at two in St. Willibrod's church hall. I'm covering it for the paper—but you should come too. We might learn something useful."

Chapter 7

After the door closed behind Bettina, Pamela returned to the kitchen, where she tidied up the dishes and tucked the remains of the crumb cake into a zip-lock bag. Then she collected her jacket and her purse and set off up Orchard Street.

Midway to the corner, a bright spot on the sidewalk ahead caught her eye. When she reached it, she saw that it was a shiny dime. She stooped for it and slipped it into her pocket. Finding money on the ground meant good luck—though perhaps it was just Pamela's innate frugality that wouldn't let her leave a stray coin uncollected.

The organizers of the tag sale at Cassie Griswold's house had been very energetic in their advertising. In her four-block walk, Pamela passed several more flyers for the sale. They were affixed to trees and power poles, the kiosk where people waited for the bus, even the mail box at the corner of Cassie's street, and they were identical to the

one on the Co-Op bulletin board except for varia-
tions in the vivid paper they were printed on.

Pamela would have known which house she was
aiming for even without looking at the addresses,
because halfway down Cassie's block several cars
were lined up along the curb on each side of the
street. Clearly, many people had been attracted by
the prospect of treasures to be found in a house
that had been inhabited for nearly half a century
by a couple as well off as an Arborvillian could
want to be. Cassie's husband had died two years
previously. He had been a college professor who
crossed the Hudson every day to teach at an institution considerably older and more prestigious than
Wendelstaff College. Cassie, in the way of things for
women of her generation, hadn't sought to com-
pete with her husband's career, but had raised her
children and done volunteer work.

The house, like many in Arborville, resembled
Pamela's—a solid wood-frame house with clapboard siding, two stories plus an attic with little
dormer windows beneath a peaked roof, and a
wraparound porch. Six wooden steps led up to the
porch, and a printed notice on the door said,
"TAG SALE TODAY. COME IN."

Pamela stepped into a parquet-floored entry
rather like her own. Off to the left—instead of the
right, as in her house—was the living room. It was
still furnished with a sofa, armchairs, lamp tables
and a coffee table, each bearing a bit of masking
tape with a price written on it, but extra tables had
been set up. As best Pamela could tell, they bore
china and crystal—perhaps the "good" dishes and

glassware normally kept in a cupboard, as well as vases and figurines and curious carved objects that looked like souvenirs of travel to exotic places. But the room was so crowded, with people elbowing each other out of the way in their eagerness to inspect the items on display, that it was hard to see what was what.

Could you tell, Pamela always wondered when she visited a tag sale after the owners of the house were gone, whether the people who lived in the house had been happy? You could study the possessions they had amassed, and even guess at their routines—ample table linens suggested they had enjoyed the ceremony of holiday dinners, for example. But was there any way to know whether the people who traveled up and down those stairs or gathered around that dining room table had spoken cheerfully to each other or with barely concealed contempt?

"Welcome," said a pleasant, elderly woman as Pamela retreated back into the entry. The woman was jacketless and wore a belt with a zippered pouch, suggesting that she was not a shopper but rather one of the people running the event.

Pamela summoned her social smile. "Lots of goodies," she commented.

"*Lots*," the woman agreed. "And it all has to go—*soon*. Are you looking for anything in particular?"

"Not really," Pamela said, "but I can't resist a tag sale. And I just live a couple of blocks away."

"You must have known Cassie then," the woman said. "Such a shame, her dying. She just got weaker and weaker, and nobody could figure out what the problem was."

"Are you a friend?" Pamela asked. She'd noticed in her tag sale adventures that people often contracted with professionals to run their tag sales when the goal was to empty a house as fast as possible.

The woman nodded. "A very old friend." She glanced toward the doorway that Pamela knew, from the layout of her own house, led to the kitchen. "Haven's in there, Cassie's daughter. She's trying to do what she can but she's quite overwhelmed. And Cassie's son lives on the West Coast. He came out for the funeral but he had to get back for his work."

The woman was distracted then as one of the shoppers approached with a crystal wineglass in each hand, and Pamela wandered into the kitchen.

The kitchen table and counters were piled with items for sale—pots, pans, skillets, griddles, bowls, muffin tins and cookie sheets, utensils in jumbled heaps. In addition, several cupboard doors were open to reveal canned goods, bottles of vinegar and soy sauce, boxes of pasta and rice, bags of dried beans, and jars and jars of jam, the latter crowded onto a shelf that bore a sign reading NOT FOR SALE. But the room was empty of people except for a tall slender woman in her forties. Haven, Pamela surmised. She could have been Pamela's double with her straight dark hair, large dark eyes, and features that didn't need cosmetics to make them attractive.

An interesting blue-speckled pottery mixing bowl caught Pamela's attention. It was a smaller version of one she'd found in an antique shop at the Jersey Shore. But her eye was also drawn to the unusual pullover sweater Haven was wearing. It had been knit in a color-block effect. The front and what Pamela could see of the back were divided into large squares in contrasting colors— red, blue, yellow, and black, and each sleeve was a different color, one green and one orange.

"You must be a knitter!" Pamela exclaimed. She couldn't imagine how such a sweater could come into being if not as an original creation of its wearer.

Haven smiled and glanced down at the sweater. "I *did* make this sweater," she said. "People usually guess that." She looked back up. "Are you a knitter?"

Pamela nodded. She tugged back the two sides of her jacket to reveal the Icelandic-style sweater with the snowflakes that she'd put on again that morning.

"Nice!" Haven smiled again. Then she added, "There's yarn. Tons of it. Mom was a bit of a hoarder." Haven gestured around the room. Cassie had indeed acquired things in multiples. There were a least six muffin tins among the items on the counter, and open doors on cupboards below the counter revealed three more, as well as four crock pots and a stack of cast-iron griddles and skillets. "It made her good at her job, I guess," Haven added. "Her volunteer job. Mom was the town archivist for Arborville."

"I'm sorry that you lost your mother," Pamela said, feeling a twinge in her throat at the thought that she herself would lose her mother one day.

"Thank you." Fine lines that showed her age

had appeared as Haven's smile subsided. "She was a good mother."

"She liked jam." Pamela nodded toward the collection of jam in the upper cupboard.

The smile returned. "Actually most of those were a gift. It's apricot, home-made as you can see by the labels, and it was really more than she could use—especially because she sort of lost her appetite when she got sick. She was always trying to give it away, in fact."

Haven pointed toward a second door in the kitchen, not the one Pamela had entered. Based on the similarity of this house to hers, she suspected the dining room was beyond.

"The yarn's all out here," Haven said. "We're bringing stuff down from upstairs. I don't like to think of people pawing through my mom's drawers."

She led Pamela into what indeed was the dining room. Spread out on a grand table, with an elegant chandelier above, was enough yarn to stock a small yarn shop—whole skeins with the labels still on them, partial skeins, random balls of different sizes, in every color imaginable. And there were knitted creations too, sweaters, mittens, scarves, and socks. Several women were clustered at one end of the table examining the offerings and making piles of their selections.

"You found the yarn," said a voice from the living room. Pamela looked through the arch that, just as in her house, separated the living room from the dining room to see the elderly woman who had greeted her.

"Marjorie Ardmore," Haven explained. "Mom's old friend. Popped up to help out when Mom got sick and she's been in and out ever since." Haven gazed at the bustle of people intent on their treasure hunting. "She's been great though. I sure couldn't have handled clearing this place out on my own."

In the living room, Marjorie accepted a few bills from a woman holding a large crystal vase and tucked them into the zippered pouch at her waist. The next moment she had joined Pamela and Haven at the yarn table.

"Cassie was so talented," she commented, picking up a red and blue striped sock. "All these beautiful things she made." She put the sock down and regarded her hands, which were wrinkled but large and well-shaped. "I can't do anything useful along those lines. But put me in a kitchen at canning season with a bushel of fruit and I'm happy as a clam." She laughed.

Marjorie was a sturdy woman, and seemingly resigned to aging, with her unapologetically gray hair worn in a utilitarian pony tail, her sensible shoes, and her glasses on a chain around her neck.

"Hello!" called a voice from the kitchen door. "Is anybody in charge?"

They all turned to see a tall young man in a leather jacket holding a cast-iron griddle.

"Can I help you?" Marjorie asked. She took a few steps toward the young man. "Interested in a griddle? There's a much nicer one."

From the living room came another voice. "Can

I leave an offer for the coffee table? In case you don't sell it for what you're asking?"

Marjorie paused on her way to the kitchen. "Haven," she said. "Can you handle that, please?"

Then they were both gone, and Pamela turned her attention to the yarn spread out before her. She didn't really *need* yarn—and she herself knew that she was on the way to amassing a hoard that Penny would have to deal with some day—hopefully far in the future. But some of the yarn laid out before her was clearly very good quality, and some of it was—she picked up a small ball of pale aqua yarn—*familiar.*

One of the yarn tails that she and Bettina had clipped from the tree-sweaters had been just such aqua yarn—and she remembered the tree-sweater. It had been a particularly beautiful one, The various colors of yarn that formed the stripes seemed less random than in some of the other sweaters. The knitter had chosen shades of blue and yellow that played off against each other to make each band of color seem particularly intense. Some of the yellows had been rich shades that veered toward . . . *mustard.*

A skein of yarn beckoned from across the table and Pamela reached over and snatched it up, provoking a disapproving stare from a woman who had been just about to claim it for herself.

Pamela summoned her social smile. "You saw it first," she said. "I'll give it back. I just want to check something." The woman acknowledged the words with a scowl.

The yarn was heavy, suitable for a rugged garment, like the mustard-colored yarn tail the woman at the yarn shop had recognized. The skein still wore the paper band that identified it as "the wool that has kept Shetland Islanders warm for centuries . . . only the best from specially bred sheep."

Pamela handed the skein of yarn back, and noticed that the woman had already collected several skeins of the same yarn. Most still wore their paper bands, suggesting that the project for which the yarn was purchased had never come to fruition.

The woman accepted the skein, added it to her collection, and looked up with another scowl. Mustard isn't a color that everyone can wear, Pamela reflected, but she kept the thought to herself.

She scanned the table. So much yarn, but clearly some of the trove that Cassie had accumulated over the decades had already been claimed—by at least one of the people who had been so busy knitting the sweaters intended to protect the trees of Arborville from the axe.

Pamela resisted the urge to add more yarn to the stockpile that already occupied several plastic bins in her attic. Instead, she returned to the kitchen. A few shoppers had drifted into the kitchen as well and were browsing among the items piled on the counter. Pamela focused her attention on the table instead, where the blue-speckled pottery mixing bowl she'd noticed earlier still sat. She picked it up, enjoying its solid heft, and turned it over. The letters USA had been pressed into the clay before the bowl was fired, as well as a word that started with the letter "E" but was otherwise illegible.

Happy with her find, and happy that she had a reason to talk to Marjorie again, she stepped back into the entry. Marjorie was busy adding up prices for a large pile of goodies a middle-aged man had accumulated, including a carved wooden hippo and a gold-framed painting of a sailing ship. "Twenty-seven dollars total," she announced, accepted the money and tucked it into the zippered pouch, and then turned to Pamela.

"It looks like you found something," she said approvingly, then added, "Not interested in the yarn?"

"I have so much already," Pamela said. "Not as much as Cassie had, but . . ." She let the words trail off, and Marjorie supplied just the response she was hoping for.

"Oh, there was more." She gestured as if to suggest an expanding mass. "Haven carried bags and bags of it away a few weeks ago. Cassie knew she was dying and that the house would have to be cleared out so it could be sold."

"Some of the yarn looks familiar," Pamela said. "Like Cassie's yarn could have been used to make those sweaters that somebody's putting on the trees."

Marjorie laughed. "Haven's definitely one of those tree-huggers, or whatever they call them. I don't know if she's putting the sweaters on them but she sure goes on about how she disapproves of cutting them down just to protect the power wires. If anything should come down, she says, it should be the power wires."

"Oh, my!" Pamela said it more to herself, but Marjorie overheard.

"Oh, my is right," she said. "I like my electric lights." A few more shoppers bearing their finds were milling about in the entry, as if eager to settle up and be on their respective ways. "Five dollars," Marjorie announced, nodding toward the blue-speckled bowl.

Pamela was dipping into her purse for her wallet when the front door opened and a man and a woman stepped in. The woman was carrying a folded note. Before Marjorie could greet them, the woman handed her the note. "Somebody outside saw us coming to the sale and said to give you this," she explained.

Marjorie unfolded the note and settled her glasses on her nose. As she read the note, she frowned. Then she laughed.

"Well, who ever heard of such a thing?" she said, holding the note up.

Handwritten in bold letters were these words: "Your tag sale signs are all over town. They are an EYESORE and they had better be gone the minute your tag sale is over. P.S. I KNOW WHERE YOU LIVE."

Cradling the blue-speckled pottery bowl in both hands, Pamela set out for home. Halfway down Orchard Street she noticed Wilfred's ancient but lovingly cared-for Mercedes turning into the Frasers' driveway. The spot usually occupied by Bettina's Toyota was empty—she'd said that her babysitting duties were likely to stretch into the afternoon.

Wilfred caught sight of Pamela as he climbed

out of his car. He waved and darted around the car to open the passenger door, whereupon Woofus sprang onto the asphalt. The shaggy creature stuck close to Wilfred as Wilfred backtracked to open the trunk. By this time Pamela was near her own house, but she crossed the street to greet Wilfred. Woofus looked up apprehensively as she approached, but Wilfred gave him a comforting pat on the head and murmured, "You know Pamela."

"It looks like you've been shopping," Wilfred said with a genial smile.

"A tag-sale treasure." Pamela held up the bowl. "I have another just like it but bigger." Wilfred lifted a large shopping bag from the trunk and she added, "You've been shopping too."

Wilfred held up the bag. "The main ingredient of our Easter feast—a hand-cured ham from Long Hill Farm, way out in Carringtown. Bettina said Penny would be home for spring break, and you'll both join us, of course."

"We'd love to," Pamela said. "What shall I bring?"

"I'll consult with the boss about the Easter menu." Wilfred raised the bag higher as Woofus began sniffing at it eagerly. "Long Hill Farms makes sausages too," he explained, "and they looked too good to pass up. That's what he smells." Wilfred gave the dog another pat and said, "You'll get your treat too." He slammed the trunk closed and Pamela turned to go.

At home, Pamela set the blue-speckled bowl on the kitchen counter to admire for a few days be-

fore she shelved it with its bigger mate. Stepping
over cats, she returned to the porch to retrieve her
mail, which consisted of nothing but catalogues
and a sheet of free address labels featuring flowers.

The talk of hams and sausages had made her realize it had been quite a while since she'd eaten,
and crumb cake and coffee don't keep one going
very long in any event. Back in the kitchen, she
scrambled a few eggs and mixed in a bit of grated
Swiss when they were nearly done. She ate them
with a piece of toasted whole-grain bread.

Her house was clean and she was caught up on
her work for *Fiber Craft*. She checked her email
and found only a message from Penny. The message
would be brief, Penny said, because she was busy
with a demanding report that had to be turned in
before she left for spring break. But she'd arranged
a ride to Arborville with her friend Kyle Logan and
unless plans changed she'd arrive a bit after noon
on Friday.

Pamela responded with the news that they were
invited to Easter dinner at Bettina and Wilfred's to
feast on a hand-cured ham that Wilfred had just
bought. Then she happily settled onto the sofa for
a few hours of knitting.

It was the first she'd worked on the lilac tunic
since Tuesday night, when the Knit and Nibble
meeting had been disrupted by the police showing
up to arrest Roland. Now she pondered the swath
of knitting dangling from her needle. It was a
sleeve, the second sleeve, and the only piece of the
project that remained to be finished. Then Pamela
would sew the pieces together and the tunic would

be ready for Penny when she arrived the following Friday.

The tunic's lacy effect resembled filigreed shells with eyelets, and required careful counting of stitches. Where in the complex pattern had she left off? She'd been so rattled by the events of that evening that she'd simply stared at her project for a bit and then tucked it away in her knitting bag.

She studied the directions in the knitting book, turned her attention back to the nearly finished sleeve that lay in her lap, then frowned as she studied the directions again. So puzzled was she that she was relieved when the ringing phone gave her an excuse to set the knitting aside and climb to her feet.

"It's me," Bettina's cheerful voice announced as Pamela put the phone to her ear. "I'd have crossed the street to visit but I'm worn out from chasing those little boys around all day. How was the tag sale?"

"I have many things to tell you," Pamela responded. "I know who bought that mustard yarn, and I'm almost positive I know who's been putting those sweaters on the trees—one of the people anyway."

"Tell me in person," Bettina said. "Come for dinner. Wilfred is cooking his Long Hill Farm sausages with apples and onions tonight."

"Shall I make deviled eggs?" Pamela asked.

"Wait till next week." Bettina laughed. "The Arborville grandchildren have a big egg-dying project planned, and I'm sure we'll end up with many more hard-boiled eggs than anyone will want to eat."

Pamela returned to her knitting project, and after she pondered a bit more her needles were clicking smoothly through the motions that produced the delicate lilac lace.

Chapter 8

On the Frasers' kitchen counter, a piece of white butcher paper had been unfurled to reveal six plump pink sausages. Wilfred was working busily nearby, his bib overalls protected by an apron. The fact that Woofus was watching serenely from his favorite corner suggested that he'd been given his promised treat and was content.

"Have a glass of wine?" Bettina asked as she led Pamela toward the scrubbed pine table that furnished the eating area of the kitchen. "Or would you prefer hard cider? Wilfred needed some for his recipe and we chilled the rest." Bettina was still wearing the turquoise tunic and leggings outfit she'd started the day in, but on her feet were furry slippers.

"I'll have wine," Pamela said, picking up an empty wine glass from the table. She recognized the glass, with its faint purple tint and elaborately twisted stem, as one of a hand-blown set Bettina had found at a craft shop. "How were the boys?"

"Exhausting," Bettina sighed. "But they're such little dears and Wilfred and I are lucky to have them so close." She looked down at the slippers. "I put my feet up and napped for a bit after I talked to you, and I'm quite myself again."

Bettina headed for the refrigerator and Pamela stepped up to the high counter that separated the cooking area of the Frasers' spacious kitchen from the eating area. Bettina fetched the wine and poured a few inches' worth into Pamela's glass.

A sizzling sound and a tantalizing aroma drew Pamela's attention to the stove, where a generous amount of butter was frothing in a large stainless steel frying pan. Wilfred was slicing an apple on a cutting board. Also on the cutting board was a small pile of sliced onions, and a bouquet of fresh sage sat nearby.

Bettina retrieved her own wine from the table and joined Pamela to watch as Wilfred poked each sausage with a fork to guard against bursting, then arranged the sausages in the pan. The sizzle immediately became more intense, and a moment later the aroma of frying pork replaced that of butter. "Well begun is half done," Wilfred observed with a satisfied nod.

"So"—Bettina raised her glass as if offering Pamela a toast—"you said you have things to tell me. Spill!"

"I think Cassie's daughter Haven is our suspect," Pamela said.

"Really?" Bettina's brightly painted lips stretched into a smile and her eyes grew wide.

Pamela nodded. "Cassie was a devoted knitter. There was tons of yarn at the sale—leftovers from projects, but also unused yarn bought for projects that never happened. Haven is a knitter too, and according to the woman running the sale—an old friend of Cassie's named Marjorie—Haven had carted away bags and bags of it a few weeks ago."

The sizzle modulated into a high, steady hum as Wilfred prodded the browning sausages with a long fork, rolling them from side to side. "Strike while the iron is hot," he murmured, then lifted the cutting board and used the fork to guide the chopped onion and apple into the frying pan. There was a dramatic whoosh as they made contact with the pan's sizzling contents, but as they settled around the sausages and began to gently fry the sounds muted.

Bettina's smile had vanished as Pamela spoke. "Lots of people are knitters," she said at last, after Wilfred had covered the frying pan and there was, for the moment, nothing to watch. "And lots of people stockpile yarn," she went on. "I don't see why—"

Pamela held up a finger. "The mustard yarn. Remember, we clipped a bit of mustard yarn from one of the tree-sweaters. The woman at the yarn shop said it wasn't a common sort of yarn, but the shop had carried some and a woman from Arborville had bought it." The expression on Bettina's face grew hopeful again. "That woman must have been Cassie. There were skeins and skeins of it at the sale. Apparently Cassie never got around to making whatever she had in mind."

Bettina laughed. "Or she thought better of the idea. Mustard *really* isn't a color that everyone can wear."

"Haven had already carried some off and used it for a tree-sweater, but there was still a lot at the sale."

Bettina nodded. "Haven is a knitter and the mustard yarn isn't a common sort of yarn, but Haven had access to it and it was used in one of the tree-sweaters."

Pamela nodded in return. "So that links Haven to the tree-sweaters—and I recognized at least one other kind of yarn from the tree-sweaters too—pale aqua." She paused. "And here's what clinches it! Marjorie said Haven really disapproves of the town cutting down those trees."

At the stove, something else exciting was starting to happen. Wilfred had set a heavy cast-iron griddle on the stove's other front burner and he was stirring up something in a large stainless-steel mixing bowl.

"Potato pancakes, dear ladies," Wilfred explained, tipping the bowl to show grated potatoes bound together with egg and milk. "I'm warming up my collard greens"—he nodded toward a small saucepan on a back burner—"and when the potato pancakes are nearly done, the cider and sage go onto the sausages, and"—he paused to drizzle oil onto the griddle—"we eat in ten minutes."

"Shall I bring the plates in here?" Bettina asked.

"Why not?" Wilfred turned from the stove, his cheeks all the more ruddy from the heat of cooking. "We don't have to stand on ceremony. After all, we're family."

"I'll put the salad on the table though," Bettina said. She stepped around the high counter, opened the refrigerator, and took out a wooden salad bowl in which cherry tomatoes offered a bright contrast to delicate mesclun lettuce and chopped cucumber. Then she waited as Wilfred dressed the salad with a swirl of olive oil, a splash of balsamic vinegar, a sprinkle of salt, and a few grindings of pepper. He finished by giving it a toss with a large spoon and fork carved of smooth wood. Bettina seized the bowl up again and proceeded toward the doorway that led to the dining room, Pamela following.

Bettina had been a willing but uninspired cook for most of her married life. When Wilfred retired, he'd happily assumed most cooking chores. But Bettina had always enjoyed setting her table with the interesting hand-crafted dishes and table linens she collected.

In the dining room, the table was already set with Bettina's sage-green pottery plates, maroon linen napkins tucked at their sides along with knives, forks, and spoons. Under the plates were colorful placemats, rustic plaid woven from shades of maroon, rust, and cream. Fresh wine glasses had been provided, crystal, with a Scandinavian flair. The sleek minimalist lines of the muted silver candleholders suggested Scandinavian influence as well, as did the silver wine coaster.

Bettina set the salad in the middle of the table

and took matches from a drawer in the sideboard to light the candles. Then she picked up two plates, Pamela picked up the third, and they headed back to the kitchen.

While they were gone, Wilfred had spooned six portions of his potato pancake batter onto the cast-iron griddle, where the low heaps of shredded potato, pale against the dark surface of the griddle, steamed and sizzled. He was watching them carefully, spatula in hand. Pamela and Bettina lined up the plates on the high counter and picked up their wine glasses, now nearly empty.

After a few minutes, the potato shreds at the edges of the potato pancakes began to brown and the tops began to look less glossy. Wielding his spatula, Wilfred lifted up the side of a pancake and bent to peer underneath. "Yes," he whispered, and expertly flipped the pancake.

He went to work flipping the other five, and soon six tawny, plump pancakes steamed on the griddle as their undersides cooked.

Wilfred lowered the flame under the griddle, turned his attention to the frying pan, and removed the lid. A cider bottle stood ready on the counter, along with sage leaves, which he'd removed from their stems and chopped. He picked the cider bottle up and sloshed a good amount of cider over the sausages and the onions and apples, now caramelized to an appealing toasty gold. An impressive cloud of vapor, fragrant with apple and onion, rose as the cider made contact with the hot frying pan. He added a large pinch of chopped sage, and then another, and replaced the frying pan's cover.

"Nearly ready," he murmured to himself, teasing a potato pancake with his spatula. He lifted the lid on the small saucepan, peeked inside, and set the spatula aside in favor of a spoon, with which he gave the saucepan's contents a quick stir.

He stepped away from the stove to open the refrigerator and take out a fresh bottle of wine. "Dear wife," he said, turning to Bettina, "will you do the honors?"

"Please let me!" Pamela reached for the wine. "I have to do *something*."

"There's a corkscrew in the top drawer of the sideboard," Bettina called as Pamela headed for the dining room bearing the chilly bottle of wine.

When she returned, the collards waited in an oval bowl on the high counter, their rich green all the deeper against the paler green bowl. Wilfred was standing at the stove holding one of the sage-green plates. The cover was off the frying pan. The contents, the browned and gleaming sausages surrounded by the supple golden slices of apple and onion dotted with chopped sage leaves, simmered and steamed.

"One sausage or two, Pamela?" Wilfred asked as he brandished a large spoon.

"Just one," Pamela said, then—transfixed by the appearance and aroma of the sausage dish—she added, "at least to start."

Wilfred nodded. He remarked, "Out of the frying pan," and scooped up a sausage. He deposited it on the plate he held, and added a heaping spoonful of sage-flecked apple and onion.

"And how many potato pancakes?" He turned toward Pamela.

"Two," Pamela said. "I can't resist."

In a moment the plate, with two of the tawny potato pancakes nestled close to the sausage and its fragrant garnish, sat on the high counter. Bettina added a serving of collards as Wilfred prepared another plate.

Soon the three of them—Wilfred still wearing his apron—had taken their places at Bettina's carefully set table, and fresh glasses of wine had been poured. It was dark outside and the room was dim, except for the flickering candles. They cast a halo of light around the table that made the meal seem an intimate ritual.

"To family and friends." Wilfred raised his glass.

"Family and friends," Bettina echoed, raising her glass. "Especially friends, tonight."

Pamela joined the toast, feeling her throat tighten. How wonderful to have Bettina and Wilfred in her life.

After the toast there was silence for several minutes—or rather, words proved insufficient to do justice to Wilfred's meal. In their place were sighs of pleasure and hums of contentment. The caramelized apple and onion, slightly sweet with a dusky hint of sage, set off the garlicky sausage, and the bitter collards balanced the sausages' richness.

After sampling the sausage and its garnish, and the collards, Pamela lifted a bite of potato pancake to her mouth. Its crisp simplicity provided a perfect foil to the other dishes.

"Haven's going to be at that tag sale again tomorrow," Pamela said suddenly, looking past the candle flame at Bettina on the other side of the table. "I just remembered." Now that her hunger was on its way to being satisfied, her thoughts had drifted to her adventure of that morning.

Bettina paused in cutting off a bit of sausage and raised her head. "So we go ask her if she killed Bill Diefenbach?"

"Nothing ventured, nothing gained," Wilfred contributed from his spot at the head of the table.

"Maybe we won't be that direct." Pamela laughed. "But we can have a little chat . . . about what she might have been up to last Monday night. You're good at getting people to talk."

Bettina nodded. "Haven does sound like our best suspect so far. Besides, I'm curious to meet her. Even if she only made *some* of those tree-sweaters, it's still quite a feat of knitting."

She resumed eating. But Pamela's thoughts remained on the tag sale. "Wilfred?" she asked. "Did you know Cassie Griswold?"

"Um?" Wilfred left off scooping a forkful of collards toward the stub that remained from his first sausage.

"She was the town archivist, and you're in the historical society," Pamela explained.

"I knew of her," Wilfred said. "But the town archives have existed much longer than the historical society. More than a century, I'm sure, and it was always a casual thing—somebody with the collecting gene, filling boxes and filing cabinets with newspaper clippings and souvenirs of town events. Then when that somebody can't do it any more, the boxes and files get passed along to somebody else."

As they nibbled on the cookies and sipped their coffee, they chatted about Bettina's adventures with her grandsons and what news the Frasers had had recently from the "Boston children," as Bettina called her other son, Warren, and his wife Greta. Their only child, a little girl named Morgan, had been born the previous fall—though being Boston academics and very modern, they had banned baby gifts that alluded to Morgan's gender, like dolls or anything pink.

"As soon as we learned the baby was to be a girl," Bettina lamented, "Wilfred started picturing the splendid dollhouse he would build her, but now . . ." Her voice trailed off mournfully.

Pamela had heard this lament many times before, but she offered a little moan of sympathy. "Perhaps something less girly," she suggested, "like a . . . a . . . theater, for puppets."

Bettina shook her head and her bright red earrings bobbed to and fro. "I'd hate for him to be disappointed, if they decided . . ." She sighed. "I was so excited about the pink granny-square afghan, and I'd made so many squares, and then . . ." She reached for another cookie and began to look more cheerful up as she bit into the sweet treat.

The pink granny-square afghan had ultimately been handed over to Nell as an offering for the Haversack women's shelter, one of her do-good projects, but Bettina still mourned the fact that it hadn't swaddled her new granddaughter.

"I wanted to send her something for Easter, like a plush bunny," Bettina went on, "but then I thought . . . is a plush bunny just a girly thing?"

the tin of ground coffee from the cupboard and arranged a paper filter in the plastic cone that fit Bettina's carafe. As she was reaching three of Bettina's sage-green mugs from the cupboard where Bettina kept her special pottery, Wilfred entered.

Whistling mysteriously to himself, he continued on to the utility room, emerging moments later bearing a platter covered in plastic wrap. Through the plastic, cookies were visible—flat round sugar cookies with dabs of deep red jam filling small depressions at their centers.

"Thumbprint cookies," Wilfred announced, his ruddy face gleaming with delight. He peeled off the plastic wrap and stood by while Pamela scooped coffee into the paper filter and waited for the water to boil. When steam began to drift from the kettle's spout, she tipped the kettle over the plastic cone and the seductive aroma of brewing coffee signaled that the boiling water was doing its work.

In a few moments, the coffee was ready. Pamela filled the three mugs and arranged them on a tray, along with cream and sugar. Then with Wilfred leading, bearing the platter of cookies before him, the two returned to the dining room.

"Oh, my goodness!" Bettina squealed when she caught sight of the cookies. She raised her eyes to focus on Wilfred's face. "I thought I smelled something yummy when I came in from babysitting. You sneaky, sneaky person!"

"Sweets to the sweet," Wilfred responded with a fond smile. He set the platter of cookies in the middle of the table. Pamela set the tray next to it and handed the coffee around.

As they nibbled on the cookies and sipped their coffee, they chatted about Bettina's adventures with her grandsons and what news the Frasers had had recently from the "Boston children," as Bettina called her other son, Warren, and his wife Greta. Their only child, a little girl named Morgan, had been born the previous fall—though being Boston academics and very modern, they had banned baby gifts that alluded to Morgan's gender, like dolls or anything pink.

"As soon as we learned the baby was to be a girl," Bettina lamented, "Wilfred started picturing the splendid dollhouse he would build her, but now . . ." Her voice trailed off mournfully.

Pamela had heard this lament many times before, but she offered a little moan of sympathy. "Perhaps something less girly," she suggested, "like a . . . a . . . theater, for puppets."

Bettina shook her head and her bright red earrings bobbed to and fro. "I'd hate for him to be disappointed, if they decided . . ." She sighed. "I was so excited about the pink granny-square afghan, and I'd made so many squares, and then . . ." She reached for another cookie and began to look more cheerful up as she bit into the sweet treat.

The pink granny-square afghan had ultimately been handed over to Nan as an offering for the Haversack women's shelter, one of her do-good projects, but Bettina still mourned the fact that it hadn't swaddled her new granddaughter.

"I wanted to send her something for Easter, like a plush bunny," Bettina went on, "but then I thought . . . is a plush bunny just a girly thing?"

"I had a plush bunny when I was a boy," Wilfred said. "I called him my E-bun. I still remember how cuddly he was."

The conversation turned to plans for Easter dinner, with the splendid Long Hill Farms ham as its centerpiece. "Based on their sausages," Pamela said, "I can't wait for Easter to come. And you must let me know what I can bring." Various ideas for side dishes were considered, with asparagus voted a definite yes.

"But you should make the dessert, Pamela," Bettina concluded. "Wilfred"—she reached over and squeezed his hand—"is an amazing baker, but he'll be busy with the ham and other things."

"Agreed." Pamela nodded.

Wilfred rose. "I'm off to my kitchen duties," he announced. "But you, dear ladies, needn't stir." He disappeared through the doorway that led to the kitchen.

Bettina leaned forward, as if to see Pamela more clearly in the flickering candlelight. Suspecting that she had something other than desserts on her mind, Pamela studied her friend's face. Its expression—a narrowing of the eyes, a tightening of the lips—mixed determination with concern. Pamela held her breath. Something was coming.

"Have you given any more thought to Richard's invitation?" Bettina asked at last.

"Why should I give it more thought?" Pamela felt her forehead crease in a frown and was grateful for the candlelight. "I told him no."

"I'm sure he'd accept a change of mind. You could just say he caught you by surprise, and you've had a chance now to look at your calendar—"

"Bettina!" Immediately sorry she'd interrupted, Pamela sighed and struggled to modulate her tone. "As if I have such a busy social life," she began, then sighed again.

"He'll find someone else," came a tiny voice from across the table, "and then you'll be sorry."

"Lemon-yogurt layer cake," Pamela said suddenly. "I'll make lemon-yogurt layer cake with cream cheese icing. So that settles that." She stood up. "And now I'll go home."

Before heading to the door, Pamela detoured into the kitchen, where Wilfred was standing at the counter rinsing dishes and slotting them into the dishwasher racks.

"That was a delicious meal," she said to his back. "Thank you so much."

He turned and winked. "Don't let the boss lady get you down," he whispered. "She has your best interests at heart." Pamela shrugged and mustered a smile.

When she returned to dining room, Bettina was gone. But Bettina met her halfway through the living room, carrying Pamela's jacket. "I can't let you go without a hug," she murmured, setting the jacket on the sofa and reaching out to enfold Pamela in her arms. "I didn't mean to upset you." Bettina was no taller than Penny, and she laid her head against Pamela's breast as if she was the one being comforted.

"Tag sale tomorrow?" Bettina said brightly as she stepped back from the hug.

Pamela nodded. Irritated as she'd been by the conversation about Richard, she was eager to find out if Haven had an alibi for the night Bill Diefenbach was killed. "Ten a.m.?" she asked.

"We can walk," Bettina said. "I know you like that." The offer seemed another attempt to make peace. "And if Haven continues to be as suspicious as she seems, I'll tip Clayborn off."

Chapter 9

Marjorie Ardmore greeted Pamela and Bettina with a hearty "Welcome!" as they stepped over the threshold of Cassie Griswold's house. She glanced first at Bettina, who made a striking figure with her scarlet hair, pumpkin-colored down coat, and jaunty cashmere scarf in shades of violet and fuchsia. Then she recognized Pamela and chuckled. "Back for more treasures?" she asked.

"I can't resist a tag sale," Pamela responded, "and I've brought my neighbor."

"Bettina Fraser," Bettina said, offering her hand. "I didn't know Cassie well, but I heard she'd been ill. Such a shame."

Pamela's gaze strayed toward the living room. The stock of vases, figurines, and travel souvenirs seemed sparser than it had been the previous day, but plenty of china and crystal remained. The crowd was sparser too—but perhaps people were at church. A solitary man was fingering a small brass Buddha and a young couple were murmuring over a delicate set of champagne flutes. There was no sign of Haven. Yesterday she'd been in the kitchen though, leaving it to Marjorie to handle most details of the sale.

The front door opened, bringing in a chilly gust of wind and a group of three middle-aged women. Marjorie turned away from Bettina and Pamela to welcome the newcomers, and Pamela rested a hand on Bettina's arm, pointed toward the doorway that led to the kitchen, and stepped across the entry's parquet, as worn as that in her own house. Bettina followed.

Haven was sitting at the kitchen table, wearing the same unusual sweater she'd worn the previous day, with its bright blocks of color and mismatched sleeves. She greeted Pamela with a smile of recognition. "The knitter," she said. "Have you decided you really *do* need some of my mom's yarn?"

As was often the case when she and Bettina embarked on one of their sleuthing expeditions, Pamela was asking herself why on earth they hadn't planned a strategy for learning what they wanted to know before setting out. They couldn't, after all, just come out and ask Haven if she killed Bill Diefenbach—as they'd realized at dinner the previous night. But in answer to Haven's question, she said, "I'm very well supplied. But I've brought my friend Bettina. She's a knitter too."

"Yes, indeed I am," Bettina said, with a burst of energy that Pamela found encouraging, suggesting as it did that Bettina was hatching a strategy. "And we're both—did Pamela tell you?—in a local knitting group, Knit and Nibble."

"There's loads more yarn!" Haven jumped up from the table. "Right out here in the dining room." She led the way, and in a moment they were standing before the grand table heaped with nearly as much yarn and nearly as many knitted creations as had been there the previous day.

Bettina picked up a skein of pale green yarn, then one of maroon, fingering them thoughtfully before returning them to the hoard. "Yes," she murmured, as if talking to herself, "we're all quite committed to the craft, but we've certainly never done anything as ambitious as dressing Arborville's trees in sweaters."

Pamela glanced quickly at Haven's face. She thought she saw a subtle rearrangement in Haven's expression, as if in an effort to substitute pleasant interest for something more intense.

"I'd love to talk to whoever's doing it," Bettina went on, now looking at Haven and speaking louder. "It has to be a *them*, doesn't it, with so many sweaters all over town."

"Bettina is a reporter for the *Arborville Advocate*," Pamela contributed.

"Oh, my goodness!" Bettina picked up a partial ball of bright orange yarn, and another of yellow. "These are exactly the colors in the sweater on the tree in front of my house."

Pamela knew very well that there was no sweater on the tree in front of Bettina's house. In fact, none of Bettina's trees were on the strip of land between the sidewalk and the street, so none had been targeted by the Arborists. But Bettina was off and running. She seized another ball of yarn, deep purple. "And this color too!" she exclaimed.

She looked at Haven again. Then, in a wondering tone that implied a sudden and startling realization, she added, "Whoever's making those sweaters must have had access to Cassie's yarn supply!"

Haven had taken a step backward, and looked as if she was fighting off whatever emotion had twisted her mouth and furrowed her brow. "There's lots of purple yarn in the world," she managed to say at last.

"Oh"—Bettina laughed, then reached out and grabbed Haven's arm—"you're just being modest. *You're* the artist, or one of them, who's responsible for this wonderful project. You're busy now, with the sale, but when can I interview you for the *Advocate?*"

"You can't . . . because, no . . . I'm really not that person, or one of them. *Really.*" Haven took another step backward.

"I know when that sweater appeared on my tree," Bettina said, with a teasing smile. "Last Monday night between eight-thirty and nine-thirty. Because at eight-thirty my husband took the garbage out and the sweater *wasn't* there. He'd have noticed, I'm sure, and said something. And at nine-thirty I took our dog out for a walk, and the sweater *was* there."

"Well, I don't even live in Arborville, so how could I have had anything to do with it?" Haven had recovered from her surprise, and signaled her self-possession by crossing her arms over her chest, which created an interesting effect with the mismatched sweater sleeves. "On Monday night I was at home in Manhattan, on deadline for a writing job. I'm a freelance writer." Her arms remained crossed over her chest. "And my husband was at his studio in Brooklyn. So I was there all alone and you'll just have to believe me. Anyway, what difference does it make? Putting sweaters on trees isn't a crime."

But as she finished speaking, her eyes widened as if a thought had just occurred to her. "You're a reporter for the *Advocate*? That's the pathetic little throwaway that people leave lying around in their driveways. I'm surprised the person who wrote the note about the tag-sale signs hasn't complained about what an eyesore *it* is."

Bettina straightened her back and lifted her chin. "The *Advocate* performs a valuable service by keeping the residents of Arborville informed about local events. Most people in town appreciate it."

Haven's eyes grew wider still and she stared at Bettina. "Bettina isn't the most common name in the world. You're the person who interviews that cop, Claymore or whatever his name is, for the *Advocate*." Haven laughed in a way that was more like a smirk. "Okay, I read the *Advocate* sometimes. My mom used to bring it in."

Then she frowned. "Wait a minute—that Diefenbaugh or whatever *his* name is was killed between eight-thirty and nine-thirty last Monday night."

Pamela heard herself murmur, "Nine p.m."

But Haven didn't hear, or didn't react. She went on, her voice rising in pitch, as if the questions she was asking were unimaginably ludicrous. "So—what? You're starting to believe that you're a cop too? And you're thinking—for whatever crazy reason—that I killed Diefenbaugh and trying to find out if I have an alibi?"

"Roland DeCamp, who's been accused of Diefenbach's murder, is a close friend of ours," Pamela said. "You were putting sweaters on the trees that Diefenbach wanted to cut down."

"I wasn't putting sweaters on trees."

Bettina picked up the ball of deep purple yarn again, and the bright orange and the yellow. Pamela and Bettina were both silent then, looking attentively at Haven. Pamela's daughter Penny had been a most cooperative child, especially after her father died, as if unwilling to cause her mother any more heartache. But in raising any child, even a cooperative child, most parents learn how usefully the silent stare can elicit information.

A few women had drifted through the arch that separated the dining room from the living room and were sorting through the pile of knitted objects that occupied the far end of the table. One held up a large green sock and the other laughed.

Haven reached out and fingered a skein of black yarn. "I don't live in Arborville. I told you that," she said. Pamela and Bettina remained silent. "I wasn't here Monday, during the night or during the day or any time at all."

"What were you writing about?" Bettina asked.

"What?" Haven stared at her.

"The writing job you were doing Monday night?" Bettina resumed the silent stare. Pamela was amused to see her friend look so stern, and struggled to look equally stern.

"It was . . . it was . . ."

A voice drew their attention to the doorway leading to the kitchen, and looking grateful, Haven paused. An elderly man stood in the doorway, holding a cast-iron griddle. "Do you have any more of these?" he asked. "They go for a lot now on eBay."

Without excusing herself, Haven darted away and disappeared into the kitchen with her customer.

More people were showing up for the sale now. Pamela could hear voices coming from the kitchen as Haven fielded questions about prices, and a few more women had been attracted to the offerings on the yarn table. A man in the living room was wrapping plates from the china set in newspaper and stashing them in a cardboard box.

"I'll just take a look in there," Bettina said. "I'm not so much of a vintage person like you are, but I see a few interesting crafty items on those tables."

As Bettina browsed among the crafty items in the living room, Pamela noticed a cluster of watercolors hanging to the left of the arch leading into the entry. She studied them one at a time, enjoying the skillfully rendered views of what had to be a charming European village with a seacoast. As she moved from one to another, she gradually drew nearer to the opening between the two rooms.

Marjorie was at her post in the entry. She was just seeing a group of shoppers out the door, thanking them for coming and congratulating them on their finds. The next voice Pamela heard was Haven's, though Haven wasn't visible from where Pamela was standing.

"You know I appreciate all your help," Haven said. "I really do. But we've got so much to clear out of here I wish you'd stop worrying about those boxes of archives till we get the rest of the stuff under control."

Pamela missed hearing Marjorie's response because the very next moment Bettina was at her side, excitedly displaying a basket—surely made by hand—with a sophisticated pattern that contrasted fibers of palest tan with those of deep russet brown.

"I'm ready," Bettina announced. "Take me away before get too tempted by that Japanese tea set." She pointed toward a tea pot and four bowl-like cups that gleamed with a burnished sienna glaze. "I'm sure the price would be more than reasonable, but my cupboards are bursting as it is."

Haven scurried off as Pamela and Bettina stepped into the entry. Marjorie turned toward them with a smile, nodded toward the basket, and said, "How about five dollars?" While Bettina was dipping into her purse for her wallet, Marjorie directed her attention to Pamela. "No treasures today?" she asked.

Pamela offered the apologetic version of her social smile and said, "No, but I love my blue-speckled bowl."

"We'll be here next Saturday." Marjorie had tucked Bettina's five-dollar bill into the zippered pouch at her waist. "Not Sunday though, because who'd come out to a tag sale on Easter?" She scanned the living room. "I don't know what we'll do after that. It depends on if the realtor's making progress finding a buyer. So much stuff to get rid of." She shook her head.

"It's awfully nice of you to help out," Bettina commented. "I guess Haven's got a busy life in the city and can only get out to New Jersey on weekends."

Marjorie nodded. "I'll be here all week though, and the following week. Some of it's just going to the Goodwill—Cassie's clothes weren't too stylish and not old enough to be vintage. We haven't sold any of them. And books! Don't people read anymore?"

"It depends on what kinds of books I suppose," Pamela said.

"Books a professor would read. Too egg-heady for most people." Marjorie shrugged. "Maybe a used-book dealer would be interested, someone who'd take the trouble to list them online."

A few of the women who had been browsing at the yarn table approached then, asking if Marjorie had plastic bags they could take back to the table to fill with their selections. Marjorie excused herself to supply them with bags, and Pamela and Bettina went on their way.

"Well?" Pamela asked as she and Bettina strolled along the sidewalk, Bettina carrying the intricately patterned basket.

"I'm proud of the writing I do for the *Advocate*." The forlorn quality of Bettina's voice contrasted with the confidence implied by her statement. "*Most* people in town like it."

Three weeks' worth of the *Advocate* waited to be retrieved in the driveway they were just passing. All three issues were still in their flimsy plastic sleeves, but two of them had been run over several times and one of them had clearly been out since before the last rain and was soggy despite its wrapping.

"I'm sure they do," Pamela said, hoping Bettina hadn't noticed the sad spectacle. "But what did you think of Haven? You were great, by the way."

"I don't believe she didn't knit any of those tree-sweaters," Bettina said. "She got too nervous when we brought it up."

"But the members of that group are all sworn to secrecy. You found that out when you researched them on the internet."

"True."

They had reached the house at the corner of Cassie's street, where the fact of having both a front yard and a side yard exposed to the gaze of passersby gave the homeowners plenty of scope to display their carefully planned and scrupulously maintained landscaping. This time of year there wasn't yet much to see, except for a riot of jonquils and an exuberant forsythia. But little nubbins rising from the dark earth marked what Pamela knew from her walks would turn into peonies and hosta, and stubby green blades marked the return of iris.

"What about Monday night?" Pamela said. "Do you believe she was at home in Manhattan on deadline for a freelance writing assignment?"

Bettina shrugged and tightened her brightly painted lips into a skeptical twist. "She acted confused when I inquired about the topic."

"She did," Pamela agreed. "But she volunteered

the alibi before she got onto the idea that we were really wondering if she could be the person who killed Diefenbach. And we were just us—then. It was before she recognized your connection with Detective Clayborn, so it wasn't like coming up with an alibi in the course of a police interrogation." Pamela paused. "Though she *was* trying to convince us she didn't have anything to do with the tree-sweaters."

"We have to find out more about her though," Bettina said. "She grew up in Arborville. Now she's living in Manhattan, writing for a living, and she's got a husband who does something that involves a studio in Brooklyn."

"Musician?" Pamela raised an eyebrow. "Artist? Sounds glamorous."

They walked on in silence for a block. At the corner of Arborville Avenue, Pamela turned to Bettina. "How about brunch at Hyler's?" she asked. "It's not quite lunch time but all I had for breakfast was one piece of toast."

"I'd love to," Bettina sighed. "I haven't had one of their waffles in ages—but Wilfred Jr. and Maxie and the boys are coming for lunch, and we're going to dye some eggs. My Wilfred boiled three dozen this morning."

They crossed Arborville Avenue and soon had reached the end of Bettina' driveway. "I'm planning to go to that memorial reception," Pamela said as she turned to head for her own house, "so I'll see you in a couple of hours?"

"Of course!" Bettina smiled. "And Wilfred too. We're not walking though, even though St. Willibrod's is just up on Arborville Avenue. Come over a little before two and ride with us." She extended a foot to display a bright red sneaker. "One walk a day is enough, and besides I want to wear nice shoes. I'll be representing the *Advocate*."

Chapter 10

"The boss is in the kitchen," Wilfred announced as he pulled the door back and Pamela stepped into the Frasers' living room. He'd set aside his bib overalls and was wearing one of the well-cut suits he'd worn when he was still going to his office every day.

"Come on back here," came Bettina's voice from deep within the house. Pamela obeyed and found her friend standing at the high counter between the cooking area and the eating area arranging colored eggs in the basket she'd brought home from the tag sale.

She'd changed her clothes since that morning, to an ensemble that featured "good shoes"—a pair of wedge heels in violet suede, a matching violet sheath dress, and amethyst earrings.

"You wore a decent coat," Bettina said when she caught sight of Pamela. "Thank goodness. Let's see what's under it."

Pamela unbuttoned the coat to show that she had dressed up in deference to the occasion as well. Her wardrobe didn't offer nearly as many resources as Bettina's, but she'd reached into the depths of her closet for a pair of black wool slacks and her low-heeled black pumps. She'd finished the outfit with an off-white pullover that featured a ribbed turtleneck and extra-deep ribbing at cuffs and hem. As a final touch she'd added her simple silver earrings and a bit of lipstick.

"The eggs turned out nice," Pamela said.

"This is only part of them. They took the rest home for the Easter bunny to hide in their yard next Sunday." Bettina picked up a deep yellow egg and added it to the cheerful heap in the basket, whose subtle brown tones were the perfect foil for the rainbow-hued eggs.

"Shall we go?" Wilfred appeared in the doorway that led to the dining room. He'd buttoned a dark wool coat over his suit and he carried Bettina's coat, lavender wool, and the violet and fuchsia cashmere scarf that had already made an appearance that morning.

Bettina tucked two more eggs, a green one and a blue one, into the basket, and they set out for the reception.

The St. Willibrod's church hall hosted many of the events that crowded Arborville's community calendar—among them pancake breakfasts, scouting activities, bingo nights, and of course the annual rummage sale. St. Willibrod's itself was a venerable structure, built of dark stone, with an angular bell tower and grand double doors of heavy wood at the top of a half-flight of broad slate steps. But the church hall had been added in the fifties, and designed more for utility than grandeur.

As they entered the heavy glass doors, a sign on an easel greeted them with the words "Remembering Bill Diefenbach." Below was a large color photo of a well-fed man in his fifties with blue eyes, a florid complexion, and thinning sandy hair. Pamela recognized it from the campaign literature that had appeared, seemingly at least once a week, in her mailbox the previous fall.

A few rolling coat racks had been staged off to the side, already bearing the coats of the small crowd clustered around the long white-covered table in the center of the room. Fluorescent lights made the room bright with a shadowless brightness, and echoing voices merged in an indistinguishable hubbub.

Their own coats added to the collection, Pamela and the Frasers approached the long table. Pamela mustered her social smile as Marlene Pepper stepped away from the crowd, dressed for the occasion too in a sky-blue pants and jacket combo. "Have some cake!" she urged. "We're just about to cut into it. And there's punch." She grabbed Bettina's right hand and Wilfred's left hand and drew them closer as Pamela followed.

The crowd parted a bit and Pamela could see that the table's white cover was actually paper. Midway between one end of the table and the other was an impressive sheet cake, iced in white with white scallops piped all around the top and base. Across the expanse of buttercream were the words "In memoriam Bill Diefenbach RIP," piped in chocolate. Below the words was a cross formed of chocolate icing.

To the right of the cake were stacks of clear plastic dessert plates and clusters of clear plastic forks. To the left was a large punch bowl containing a liquid whose pink hue reminded Pamela of nothing so much as a pink Easter egg. Stacks of plastic cups awaited servings of punch and stacks of napkins awaited lips and fingers sticky with cake.

A woman who Pamela recognized from Borough Hall, the friendly woman who sat at the desk behind the counter where people paid their property taxes, picked up a knife in one hand and a cake server in the other. Bettina and Wilfred had been drawn close to the table, and to the cake, by Marlene Pepper, but Pamela lingered at the edge of the crowd.

Many people looked familiar, besides Marlene Pepper and the friendly woman from Borough Hall. Pamela recognized several people she had seen eating lunch at Hyler's, though she didn't know their names. And Brandon MacDonald, the former mayor, was standing at the far end of the table. Pamela recognized him from Hyler's too. During his many terms as mayor he had been a regular there, often holding court as lunchtime stretched into afternoon coffee break time. He was holding a plastic cup filled with pink punch.

MacDonald was a rumpled looking man, dressed in jeans even for the memorial event, unlike Diefenbach, whose precisely cut hair and well-tailored clothes had signaled his fellow feeling with the business community. Several men stood near

MacDonald, accepting cups of punch being ladled out by one of their number. Another of the men was topping up the servings of punch with a clear liquid that he poured from a flat, pocket-sized bottle. That man resembled an aging hippie, with his luxuriant moustache, faded blue jeans, and fringed suede jacket.

Finally he added a substantial dollop of the clear liquid to his own plastic cup and raised the cup in a toast. "To Bill Diefenbach," he exclaimed in a gravelly voice, "May he rest in peace." He took a deep swallow from his cup and asked, in mock-pious tones, "Shall we cut down a tree in his honor?" adding a vulgar word.

This remark provoked a round of hearty laughter, though MacDonald stopped laughing sooner than the others and said, "Come, come. Let's put hostilities aside for the day. He's leaving behind people who cared for him."

"Like who?" asked one of the other men. Pamela recognized him as the proprietor of Arborville's hardware store. MacDonald tipped his head toward a woman who had just come in and had paused by the coat racks to remove her coat. He raised his brows meaningfully.

"Whew!" the mustachioed man's moustache expanded above an amazed smile. "I can't believe *she's* here."

Someone said "Pamela," and Pamela turned to see Bettina, holding two plastic plates containing slices of cake with plastic forks tucked alongside. "I tried to get two pieces from the corners," she said, "but there are only four corners. At least I got them both from a side, so there's more icing than just on the top, and some of the extra buttercream decoration." Pamela thanked her and accepted a plate. Beneath the white icing, the cake itself was yellow. "Wilfred found someone from the historical society to talk to," Bettina added.

The crowd had doubled by now, and the room was abuzz with conversation. Many people had drifted away from the table and formed small groups, some holding plates with cake and some holding cups of punch. Others, determined to have punch and cake simultaneously, were standing along the edges of the long table and resting plates and cups on it.

Pamela used the plastic fork to carve off a bite of the cake and lifted it to her mouth. The yellow cake was light and moist, and the icing was a fluff of intense sweetness. As she and Bettina stood there surveying the proceedings, Marlene Pepper detached herself from the group she was talking to and strolled toward them, carrying a plastic plate with a partial slice of cake on it. Marlene was the same size and shape as Bettina, and shared her fondness for sweet goodies.

"It's turning out nice," she said. "Don't you think? Lorinda did most of the organizing. She's the one cutting the cake—she ordered it from a bakery in Haversack." Marlene teased off a forkful of cake, conveyed it to her mouth, and smiled as she chewed it. When it had been swallowed, she leaned toward Bettina and whispered (though with the din in the room, whispering was hardly necessary to keep a communication private), "I can't believe *she's* here." Marlene pointed to the same woman MacDonald had indicated when he remarked about Diefenbach leaving behind people who cared for him.

With her coat removed and hung up, and standing away from the coat racks, the woman was revealed as being quite amazingly turned out.

"That's a Chanel suit." Bettina's tone was reverent. "The real thing, I'm sure." The suit, with a slim skirt and boxy collarless jacket, was made from a nubbly tweed check in black and white. "And that handbag," Bettina went on with a sigh. "Handbags like that cost thousands." The handbag, made of smooth black leather, was shaped rather like an old-fashioned lunchbox, but with a complicated gold metal clasp. The woman herself was middle-aged and not model-thin, but her smooth blonde hair and careful makeup fit with the pedigree of the outfit.

"It's Eloisa Wagner," Marlene explained.

"Is she an heiress?" Pamela asked, curious despite her lack of interest in fashion.

Marlene laughed. "The suit and bag are from her shop, I'm sure. She owns Not Necessarily New in Meadowside. It's all consignment. Rich people from places like Timberley bring in clothes they've gotten tired of and Eloisa sells them and splits the proceeds with the owners.

Eloisa had moved toward the long table as they were talking and was cutting herself a slice of cake. The cake, which was more than half gone now, had become a serve-yourself affair, and Lorinda had joined a group of other women who were finding quite a bit to laugh about despite the gravity of the occasion. Additional laughter, louder and more raucous, was coming from the group composed of MacDonald and his supporters, who were still lurking near the punch bowl, their tongues apparently loosened by the clear liquid in the flat bottle.

The level of punch in the punch bowl had sunk—though not as low as one would expect from the many cups of punch that had been served. As Pamela watched, Lorinda detached herself from her friends, slipped around the back of the table, and lifted a huge plastic bottle of pink liquid from a cooler that Pamela hadn't noticed before.

Then Pamela heard the words "wasn't supposed to lose," muttered in a deep masculine voice, and turned her attention from Lorinda to the group of men clustered nearby. Some of the men were still laughing, but it was clear that MacDonald wasn't amused. "The guy was a crook," he growled. "One week before the election, the Wendelstaff College poll had me leading by twelve points."

"What happened to 'hostilities aside for the day'?" The mustachioed man grinned and jabbed MacDonald with an elbow. The action set in motion the fringe on the man's jacket, which extended even down the sleeves. Then suddenly, he called, "Hey!" He glanced over at Pamela, extracted the flat bottle from his jacket pocket, and held it toward her. "You'll hear better if you come right on over," he said. "Have a drink and join the party."

Pamela rarely blushed, but she felt her cheeks grow hot. Yes, she'd been staring, and eavesdropping shamefully. She mumbled, "No thanks," and retreated, backing up until she encountered an obstacle. The obstacle turned out to be Bettina, who was chatting with Marlene Pepper. Bettina laughed good-naturedly. "You're all pink," she said.

"Hot flashes," Marlene said. "It happens to us all." And she grabbed Pamela's arm in a gesture of female solidarity.

"What's going on?" Bettina asked, suspecting that Pamela's flush had another cause.

"I'll tell you later," Pamela mouthed, because Marlene was standing right there, and Marlene had the eager look on her face of someone who had been interrupted in mid-sentence and was longing to complete her thought.

Bettina turned back to Marlene with a smile that invited her to go on. "So," Marlene said, "like I was saying, he told her that one marriage was enough for one lifetime and he didn't plan to repeat the experience." Marlene tipped her head forward in a satisfied nod, as if confirming his (*whose?* Pamela wondered) satisfaction in making his position clear.

"She must have been crushed!" Bettina's mobile features usually radiated cheer, but when sympathy was called for, her forehead creased and the corners of her mouth sagged.

"She was!" Marlene agreed. "Seven years of her life, and helping him through the campaign, and then he wins—and the very next thing, he tells her that marrying her is not on his agenda and never will be."

"Hmmm." Bettina pondered for a moment, nibbling her lip. "Getting involved with a divorced man can be sad," she observed. "The first time around wasn't good for him, and so of course—"

"Oh, he wasn't divorced," Marlene cut in. "He

was a widower. Unhappily married, but he stuck it out. I give him credit for that, I guess. The kids turned out okay."

"That's important," Bettina said. "I think children know though, when their parents aren't happy together."

"True." Marlene nodded.

The conversation was winding down, and Marlene had finished her cake. She glanced toward the long table, studied her empty plate, and said, "I think there's quite a bit left. It would be a shame for it to go to waste." She smiled at Bettina and then at Pamela. "Care to join me?" she asked as she took a step toward her objective.

"No more for me," Pamela said quickly and grasped Bettina's arm. She was pretty sure she knew whose romantic misadventures Marlene had been so eager to discuss, but she wanted Bettina to confirm her impression. And if they were whose she thought they were, a new possibility for freeing Roland came into view.

"You're sure?" Marlene inquired.

"I'll have more a little bit later," Bettina said. "You go ahead."

Pamela waited until Marlene was several yards away, and for good measure she tugged Bettina toward a quiet corner of the echoing room.

"Diefenbach and Eloisa?" she asked then.

"So sad." Bettina looked as woeful as if she herself had been the jilted girlfriend. "I just can't imagine, loving someone so much and then he just . . . rejects you. I don't know what I'd do."

"Maybe you'd kill him," Pamela said.

Bettina gave a start that set the tendrils of her

hair a-quiver, and the woeful expression was replaced by alarm. "Oh, I couldn't!" she exclaimed. "I would never do anything like that!"

"Bettina!" Pamela tipped her head forward to meet Bettina's gaze. "*Someone* killed Diefenbach, and it wasn't Roland. It might have been Haven, but she might have an alibi. So we have to consider who else it could have been, like a woman who waited seven years for a proposal and then was told marriage was never going to happen."

"Eloisa?" Bettina whispered.

"Eloisa." Pamela nodded. "Or—she couldn't resist a teasing smile—"it could have been someone else right here in this room. I've been eavesdropping. But we'll get to that after we talk to Eloisa. Come on, and let's get rid of these plates while we're at it."

With Pamela leading the way, they headed for the long table, where a collection of used plates, forks, and cups had been accumulating at one end. Then they scanned the room for a blonde woman in a black and white checked Chanel suit, bobbing their heads this way and that as people milled about and chatting groups rearranged themselves. Pamela caught a glimpse of Harold and Nell, and made a mental note to say hello at some point.

"I don't see her," Bettina said at last.

"I don't either." Pamela sighed. "But just to make sure—I noticed her hanging her coat up when she first came in. It was a tan trench coat, and she was at the coat rack nearest the door. Let's go check if it's gone. If it's still here then she's around somewhere."

But the tan trench coat was gone.

"We never had the punch," Bettina said as they turned away from the coat rack.

Wilfred intercepted them when they were halfway to the punch bowl. "Dear ladies," he greeted them with a courtly bow, looking quite handsome in his well-cut suit and with his thick but well-trimmed white hair. "Quite a nice crowd," he added. "Almost everyone from the historical society is here, and Harold and Nell, and the library director. And MacDonald, though I was surprised to see him, given that the campaign was so acrimonious."

"We're getting punch," Bettina said.

"I will accompany you." Wilfred fell into step. A minute later he had ladled out three plastic cups of the pink liquid and they were each taking a first tentative sip. Brandon MacDonald and his group had retreated from their post at the end of the table and were no longer drinking punch, having perhaps used up all of the liquor with which they'd been spiking it. They were still within earshot, though it was hard to make out what they were actually saying. MacDonald still sounded angry, however.

Bettina, however, was staring fixedly at them, punch forgotten. "Pamela," she whispered after a time, "that other person, right here in this room, who you said could be another suspect. Did you mean . . . *him?*" She gestured toward MacDonald with the hand that held the cup of punch. The punch sloshed to and fro.

"I did," Pamela whispered back. Realizing there was no real reason to whisper, she continued in a normal tone of voice, explaining that MacDonald was still quite angry about losing the election to Diefenbach—at least based on what she'd overheard earlier—and that he thought the loss was due to Diefenbach being a crook.

"And MacDonald's house is right next to Diefenbach's." Bettina leaned closer to Pamela and the words rushed out. "The only car anybody saw around nine p.m. was Roland's Porsche, but living right next door, MacDonald could have popped over on foot. He could even have gone out his back door and gone in Deifenbach's back door— lots of yards in Arborville just flow into each other without fences. The argument was in the kitchen, and kitchens are usually at the back of the house."

"Now, now, now." Wilfred emphasized the words with a rhythmic gesture that mimed warding off an unwelcome visitor. "Brilliant reasoning, sweet wife, and you know I support your detecting efforts wholeheartedly. But MacDonald wasn't at home last Monday night."

Bettina's voice overlapped with Pamela's in a confused jumble as Bettina said, "He wasn't?" and Pamela said, "How do you know?"

"Historical society," Wilfred explained, intuiting the question despite the jumble. "The historical society met that Monday night and he's the secretary."

"But you're in the historical society," Bettina said, her brow wrinkling, "and you're always back home by nine."

"Some of the guys go out for beer afterwards," Wilfred said. "I don't, usually, but MacDonald's always game for a beer or two."

Pamela and Bettina looked at each other as Wil-

fred aimed a jaunty salute in the direction of Mac-
Donald, who had caught sight of him and boomed
out a hello.

"Now I'm ready for another piece of cake," Bettina said, setting down her empty cup.

The three of them circled back toward the middle of the table, where the remains of the cake still
beckoned to late arrivals and those in search of a
second helping. On the way, they encountered
Harold and Nell, Nell in the somber gray suit that
Pamela recognized as her funeral outfit. Pamela
and Wilfred lingered there as Bettina excused herself, saying she'd be back in a minute.

"That cake *is* tempting," Nell commented, her
kindly expression suggesting she sympathized with
those unable to resist temptation.

"She had a bit herself," Harold said with a
hearty laugh. "Don't let her fool you."

"The world would be better off without refined
sugar," Nell said primly.

"Hello! How are you?" said a voice behind
Pamela. The words were apparently aimed at Nell
and Harold, who gazed past Pamela to return the
greeting with smiles and a cheery "Just fine" on
Harold's part.

"Do you know Albertine Hutchins?" Nell asked,
as Pamela stepped back to admit the newcomer to
the group. Bettina was approaching too, with her
fresh slice of cake, and she slipped in between Wilfred and Harold.

Nell introduced Pamela, Bettina, and Wilfred.
Albertine extended her hand and said, "I'm the library director."

"I've seen you in there"—Pamela shook the offered hand—"and now I know your name." Albertine was a delicate, slender woman whose slightly bohemian style extended, today, to a long, gauzy dress the color of charcoal. The dress had been given a semblance of shape with a belt fashioned of macramé and beads.

"Two deaths in town," Albertine observed with a mournful shake of her head, "and both people who contributed so much to Arborville"—she paused—"though I can't say I was always in agreement with Mayor Diefenbach's initiatives."

"A lot of people weren't," Nell said. "A lot of people right here in this room right now weren't."

"Cassie Griswold though—such a valuable service, maintaining the town archives." The opportunity to praise someone restored a bit of cheer to Albertine's expression. "The library will be drawing on that material for our upcoming exhibit."

"What's the exhibit about?" Pamela asked.

"The title is 'Suburbia: American Dream, American Nightmare,'" Albertine said with a wry smile. "All about murders and such. It's a bit macabre, but the exhibit is a master's degree project for one of our interns. He's getting a library science degree from Wendelstaff College."

A gray-haired woman who Pamela recognized as one of the library volunteers touched Albertine's arm and gestured toward another group. "Duty calls," Albertine explained with an apologetic shrug and allowed herself to be led away.

The reception was winding down now. The punch bowl was finally empty and all but a few misshapen heaps of crumbs glued together with icing remained on the flat foil-covered rectangle that had held the cake. The coat racks were emptying as people retrieved their coats and trickled out through the heavy glass doors, waving and calling goodbye to those who remained.

Wilfred and Harold, however, seemed oblivious to the fact that the crowd had thinned out. They were immersed in a conversation evidently sparked by the reference to the town archives—and the loss of the town archivist—exploring ways that the historical society could take over the archiving task.

"Did you know Cassie?" Bettina asked suddenly, aiming the question at Nell.

"Not as a close friend," Nell said, "but we were acquainted, certainly. Her daughter overlapped my youngest in school."

"Haven?" Bettina mentioned the name so off-handedly that Pamela wasn't sure about her friend's motive. Was Bettina simply making conversation until the men could be carried away to their respective homes? Or was she probing to see what Nell could tell them about Cassie's daughter that might be useful in their detecting?

"Oh, my!" Nell clasped her hands before her and looked past Pamela and Bettina, her lips parted, as if seeking inspiration. "Where to begin? Haven Griswold was the queen of the neighborhood—brilliant, beautiful, environmentally conscious, multi-talented, with a glowing future ahead. Just a very very impressive young woman."

"That's quite a compliment, coming from you especially," Bettina said. "I guess she would have been in high school in the nineties?"

Nell nodded. "Then she went off to Bennington for college and married a sculptor, Axel Crenshaw.

We were all so grateful that Cassie kept Arborville up to date on Haven's accomplishments."

Pamela thought she detected a hint of irony in Nell's final sentence, but she wasn't sure. Nell's own children had turned out very well, and Nell wasn't the type to begrudge others their good fortune.

Chapter 11

"Queen of the neighborhood," Bettina announced from the front seat after they'd settled themselves into Wilfred's ancient Mercedes for the short drive home. "Would the queen of the neighborhood kill a person? Even to save a tree?" She turned and regarded Pamela over the seat back.

"Nell said she was environmentally conscious, even back in high school," Pamela said.

"It was an argument." Bettina swiveled in her seat to face Pamela more directly. "It's not like the killer went there intending to kill him. The whole thing could have started as a discussion. Then it turned into an argument. Then it got out of hand."

"We only have Haven's word that she was in Manhattan finishing up a writing job. But now we know she was the queen of the neighborhood."

The drive from St. Willibrod's was very short.

They were already turning onto Orchard Street. At the end of the street, to the west, a pink tint was spreading in the sky as sunset approached.

As they neared the Frasers' driveway, Pamela went on. "I think I need some new clothes," she said. In response to Bettina's amazed look, she amended the statement. "Not *new* new though. I'm thinking of a shopping trip Nell would approve of—like a visit to . . ." She paused, unable to control the teasing smile she felt creeping over her face.

The smile was contagious. Bettina's face mirrored it, though not so teasing. "Not Necessarily New," she pronounced with a giggle.

"Tomorrow morning," Pamela said. "Ten a.m. I'll drive."

Pamela and Bettina lingered outside chatting after Wilfred went into the house. As they stood there, an olive-green Jeep Cherokee approached from the east. It slowed and then turned into Richard Larkin's driveway. The vehicle itself was familiar, as was the tall blond man who climbed out. Unfamiliar, however, was the woman who emerged from the door on the passenger side after Richard opened it and took her hand to assist her.

Anyone watching Pamela and Bettina at that moment, or eavesdropping on their conversation, would have been forgiven for thinking that it was Bettina who harbored romantic feelings for the handsome man across the street.

"That's not Laine," Bettina whispered, mentioning one of Richard Larkin's daughters, "and it's not Sybil." Sybil was the other. Every vestige of cheer had fled from her expression, which seemed frozen in an imitation of a tragic mask. "Oh, Pamela!" she moaned, grasping for Pamela's hand, "He's found another girlfriend."

Pamela was processing her own reaction too, though not as visibly or audibly. The woman, who Richard was now escorting toward his porch with a chivalrous hand on her back, looked indeed like a suitable age for him, and a suitable type. She had thick black hair plaited into a fashionable side braid, and was wearing a chic camel-colored wrap coat and sleek black boots tall enough to be hidden by the hem of the coat.

"Another?" Pamela asked. "I didn't know he had—"

Bettina interrupted with a shriek that turned into the words, "What have you done?" Even in the fading light, Pamela could see that Bettina's frozen expression had thawed and in fact her face was rosy with anger. "That . . . *lovely* . . . man has been interested in you since the day he moved into that house almost two years ago. And you know you find him attractive—you've told me as much. But you're *afraid*, of what I don't know. Now, *finally*, he's given up and decided to look elsewhere. And he obviously didn't have to look very far, because he's very eligible."

Pamela studied the asphalt beneath her feet. Of course, she couldn't blame Richard Larkin for looking elsewhere. He'd been friendly, and she'd been friendly—but like a neighbor would be—then he'd made his interest in her clear, and she'd turned him down. So what had she expected? That he'd wait around for years and years and years?

"Tomorrow at ten?" Bettina's voice disturbed her reverie.

"Yes, yes," she said with a flustered shake of her head. "Tomorrow at ten."

She was greeted in her entry by milling cats, requesting their supper with plaintive meows. She hurried to the kitchen, opened a can of the chicken-fish combo that seemed to be their favorite, scooped a generous serving into a fresh bowl, and placed the bowl in the corner where one set of cabinets made a right angle with another set. Leaving Catrina and Ginger nibbling delicately at their meal, she proceeded upstairs to check her email and change her clothes.

A light was on in Richard Larkin's kitchen window, which directly faced Pamela's kitchen window. Had he brought the woman home to cook dinner for her? Or was she going to cook dinner for him? At present no heads were moving about in the brightly lighted space. Perhaps Richard and the woman were sitting in the living room drinking wine and laughing. Perhaps cooking would come later. Perhaps they would do it together, slightly befuddled by wine. Pamela admonished herself that her neighbor's date was absolutely none of her business and set about preparing her own dinner.

The pot roast she'd cooked Thursday night had been sumptuous, and there was plenty left, along with the rich sauce it had generated as it simmered. Pamela took the pot roast's remains from the refrigerator and carved off two slices. She spooned a goodly amount of the sauce, now congealed, into a small skillet and set it to heating on the stove. As the sauce melted and spread out, she slipped the pot roast slices into the skillet and turned them over a few times to coat them with the sauce. Then she covered the skillet and turned the flame under it to low.

While the meat was warming, Pamela peeled half a cucumber and sliced it into a small bowl. She added cherry tomatoes, cut in half and sprinkled with sea salt to bring out their flavor. A dash of olive oil and a few grinds of pepper completed the salad.

She checked the contents of the skillet, which were warming nicely. The plan was to serve the pot roast and sauce on a slice of toasted whole-grain bread, so when she judged the meat just hot enough, she slipped a slice of bread into the toaster.

The chair Pamela usually occupied faced her kitchen window and Richard Larkin's kitchen window beyond. Abandoning her usual spot, she ate her meal sitting on the side of her kitchen table usually occupied by Bettina. After her meal, she repaired to the sofa to work on the sleeve for the lilac tunic. Trying to avoid any programming that would touch on love or marriage, she opted for the nature channel. To her chagrin, that night's episode dealt with the courtship rituals of the bower bird.

*   *   *

On Monday morning, after her usual breakfast of coffee and whole-grain toast, Pamela ascended to her office. Bettina wouldn't arrive until ten, so still in her robe and slippers, Pamela pushed the button that would awaken her computer. A few whirs and clicks brought its icons up on the screen and soon she was watching as one message after another arrived in her inbox, for total of five.

One was from Penny, and Pamela reserved the pleasure of reading that one until she had checked the others. Three were eminently delete-able, and the fourth, complete with an attachment, was from her boss at *Fiber Craft*.

"Nothing pressing," the message read. "If we accept it we won't use it till next winter, but let me know sometime this week if you agree with me that 'Making a Difference: How Women's Weaving Collectives Lift Peruvian Villages Out of Poverty' will be a big hit with our more socially conscious readers. The author has devoted her life to empowering women—quite an impressive website. "

Penny's message was even more succinct. "Maybe closer to three or four Friday. Kyle has a test."

Pamela was about to turn the computer off and cross the hall to find an outfit suitable for a visit to a consignment shop when a thought occurred to her. The author of 'Making a Difference: How Women's Weaving Collectives Lift Peruvian Villages Out of Poverty' had a website—an *impressive* website. Haven, as a freelance writer, was bound to have an internet presence: a website, a Facebook page . . . all sorts of things.

Had she kept her birth name, Griswold? Pamela

wasn't sure, but she Googled first on "Haven Griswold." Nothing at all came up. Haven Griswold was an unusual enough name that there weren't even any posts with headings like "Haven Griswold of Omaha, deceased at age 92." Next she tried "Haven Crenshaw," but the results were similarly unsatisfactory. Since it was barely nine a.m., Pamela opened the attachment from *Fiber Craft* and immersed herself in the world of Peruvian craftswomen and the traditional designs that were bringing new wealth to their villages.

The first thing Bettina said upon stepping into Pamela's entry was, "At least she didn't stay too late." Then she added, "I won't take off my coat, since we'll be leaving in a minute." The morning was chilly, and Bettina was bundled in the pumpkin-colored down coat that was her everyday cold-weather wrap, though her head was bare. The bit of lavender scarf peeking from her neckline echoed the color of her kitten heels, and her Faberge egg earrings dangled from her earlobes.

"Who didn't stay too late?" Pamela asked, puzzled.

"That woman, of course." Bettina pointed toward the entry window through which Richard Larkin's house could be seen.

Without answering, Pamela turned toward the closet and pulled out her jacket. Neither spoke again until Pamela braked her car for the stop sign at the corner of Orchard Street and Arborville Avenue. "I wonder if Eloisa's shop takes credit cards," Bettina commented. "Sometimes those kinds of places don't."

"I'm sure it does," Pamela said. "Places that sell Chanel suits, even used, would have to take credit cards."

Monday morning was a good time to seek parking along Meadowside's main shopping street, which offered many more destinations than Arborville's small commercial district: a shoe-repair shop, a florist, several restaurants, a fish monger, two bars, and an optometrist among them. Often, later in the day or on weekends, one had to cruise several blocks past one's target before coming upon an empty curbside spot. But today Pamela slipped easily into a space right in front of Not Necessarily New.

Below an awning with the shop's name spelled out in a quirky but elegant script, the shop window featured three mannequins dressed and posed as if chatting at an upscale daytime event (perhaps a charity luncheon), in simple but obviously expensive sheath dresses, sleek high-heeled shoes, status handbags, and statement jewelry.

Even from the doorway it was clear that Eloisa was very discriminating in the garments she accepted for consignment—or perhaps it was just the muted lighting that made the colors and textures of the clothing on display seem so luxurious.

At the back of the shop, a row of curtains indicated that fitting rooms were available, and racks punctuated by long mirrors in ornate frames occupied both sides of the room. The left side of the shop was devoted to dresses. On the right side, blouses and jackets occupied an upper rack and pants a parallel lower rack. In the center of the shop was a sort of island, waist high, with handbags and shoes carefully arranged on its top and folded sweaters stacked on the shelves that formed its sides. Directly to the right of the entrance was a counter with a computer screen, a cash drawer, and a credit-card reading device. Beneath the counter's glass top was a display of jewelry.

Eloisa herself was nowhere to be seen.

"Look at this!" Bettina exclaimed. "People even consign wedding gowns." She stepped closer to the rack on the left, tugging Pamela with her.

Indeed, the first several of the dresses on display were wedding gowns, mostly full length, their hems skimming the floor. There were fanciful organza confections, svelte columns of heavy satin, and exuberant bouffant creations fashioned from taffeta. Their hues ranged from icy white through cream to rich ivory. Some designs involved pearl beads or sparkly touches.

One of the curtains at the back of the store rippled and a woman stepped out. She was wearing a wedding gown—of the svelte column type—and a veil that hid her face, and she was carrying a bridal bouquet that seemed fashioned of oversized white peonies.

"The peonies have to be silk," Bettina whispered, "at this time of year."

With slow, rhythmic steps, moving to music that only she could hear, the woman made her way toward one of the long mirrors. There she posed, the bouquet clutched with both hands at waist level. She turned slightly to the right, glanced back at the mirror as if studying the effect, then repeated the process with a turn to the left. Finally she turned all the way around and twisted her head as far as it would go to contemplate the effect of the gown and veil when seen from the rear. Facing the mirror again, she tossed the veil back with one hand and raised her face as if expecting to be kissed.

Then Pamela and Bettina realized they had been observing Eloisa Wagner herself, not a bride-to-be economizing for her big day by shopping for a pre-owned wedding gown. And Eloisa noticed them.

"Oh," Eloisa said, flushing. She stared at the bouquet in her hand, looked around confusedly, took a few steps, and placed it atop a pair of shoes on the island in the middle of the shop. "A little prop, for the convenience of the shoppers, so they can picture . . . picture . . . how things will look. At their wedding." She glanced down at the dress and added, "I like to try them on. Not just the bridal gowns. Everything really. Sometimes things look nice on the hanger, but they just don't . . ."

"That's an excellent idea," Bettina said, stepping forward. "I don't know how many times I've stood in a fitting room at the mall and looked at myself in the mirror and wondered how on earth whoever designed this garment could have thought it would flatter a real human being." She took another step. "You have a beautiful shop here. I can see that you put your heart and soul into it, and"—she paused and studied Eloisa's face—"you look so familiar. I can't think where I've see you, but—do you live in Arborville?"

"No." Bettina's agreement that modeling the wedding gown made complete sense—along with her praise of the shop—had had the desired effect. Eloisa smiled and went on. "I live right here in Meadowside, not quite above the store but close."

"I know!" Bettina crowed. Her eyes widened and she clapped her hands excitedly. The reaction struck Pamela as overly theatrical, but Eloisa simply waited with a pleasantly curious expression on her face. "You were in Arborville yesterday—at the memorial reception for Mayor Diefenbach!"

"Why, yes . . . yes, I was." The pleasantly curious expression that had flattered Eloisa's middle-aged features vanished. Her face sagged and she bowed her head, dislodging the headband that had held the wedding veil in place. The veil cascaded to the floor in a heap of netting.

"You must have been a friend." Bettina laid a sympathetic hand on the ivory satin sleeve that encased Eloisa's arm and stooped to retrieve the veil.

"I was. I was a . . . friend." Eloisa blinked, perhaps feeling tears beginning to form. Her voice quavered. "I really cared for him. Who wouldn't? He was such an attractive man."

Pamela, meanwhile, had decided Bettina was best left to her own devices and was browsing along the rack containing blouses and jackets. A jacket might be useful, she was thinking, a blazer-type jacket to wear with pants when an occasion called for more than a sweater and jeans.

She checked the price tag on an attractive indigo jacket in smooth, light-weight wool and was startled to see a three-digit figure. She returned it to the rack and reached for its neighbor. Perhaps the indigo jacket was the creation of a famous designer and had started out costing ten times its current price. Meadowside wasn't Timberley, after all—certainly Not Necessarily New priced most of its offerings with an eye to its local clientele.

But the conversation drifting her way from further back in the shop distracted her from these musings. The words "Cassie Griswold" caught her attention and she edged a few feet closer to where Bettina and Eloisa still stood near the long mirror.

"More than twenty years older than he was," Eloisa was saying, "and even she was smitten. Right down the block from him and a real pest—always trying to give him things, jam and whatnot." She stopped. "I've got to get out of this dress," she said. "Monday mornings are slow. I wasn't expecting any business first thing, but people start dropping by when it gets on toward lunchtime."

Pamela joined Bettina as Eloisa headed toward the curtains at the back of the shop, carrying the veil. Pamela waited until Eloisa vanished into one of the curtained cubicles before making a sound, and then she whispered, "We already knew she liked him. What about last Monday night?"

"I'm getting to that," Bettina whispered back. Raising her voice, she said, "Now I'm going to do what I came in here for: shop!"

She turned toward the closest rack and began to work her way through the blouses, which were arranged in categories of small, medium, and large. On her way back to the jacket section, Pamela discovered a row of suits—jackets hanging with their matching skirts or trousers. Among them, she noticed to her amusement, was a boxy jacket fashioned from nubbly tweed check in black and white, paired with a narrow skirt of similar fabric. It was the Chanel suit Bettina had admired at the memorial reception. The price tag read $500.

A few women had entered and were looking through the dresses along the other wall, conferring with each other from time to time, and Bettina was busy among the blouses.

"Look at this," Bettina called suddenly. She held up a classically styled shirt fashioned of heavy silk printed with giant magenta blooms, their leaves and stems a vivid shade of green. "Wouldn't this be perfect with wide-legged pants in the green color? And magenta shoes?"

Before Pamela could respond, a voice trilled out, "Perfect!" Eloisa had emerged from the curtained cubicle, dressed more suitably for her current role in a pale blue sheath dress that flattered her blonde hair and fair skin.

"I absolutely have to have this blouse." Bettina took a few steps toward the front of the store as if to show that she was ready to settle up. "No need to try it on. I'm sure it will fit—and I'll certainly be back for more."

"I get new things all the time," Eloisa said. "I'll be putting some out tomorrow." She led the way to the counter.

"What a lot of work a shop like this must be," Bettina said. "Pricing things, sorting out garments when the seasons change, making sure blouses are hanging with blouses and jackets with jackets after people have been pawing through them all day . . ." She opened her purse and drew out her wallet.

A few more customers, very well-dressed older women, stepped in and Eloisa greeted them in a way that suggested they were regulars.

"Saturdays and Sundays are crazy," Eloisa said. "Shoppers, of course, and a lot of the things for consignment come in then too. So Monday when the shop's not busy I go through the new arrivals, and Monday's often a late night. I close at six, but then I just stay here and work."

Bettina plucked a credit card out of her wallet and inserted it into the card-reading device.

Eloisa had been busily folding the colorful blouse, but she looked up with a stricken expression. "To think I was here working away," she said mournfully, "while someone was murdering Bill Diefenbach."

Chapter 12

"Too late for waffles at Hyler's," Bettina said, consulting her watch. They had returned to Pamela's car. "But we could go there anyway."

Pamela was waiting for a break in the traffic so she could pull out, but she nodded. "It won't be too crowded yet, and we have a lot to talk about."

So, fifteen minutes later they had settled into one of the booths that, with their burgundy naugahyde upholstery and worn wooden tables, marked Hyler's as a longstanding Arborville institution. The pleasant middle-aged woman who had handed them the oversize menus that listed Hyler's many offerings was something of an institution too. She had been a fixture at Hyler's ever since Pamela and her husband first moved there.

A few people were drifting in and taking seats in the booths, at tables, or at the counter, but the real lunch-time crush wouldn't happen till noon, when

Arborville's bankers and realtors and office work-
ers, and the people who staffed Borough Hall and
the rec center would begin to arrive.

"French dip sandwiches!" came Bettina's voice
from behind the menu. All that could be seen of
her was a fluff of scarlet hair, but her voice conveyed her enthusiasm. "They're the special today.
That's what I'm having, and a vanilla milkshake."

"Sounds good." Pamela closed her menu and
laid it on the paper placemat, centered between
the fork on one side and the knife and spoon on
the other.

"So"—Bettina had lowered her own menu and
was once again visible—"do you believe that Eloisa
was really in her shop processing new arrivals last
Monday night at nine?"

"We're not the police," Pamela said.

"I didn't think you were." They looked up to see
the server standing at the end of the booth. "Are
you ladies ready?"

Feeling vaguely silly, Pamela let Bettina order
for both of them. Once the order for two French
dip sandwiches and two vanilla milkshakes had
been placed and the server sent on her way,
Pamela went on to explain what she'd meant.

"Eloisa doesn't know we know as much about
her as we know," she explained. "So she doesn't
know we think she could have a motive for killing
Diefenbach. She volunteered the information about
where she was Monday night. It wasn't like she was
being questioned by the police and had to scramble
to come up with an alibi."

Bettina frowned for a minute, then said, "Clayborn must have known about the relationship with Diefenbach though. The police questioned so many people, and someone—lots of people even—must have told them that Eloisa had been Diefenbach's girlfriend for all those years, and that he had just broken up with her. And they must have questioned her."

"I guess they were satisfied with what she said." Pamela shrugged. "Otherwise they wouldn't have arrested poor Roland."

"Eloisa told us he was a friend, and that she cared for him." Bettina screwed her lips into a puzzled knot. "I guess she felt like she had to explain why she was at the memorial reception."

"It seemed like the 'caring for him' part kind of slipped out," Pamela said, "and I'm sure she didn't mean to almost start crying. Then she tried to cover up by saying *anyone* would have cared for him—even an ancient person like Cassie Griswold."

Bettina giggled. "Eavesdropper!"

"I looked like I was shopping," Pamela said, "but I was really listening."

Bettina was distracted then by the milkshakes. They arrived in tall glasses filmed with condensation and crowned with a froth of bubbles, accented by straws inserted at a jaunty angle. She pulled her milkshake toward her and sampled it with an eager sip.

"French dip sandwiches coming right up," the server assured them and turned back toward the counter.

But Pamela was still pondering the encounter

with Eloisa. "She didn't want to let on *how much* she had cared for Diefenbach. Maybe she didn't let Clayborn know either. Maybe she just said they'd grown apart."

"But he'd still want to make sure she had an alibi." Bettina's milkshake was half gone and her lipstick had left an imprint on the tip of her straw.

"I can see why she didn't want us to know she was in love with him," Pamela said. "You wouldn't tell a stranger that—and as far as she knew we were just strangers who wandered into her shop—because then you'd have to admit you'd been jilted."

"I wouldn't want to admit that." Beneath lids brushed with a delicate touch of lavender shadow, Bettina's hazel eyes looked as tragic as if she herself had suffered Eloisa's fate. They brightened, however, as the server delivered the oval platters bearing the French dip sandwiches.

Paper-thin slices of rare roast beef spilled from the edges of crusty mini-baguettes that had been split end to end. The sandwiches shared the platters with small heaps of golden-brown fries, fluted paper cups of slaw, and small bowls of dip made from the juices collected as the beef roasted.

Conversation ceased, at least for a time, as Pamela and Bettina sampled the feast that had been set before them. Each bite was a ritual, as the baguette, with its cargo of rare beef, was first dipped and then lifted dripping to the mouth. The meat juice, absorbed by the baguette and moistening the sliced beef, imparted a satisfying depth to each bite. After several bites, Pamela tasted her milkshake for the first time, enjoying the contrast of the cool and slightly bland sweetness with the rich meatiness of the sandwich.

When they'd reached the stage of picking at the few fries that remained on the platters, and nothing remained of the sandwiches but nubs of bread and empty dipping bowls, Pamela arranged three fries in a row at the edge of her plate.

"We had three possible suspects," she said. "Mac-Donald, Eloisa, and Haven."

Bettina nodded, setting the Faberge egg earrings to bobbing.

Pamela went on. "MacDonald had a good reason to want Diefenbach out of the way, and he lives right next door to Diefenbach's house, but according to Wilfred he would have been out drinking beer with the guys from the historical society at the time Diefenbach was being killed."

"I'm sure Wilfred is right," Bettina said. "So only two French fries left."

Pamela ate the fry and continued. "Eloisa has an alibi. She volunteered to us that she was in her shop, and Detective Clayborn may even have checked with neighbor shops about whether people saw her that night."

"I'll take this one." Bettina reached for the second fry and popped it into her mouth.

Both stared for a moment at the remaining fry then they spoke in unison: "That leaves Haven."

"As far as alibis go, we have only her word," Pamela added.

"And Clayborn didn't interview her because in his mind she's not a suspect."

"*Yet*," Pamela said.

Bettina frowned, squinted, and tightened her mouth into a thoughtful line. Then she spoke. "If we could figure out where she lives in Manhattan, we could go there. Manhattan apartment buildings are full of nosy people—and there are doormen. It might not be hard to find out if she was really at home Monday night."

As Bettina was talking, the server had appeared. "Are you ladies finished?" she asked. They both nodded, though Bettina made a grab for the Haven French fry before that platter was borne away.

Hyler's was beginning to fill up and Pamela recognized a few faces from the memorial reception. The noise level was rising—and she imagined Diefenbach (and Roland) would be a popular topic with today's lunch crowd. Pamela was glad she and Bettina had chosen the relative seclusion of a booth.

Pamela hadn't told Bettina about her morning internet search for Haven, since it hadn't revealed anything useful. But now she brought it up—to explain that Haven, for some reason, seemed unfindable online.

"Everybody has a Facebook page now," Bettina pointed out.

"We don't," Pamela said. "But I'd have thought a freelance writer would have a website, and a Facebook page, and be listed on those business networking sites."

"I'd have thought that too," Bettina said. "And don't the Yarnvaders have Facebook pages where they discuss their activities?"

"I think people can make those private now, so a Google search wouldn't attach a person's name to a group like that. And remember, the Yarnvaders want to be anonymous."

The server reappeared at the end of the booth and slipped the check onto the table.

"Did you look for Axel Crenshaw?" Bettina asked. Pamela shook her head no. "Let's do it then." Bettina pulled her phone and her wallet from her purse.

"We can sit in my car," Pamela said. "They'd probably like to give our booth to somebody else."

Pamela had parked in the lot that served Arborville's municipal complex and the town park. A narrow passageway between Hyler's and the hair salon connected that lot with the sidewalk that ran along Arborville Avenue, so after they paid for their lunch they walked single-file through the passageway and were soon sitting in Pamela's car. The grass in the park was beginning to turn green, but the weather was still too chilly for the tennis courts or the kiddie playground to be in use.

Bettina set to work with her phone. "He's everywhere," she announced after a few minutes. "Quite the impressive guy." She handed the phone to Pamela. On the small screen was the image of a brooding, swarthy man, accompanied by the words "SeaWall."

"Recipient of a genius grant," Pamela murmured, and she quoted, "Axel Crenshaw is the recent recipient of a prestigious genius grant for his work in progress, SeaWall, a monumental piece to be erected in lower Manhattan as a reminder of the rising sea levels." She handed the phone back and Bettina went to work again.

"He has a studio," Bettina reported shortly. "And here's its address, but in DUMBO?"

"It's part of Brooklyn," Pamela said, "The letters stand for Down Under the Manhattan Bridge Overpass. His studio should be easy to find. People like that want to be found."

"I'll just let Wilfred know not to look for me till mid-afternoon," Bettina said, her fingers busy on her phone. "Then I'll navigate."

Chapter 13

The route to DUMBO led across the George Washington Bridge and down the West Side Highway. "Nothing happens till Exit 1," Bettina announced as they skimmed along the edge of the Hudson River, with New Jersey across the water to the west. "Just keep heading south." The day was bright and the river reflected the clear blue of the sky, with whitecaps raised by the breeze scalloping the water's surface.

They chatted about the upcoming Knit and Nibble meeting, to be held at Holly's the following night, deciding that very likely Roland wouldn't appear. Then the conversation turned to Easter, and Penny coming home for spring break—to think she was in college already!—and Bettina reminisced about when her own sons were small and still thought a giant rabbit delivered baskets of goodies to good children on the night before Easter.

"It's coming up," Bettina said after twenty minutes had elapsed and they were approaching the lower tip of Manhattan. "Get into the left lane so you're ready."

Pamela held back to let a van and an SUV speed past, then switched lanes, slipping ahead of a beat-up compact. She made the turn and then they were heading east on Chambers, a busy two-way street flanked by stolid buildings dating from an era when a building's height was limited by the human tolerance for climbing stairs. Ranks of narrow windows marked upper floors of structures that rose only four or five stories, crisscrossed by fire escapes, with shops at street level. Lively signage and vivid displays competed for attention, and sidewalks bustled with commerce. Traffic sped up and stalled, punctuated by staccato honks, as traffic lights changed from red to green and back to red again.

After several blocks of nerve-jangling stop and go, Bettina said, "Centre Street is the next corner. Get ready to turn."

The scene had changed. Instead of storefronts, the view on the right was of a park, foliage the pale green tint of early spring. Rising out of the park was a grand structure glowing white, with magnificent columns. "A courthouse, I think," Bettina murmured, consulting her phone.

After the turn, their route took them along the side of the park, and after another quick turn they were gliding up the ramp that turned into the Brooklyn Bridge. Ahead loomed an angular stone tower, golden buff in the sunshine, with two tall pointed arches marking the roadways. Soon they were speeding along as the bridge deck rose, with a view of girders and struts, and the water and the crowded shore of Brooklyn beyond. They descended and left the bridge behind, coasting down the long slope of the ramp that led toward downtown Brooklyn.

"Turn right," Bettina said, and they looped around till they were heading back in the direction they'd just come from, but street level now and parallel to the ramp that had carried them off the bridge. Then they veered right and the sunlight dimmed as the road passed under the bridge ramp into shadows that echoed with traffic passing overhead.

They emerged into a neighborhood of low buildings formed of aged bricks glowing deep rose, as if lit from within—old factories and warehouses now marked by signs that identified galleries, cafes, and wine bars. "Fashionable," Bettina commented, her head swiveling from one side to the other. After a few blocks, the street's smooth surface was replaced by cobblestones, and Pamela's tires responded with a conversation-dampening *thumpa thumpa.*

Another shadow loomed ahead. "This is the real overpass," Bettina reported, studying her phone, "the DUMBO overpass. So we must be under the ramp that goes to the Manhattan Bridge."

On the other side were more of the low brick buildings, set off from the street by narrow sidewalks. Young people in skinny jeans and sleek jackets that skimmed their skinny bodies crowded the sidewalks, darting in and out of doorways through which the airy, wood-floored interiors of shops and restaurants could be glimpsed.

With Bettina guiding her to the parking lot that was their target, Pamela maneuvered through traffic that started and stopped as bicyclists popped out of cross streets and pedestrians lunged from between parked cars.

At last they arrived at an underground lot. Pamela coasted down the ramp into a dim subterranean chamber that smelled of exhaust and housed neat rows of cars with tickets fastened beneath their windshield wipers. A stocky Hispanic man emerged from a cubicle in the front corner, accepted Pamela's car key, and handed her a ticket.

Back above ground, they paused to get their bearings, breathe air freshened by the nearby East River, and admire the view of the Brooklyn Bridge, which was framed against the sky at the end of a street lined with charming brick buildings. Axel Crenshaw's studio was in one of those buildings, and they paced along calling out numbers till they reached their destination halfway down the block. A directory inside the main door listed Axel Crenshaw's studio as 4C.

The building was very old, to judge by its faded bricks and creaking wooden floors, and might once have been a warehouse, storing goods that arrived via the East River. But it had been subdivided into many separate units, units whose doors opened off a long hall that stretched from the main door to the back of the building. And Bettina was delighted to note that an elevator had been installed.

She pushed the button that would summon it to the first floor and they waited as its arrival was announced by an ominous series of clanks and squeals. Battered metal doors parted with a resentful screech. Bettina looked uncertainly at the gap between the floor they stood on and the floor of the elevator then took a deep breath, lifted a foot shod in delicate lavender with a kitten heel, and hopped across. Pamela joined her. A young man who had been waiting for the elevator stepped in after them. He pushed the button for the third floor and turned inquiringly to Bettina, who murmured, "Four please." He complied and the elevator began its shuddering ascent.

"Birdbaths are down the hall on the right. Wind chimes on the left."

The man who greeted them from the shabby armchair was swarthy and hairless, except for the days' worth of dark stubble that shadowed his gaunt face and his shaved head. His jutting nose and chin gave him an eager, predatory look.

"Axel Crenshaw?" Pamela asked, taking a few steps across the scarred wooden floor.

"You wouldn't like his work," the man said, leaning back lazily in the armchair, his lazy tones matching his posture. He held a spiral-bound sketch pad and a thick pencil. Crumpled sheets of paper littered the floor on both sides of the chair. "Go down the hall and pick out a birdbath to take back to the burbs with you. Or some wind chimes."

"Ohhh!" A delighted squeal escaped from Bettina, who was still lurking in the doorway. "This is it, right here!" She squeezed past Pamela and bounded toward a makeshift wooden stand that held an object modeled from clay, a long pleated rectangle like a freestanding curtain with no need of a rod to support it. After studying the object for a minute, she turned to Pamela. "It's SeaWall," she crooned. "I can't believe I'm seeing it in person." Then she turned to the man in the armchair. "You're him, aren't you? Axel Crenshaw. You look just like your pictures . . . or maybe even more handsome."

It would have been hard to conjure up a more incongruous image than Bettina—in her pumpkin-colored down coat and lavender kitten heels, with her Faberge egg earrings dangling from her earlobes—chatting with Axel Crenshaw in his studio. The studio was a long and narrow room with a high ceiling formed from iron girders. At the far end, the studio's only window was centered in a brick wall. Besides the shabby armchair, the studio was furnished with a rumpled daybed, a wooden table where the remains of several take-out meals shared space with a mound of clay, a huge cast-iron sink with a bucket beneath it, and a drawing board. Tacked to the walls were sketches of massive, angular sculptures.

In the armchair, Axel Crenshaw smirked, but he pulled himself into a more upright position and squared his broad shoulders, as if flattered despite himself. Pamela had often noticed that, when it came to accepting flattery, men didn't seem to ask themselves first whether an ulterior motive might be lurking in the mind of the flatterer. Clearly Axel Crenshaw, despite his blasé attitude, was no exception.

Apparently not content to display his physique from the comfort of the armchair, Axel Crenshaw suddenly leapt to his feet and joined Bettina next to the stand that held the clay object, towering over her. "This isn't really it," he said with an indulgent chuckle. "This is a model."

"Oh, I know *that*." Bettina craned her neck to meet his eyes. "The real SeaWall is going to be *huge*." Her tone and the way she batted her eyelashes implied that the word "huge" was not only a description of SeaWall's actual size but also a complimentary reference to the size of its creator.

"It's down at the fab yard"—he paused in the face of Bettina's puzzled expression, then resumed—"fabrication yard, in Gowanus. Metal work. I don't do that myself."

"Of course not," Bettina said, gazing up at him in awe. "You're the artist."

"What brought you here?" Axel Crenshaw asked, apparently coming out of the daze created by Bettina's flattery.

"Haven Griswold," Bettina said. "I'm an old friend of the family and I've been out of touch for ages. Cassie's dead now, you know, but for the longest time she kept me up to date on Haven's doings, marrying an artist and all that." Bettina punctuated the statement with a flirtatious wink. "I'd love to see Haven again, catch up with things, but I didn't have a current address and I couldn't seem to track her down. Then I remembered . . . she married Axel Crenshaw. So *you*, of course, with the genius grant, *you* were easy to track down . . ."

Bettina's voice trailed off. Axel Crenshaw was making an odd face. Was it the thought of Haven Griswold? A suspicion he'd been manipulated? Both?

"*Haven?*" he said at last. "Yeah, she was fun, for a while." The lazy offhand tone had returned.

"You're not married to her?" Pamela blurted out. Axel Crenshaw looked startled and Pamela realized she'd been nearly invisible for the past several minutes.

"Not for years," he said.

"So you don't know where she is." Bettina took over, sounding too disappointed to even make the words a question.

"Why would I?" Axel Crenshaw shrugged. "There weren't any kids."

"The last we heard she was living in Manhattan and working as a freelance writer," Pamela said, not quite willing to give up yet.

An explosive laugh prefaced Axel Crenshaw's response. "Manhattan? On a freelance writer's earnings? Are you nuts?"

Behind them, the studio door creaked. A lilting female voice called out, "I hope I'm not disturbing anything." Axel Crenshaw's gaunt face brightened and his mouth formed a close-lipped smile. Pamela and Bettina turned toward the door, which was open now. Framed in the doorway was a young woman who looked to be Penny's age, surely no older. She was wearing a cropped black leather jacket over a filmy white ensemble and carrying a large paper bag.

I brought you some foodies, sweetkins," she announced and stepped lightly across the scarred wooden floor. Her filmy skirt ended in jagged points that swirled around her calves.

Back in the hallway, Bettina paused outside the door of the studio they'd just left. "I don't know why he thought we'd like birdbaths and wind chimes," she commented. "But let's just pop in for a minute."

When they emerged from the elevator half an hour later, Bettina was carrying a shopping bag that contained a carefully wrapped set of wind chimes. She consulted her watch as they walked toward the door that led to the sidewalk. "We could have coffee and a little nibble," she said. "It won't be dark for a couple of hours."

They strolled past buildings similar to the one they'd just left until, after a few blocks, they reached a cross street that had more of a commercial feel, with signage identifying restaurants providing vegan fare, artisanal pizzas, or grain bowls made to order. A signboard a few doors from the corner used curly script to list the day's specials in colored chalk. One restaurant, more hopeful than realistic, was already offering outdoor seating, with chairs and a few small tables ranged along the sidewalk.

"Something looks promising in this direction."

Pamela pointed to the right. "See that place with the big arched window? And up above it says 'Coffee Break'?"

"Sounds like they have coffee," Bettina said.

A few minutes later they were standing at a tall curving bar, polished wood with a silvery metal top, that could have been as old as the building that housed it. At one end of the bar, a broad glass dome sheltered trays of various sweet goodies. The same polished wood paneled the wall behind the counter, interrupted by shelves that held cups and saucers and glassware. A giant, gleaming espresso machine crouched on a lower shelf, tended by a young woman. With a satisfying hiss it was serving up a latte, which she then deposited on the counter in front of her waiting patron.

The sight and aroma of coffee mellowed by steamed milk was all the advertisement needed. When the barista turned to them, they both ordered café latte, and as soon as their order was launched, Bettina edged toward the goodies on display further down the bar.

"There's tiramisu," she announced delightedly.

The spacious room was bright with afternoon sun pouring in the arched window. Side by side at a long table that flanked the window, with table-mates absorbed in their smart devices or laptops, Pamela and Bettina at first concentrated on sipping the sweet, rich latte and nibbling squares of tiramisu. Each bite of tiramisu was a cool, smooth mouthful. Ladyfingers moist with espresso and a touch of rum had been layered with ricotta beaten to a creamy cloud. The dusting of cocoa powder on top added a hint of bitterness that enhanced the sweetness of the rest.

"So"—when her square of tiramisu had been reduced to a sliver, Pamela turned to Bettina—"what about Haven?"

"Axel's version certainly didn't match what Nell said about Cassie's reports on Haven's doings." Bettina shook her head. "It sounds like he got tired of her and just cast her aside." Clearly, female solidarity demanded a mournful expression, but Bettina's face was still aglow with the enjoyment produced by the tiramisu. Nothing remained on her plate except for a smear of ricotta and a few ladyfinger crumbs.

"I'm even more curious about her now though," Pamela said, after a thoughtful sip of latte. "She lied to us. *Maybe* she's found some way to survive in Manhattan on a freelance writer's income—after all, if he hasn't seen her for ages, how does he know where she's living?"

"He just wanted to say something mean," Bettina agreed.

"But," Pamela went on, "she specifically mentioned her husband, and said he was at his studio in Brooklyn."

"Do you want that?" Bettina asked, eyeing the bit of tiramisu left on Pamela's plate. Pamela nudged the plate in Bettina's direction.

"Maybe she's married to someone else now," Bettina said, shaving off a tiny bite of the tiramisu sliver. "Some other artist, who also has a studio in Brooklyn."

"There are a lot of them." Pamela nodded and attacked the tiramisu sliver from the other end. "But even if this other one exists, we don't know his name. I just don't see how we can figure out where she lives. And unless we can do that, we'll never know if she was really at home the night Diefenbach was killed."

They sat in silence for a while, nibbling at the tiramisu sliver from each end and sipping the remains of their lattes, barely warm now. Out on the sidewalk, young people hurried along, more of them than before, as the workday wound down. The sun's angle had shifted too, and the room was less bright.

"We should get going," Bettina said, checking her watch. "As it is, we're going to get home late, with the rush hour traffic." She looked around and smiled. "This was fun though, even if we didn't find anything out. It's nice to get away from Arborville once in a while."

"I just thought of something," Pamela said as she stood up. The words came out in an excited burst. "The estate sale goes on again this Saturday. Haven will be back then. We'll follow her when she leaves."

"I can't wait!" Bettina was on her feet too, fastening up her pumpkin-colored coat. She groaned. "Too bad it's only Monday."

It was late, and dark, by the time Pamela nosed into the Frasers' driveway. The porch light was on, and no sooner had Pamela turned off her engine than the front door flew open and Wilfred stepped out. Woofus stood in the doorway, gazing after him.

"Oh, dear!" Bettina exclaimed. "He's been worried. I should have called him." She swung the car door open and climbed out.

Pamela watched as Wilfred hurried along the walk that led from the porch to the driveway. "Dear wife," he called, relief and distress mingling on his normally cheerful face. "Better late than never, *much* better, but . . ." They met in front of Pamela's car, where her headlights illuminated the grateful hug with which he welcomed his wife home.

Once parked in her own driveway, Pamela unlocked her front door and stepped over her threshold into her dark house. She was greeted only by two hungry cats, seemingly determined to trip her as she walked across the worn but lovely Persian rug that covered her entry's aged parquet. She hung up her jacket and proceeded to the kitchen, where she opened a can of chicken-fish blend and served generous scoops in a fresh bowl. She replenished the cats' water as well.

As far as her own dinner went, an omelet sounded appealing, after the rich afternoon treat and recent dinners that had included pot roast and its remains as well as Wilfred's magnificent sausage feast on Saturday night.

Later she settled onto her sofa, with Catrina curled up along one thigh and Ginger along the other, and began to stitch the first long seam that would join the back and front of the lilac tunic. A

British mystery unfolded on the screen before her, but the day's driving and walking had taken their toll. She dozed off with a only a few inches of sewing completed and before the genteel lady who was the mystery's sleuth had even been summoned to the crime scene.

Chapter 14

It was Tuesday morning. Pamela was sitting at her kitchen table sipping her second cup of coffee and checking back through the *Register* to see if she'd missed anything interesting the first time around. Catrina and Ginger had finished their breakfast and wandered off. The *Register* had been especially dull that day, and Pamela was glad for the distraction when the doorbell chimed.

She was still in her robe and slippers, but an unannounced early morning caller usually proved to be Bettina, and that was the case today. Through the lace that curtained the oval window, Bettina's pumpkin-colored coat was vivid against the winter-weary landscape. Catrina was dozing in the sunny spot on the entry carpet she sought out every morning. As Pamela pulled the door back and Bettina stepped inside, Catrina cast a lazy glance at the visitor, then returned to her nap.

Bettina's hazel eyes were bright with purpose,

and she began to speak before Pamela even had a chance to say hello. "I spoke to Melanie this morning," Bettina said, a bit breathlessly. "She called me first thing to say Roland won't be at Knit and Nibble tonight and he didn't want us to be waiting for him and wondering where he was."

"Oh, dear." Pamela sighed. "Leave it to Roland. The poor man! He *is* conscientious! I doubt many people in his position would think of making sure their knitting group knew they weren't coming."

Bettina nodded in agreement. "He's interviewing lawyers. Roland *is* a lawyer, of course, but not that kind, the kind that defend criminals. He's got contacts though."

"We've got to keep going on this Haven thing," Pamela said. "If only there was some way to follow up before Saturday. Haven is our only real suspect." She took a step toward the kitchen. "I can make more coffee . . ."

"I'd *love* some"—Bettina conveyed her enthusiasm by opening her eyes so wide that Pamela could see white around her irises—"but I can't stay. I'm on my way to the *Advocate* office." She grabbed Pamela's hand. "But Melanie said Roland would welcome a visit. He hasn't been going to his office and he's just been sitting at home knitting. He thinks people are afraid of him now because they think he's a murderer."

"I've got work for the magazine today," Pamela said (her morning email had brought four articles to evaluate), "but I can take a break."

"After lunch then? I'll let Melanie know we're coming." Bettina turned toward the door.

"After lunch," Pamela agreed. "I'll be ready."

The quarter cup of coffee remaining in the wedding china cup had grown cold by the time Pamela returned to the kitchen. She'd had enough coffee though, she decided, and rinsed the cup at the sink. Then she headed upstairs to get dressed and start her work day.

The first thing Pamela noticed when she and Bettina stepped through Roland's front door was the swath of knitting that stretched halfway across his living room. It featured angora yarn the color of pistachio ice cream, and it was evidently a work in progress.

It hung from knitting needles clicking busily away in Roland's lap as he sat in the low-slung turquoise chair that faced the coffee table, and it curved up over the coffee table to land on the low-slung turquoise sofa, where it formed a fuzzy angora mound. Pamela had seen the yarn before, at the Knit and Nibble meeting from which Roland had been so suddenly removed.

"It was going to be a sweater for his mother," Melanie explained. She tried to muster an indulgent smile but gave up, and her pretty face sagged. "He had already started on the back, but then he just kept going. The knitting gives him something to do besides sit there and worry, but he can't focus on directions. Fortunately he bought a lot of yarn when he started the project."

Roland was dressed, as he had been on Pamela

and Bettina's last visit, in dark slacks with a sharp pleat and a luxurious wool sweater. The sweater's V-neck revealed the collar of a crisp white shirt, aggressively starched. Melanie, on the other hand, looked even more disheveled than she had been at their last visit. She was still in her robe and slippers, and her blonde hair hung in limp strands that looked in need of a shampoo.

"You poor thing!" Bettina reached out and pulled Melanie toward her for a hug. Then she stepped back and studied Melanie's face. She turned and applied the same scrutiny to Roland. "Have you been eating?" she demanded. "Either of you?"

"Some crackers," Melanie whispered. "I just can't . . . and he . . ."

"What about Ramona? And Cuddles?" Bettina sounded alarmed. "Are you feeding them?"

"Of course, we're feeding them." Roland spoke without looking up from his knitting, his fingers busy with thrusting needles and looping yarn. "What do you think we are?" As if recognizing his name, Cuddles, who lay cozily tucked up next to Roland's thigh, raised his head.

"Well, I'm going to feed you humans," Bettina exclaimed and headed for the hallway that led to the DeCamps' kitchen. For a moment Melanie seemed uncertain what to do, glancing toward Roland and then toward Pamela. Finally she turned and followed Bettina.

"I don't know what you'll find in there," Pamela heard Melanie say. "Neither of us has been to the Co-Op since . . . since the night it happened."

"And all I bought was cat food," Roland added, not in a voice loud enough to reach the kitchen, but as if rehearsing Monday night's events to himself. "And that *is* the reason my car was seen near Diefenbach's house."

"We believe you," Pamela said. From the kitchen came the sound of rattling pots and the opening and closing of the refrigerator. "And you have access to good legal advice . . ." She edged over to the turquoise sofa and perched at the end not occupied by the heap of pistachio-colored angora.

Roland continued to knit. "The police have what they think is solid evidence. I *did* argue with Diefenbach that day and my car *was* in front of his house that night. They didn't find the murder weapon, so that means there's no way to say my fingerprints aren't on it. And any other people who might have had motives also seem to have alibis. I understand there was a jilted girlfriend. And then there's MacDonald, of course. I suppose he came up with a credible alibi, at least credible to his pals on the police force. And don't tell me a guy who was mayor as many terms as MacDonald was doesn't have pals on the police force."

Pamela was about to mention Haven, but she bit her tongue. Roland didn't need to have his hopes raised only to be dashed—assuming he'd even take seriously the idea that Pamela and Bettina could successfully challenge the results of a police investigation. And they wouldn't be able to follow up their suspicions about Haven for several days.

So she didn't mention Haven. Rather, she said, "You must have been near his house right when the murder was happening. You told us you stopped at the stop sign on his corner. Did you notice anything? The police must have asked you that . . ."

Roland shook his head, his lean face intent on the motions of his busy fingers. "I didn't," he said, "and they didn't."

There seemed nothing else to say. Roland continued to knit, drawing yarn from a skein that had diminished noticeably even in the short time since Pamela and Bettina had arrived. Cuddles dozed against his thigh. Pamela leaned back on the sofa and surveyed the DeCamps' stylish living room.

After several minutes, Bettina appeared in the entrance to the living room. "Luncheon is served!" she announced. She stepped across the carpet and stooped toward Roland. "Now you just put that knitting aside and sit down in your dining room and eat something," she said in a motherly voice that Pamela recognized as the voice she used with Woofus.

Roland complied, lowering needles and work in progress to the floor. He stood up, stretching as if stiff from sitting in the same position for a very long time. Melanie's voice floated in from the dining room across the hallway. "It's scrambled eggs and toast," she called. "Your favorite."

"Eggs!" Roland said suddenly. "I *did* notice something that night, something on Diefenbach's porch. It was a basket of eggs. Colored eggs, like something the Easter bunny would deliver."

Half an hour later, after giving Ramona a very welcome walk, Pamela and Bettina settled themselves back into Bettina's car. "Clayborn didn't mention any eggs," Bettina commented as she made a U-turn in the cul-de-sac at the end of the DeCamps' street. The Farm featured many cul-de-sacs, intended to discourage through-traffic and insure the privacy and safety of the development's residents. "I'll ask him though. Unfortunately he can't fit me in this week until Friday."

They were circling back past the DeCamps' house now, on their way to the corner that marked the entrance to The Farm. "Poor things," Bettina mused. "If I'd only known they weren't eating . . ."

"Maybe Diefenbach took the eggs in before the killer arrived," Pamela said. "Let's say Roland drives by a tiny bit before nine. Diefenbach takes the eggs in a few minutes later. The killer shows up a few minutes after that . . ."

"Colored eggs, Roland said, like for Easter," Bettina murmured. "Somebody making some kind of a statement. But what?"

"If the eggs were inside the house, the police would have found them. Or the crime-scene people from the county would have." They were passing by some of the sweater-wearing trees now, in the yards of the old Arborville houses, sturdy wood-frame, brick, and stone. Pamela turned to Bettina. "Would you mind stopping at the Co-Op?" she asked. "I've been living on leftover pot roast and eggs, and I'm in the mood for some salmon."

"I need a rotisserie chicken," Bettina said. "Wilfred isn't cooking tonight." In her years of cooking for her family, Bettina had rotated through the same seven menus, one for each day of the week.

With Wilfred retired, and an enthusiastic cook, she'd been freed from most kitchen duty, but when called upon to put dinner on the table she still relied on her old standbys. "Salmon is Thursday," she added. She swung the steering wheel to the right at the next corner and then veered left after a block.

"This is Diefenbach's street," Pamela observed as they cruised along. "And we're coming up on his house. The crime-scene tape that was all over it in that *Register* photo is gone already."

"The *Advocate* had a photo of his house too," Bettina pointed out. "A better photo, I thought." She braked as they approached the corner.

"Here's the stop sign Roland mentioned," Pamela said. "Just stay stopped for a minute. There's nobody behind you." She twisted her head and peered out the passenger-side window. "There's a good view of Diefenbach's porch from here," she said. "A basket of eggs sitting by the door would be easy to spot."

Diefenbach's house didn't feature a spacious porch accessed by a half flight of steps, like Pamela's and so many other houses in Arborville. Instead, it was a Dutch Colonial like Bettina's, though not as old, and its porch was a wide expanse of stone only a few steps up from the ground.

After studying Diefenbach's porch for a minute, Pamela turned back to Bettina. "You know," she said slowly, "the killer could have put the eggs there and then taken them away again when he left."

"Why?" Bettina screwed her mouth into a puzzled knot. A furrow appeared between her carefully shaped brows. "Why bring them? Why take them away?"

Pamela shrugged. "Some kind of a taunt. Then there's the argument—remember, the killing probably wasn't premeditated. And after Diefenbach is dead, the killer realizes the eggs could be traced back to . . . *him?* . . . and grabs them and dashes away."

"Would Haven do that?" Bettina asked. "Dye eggs and put them on his porch . . . some kind of nature ritual connected with protecting the trees?"

"I don't know," Pamela said. "I just don't know."

"I'm going to make sure Roland and Melanie have food," Bettina said as she and Pamela stood in the Frasers' driveway saying goodbye. Pamela was carrying a small white parcel containing half a pound of salmon, and Bettina was carrying a Co-Op bag from which emanated the tantalizing aroma of rotisserie chicken. "I'll call When in Rome tonight and order a pizza to be delivered to them, and tomorrow I'll take them something or have something else delivered."

"I'll help," Pamela said. "I'll do meatloaf tomorrow. One for myself and one for them."

Back at home, Pamela returned to her office. So far she had read three of the articles that had arrived that morning. The one dealing with Hmong story cloths and the Kansas City Hmong community was a definite yes, not least for the exquisite photographs the author had supplied, as was "Tradition and Innovation in the Maori Feather Cloak," also stunningly illustrated. The text of the article on bark cloth was highly informative but, perhaps spoiled by the illustrations in the first two articles, Pamela suggested that it be returned to the author with advice to use photos or drawings to give the reader a clearer sense of what bark cloth actually looked like.

Now she turned her attention to a discussion of the indigo trade. The article was longer than submissions to *Fiber Craft* generally were, and the author's language unnecessarily convoluted. But the discussion touched on the human side of indigo production and the frequent exploitation of those who produced it, and for that reason Pamela wanted to give it a fair reading and make any suggestions she could that would bring it up to *Fiber Craft's* standards.

Thus, by the time she prepared her evaluation, added it to the evaluations of the other three articles, and clicked on SEND, it was nearly five o'clock—though the sky behind the curtains that covered her office windows was darkening in a way that made it seem later. She pushed her chair back from her desk, straightened her spine, and raised her arms in a luxurious stretch. Then she scooted her chair toward the window that looked out into her back yard and pushed the curtain aside. That afternoon's visit to Roland and Melanie's house had been accomplished beneath a clear blue sky. But as Pamela was pondering the article on the indigo trade, clouds had gathered and the sky now resembled a pale gray mass of carded wool waiting to be spun.

Bettina would be at the door a little before seven to collect Pamela for the short drive up the hill to Holly's. It was time to think about dinner, for cats as well as their human mistress.

Down in the kitchen, Catrina and Ginger were staring expectantly at the empty bowl that sat next to their water dish in the corner where their food was accustomed to appear. Pamela opened a fresh can of chicken-fish blend, enjoying the tickle at her ankles as they milled around her feet sensing that dinner was on its way. She scooped two portions of the pinkish mixture into a clean bowl and substituted it for the one left from breakfast.

Her own dinner would simply be fish—the salmon she'd bought earlier that day from the Co-Op—with no admixture of chicken. But before she prepared her own dinner, a chore awaited. Tuesday night was recycling night. The Arborville DPW started their pickup rounds very early Wednesday morning, and a person whose paper or containers (depending on the week) didn't make it to the curb in time would pay the price with bins that overflowed before the next recycling day.

This week, according to the town recycling calendar tucked next to the refrigerator, was paper recycling. The bin along the side of the driveway already contained most of the junk mail and newspapers that had arrived in the past two weeks, but on her way through the entry Pamela grabbed that day's *Register* and headed out the door.

A tall and thick hedge, green and bushy all year

round, separated Pamela's driveway from Richard Larkin's property. So as she wheeled her recycling bin toward the street she had no way of knowing that Richard Larkin was on a parallel journey with his own bin.

Chapter 15

It wasn't until she reached the sidewalk and heard a voice say, "Pamela!" that she realized her neighbor was standing a few feet away. She turned and summoned a faltering version of her social smile. He was looking at her in that intense way he had, his strong features stern and his height making his presence all the more imposing.

"I guess we both had the same idea," she offered after a few moments of uncomfortable silence.

"Recycling night," he agreed, still looking at her. He shifted his gaze to the sidewalk. Then, as if realizing that nothing about the worn concrete offered any pretext for study, he glanced up and down the street. Finally, tilting his head back and looking upward, he observed, "Looks like we're going to get some rain."

Pamela nodded. "It *is* April."

"April—yes, indeed." He was looking at her again. "Soon it will be gardening season."

A vision rose in Pamela's mind, uninvited. She closed her eyes, as if doing so would blot out the recollection of Richard Larkin working in his yard the previous summer, the cling of his faded jeans and T-shirt making clear just how fit he was.

"So . . . you've been okay?" Pamela asked, though she'd last spoken to him only a few days ago.

"Very," he said. "Yes, very." He looked around confusedly, focused on his recycling bin, and added, "I'd better get this to the curb."

"I . . . yes," Pamela said. "So . . . have a nice evening."

She resumed her journey with the bin but had gone only a few yards when Richard spoke again.

"Pamela?" His voice was tentative.

She turned to find him frowning, first at her, then at the sidewalk. "I understand about your husband," he said at last, addressing the sidewalk. "I loved my wife, then she left. What I thought we had will never come back."

"Thank you," Pamela said, "for not saying I should move on."

He looked up, and she noticed a slight twitch in his lip as if he was suppressing a smile. "That's a speech I've been giving myself."

"Oh . . . well, yes." She blinked. "You should . . . move on." He *was* eligible. Bettina was right about that.

"Life is short—sometimes even shorter than we expect." Was that part of the speech he'd been giving himself too? Pamela wondered.

"I know." She nodded.

"So . . . I guess I'd better get this bin to the curb."

"Yes. Me too." Pamela felt her throat tighten as Richard resumed his chore. But once his bin was settled in its spot near the curb, he took a few long steps and was once again standing near her.

"I was willing to wait," he said. "I *did* wait, a long time."

"I know." She couldn't bear to look at him and she knew the words were barely audible.

As she wheeled her own bin into its position on the grass near the tree with the sweater, she heard Bettina's voice from across the street. "See you in a little while," Bettina called, stepping away from the recycling bin she'd just deposited at the curb.

Back inside, Pamela baked her salmon and made a pot of brown rice. She ate half the salmon and half the rice with a salad of cucumbers and mini-tomatoes, and saved the leftover salmon and rice for another meal.

Her outfit that day had been her usual jeans and loafers with a not-favorite old sweater over a cotton turtleneck. Knit and Nibble required something at least a bit nicer, so upstairs she pondered the contents of her closet. From the stack of sweaters on her closet shelf, she took down a cowl-necked pullover in a forest green alpaca blend, knit with extra-large needles that created a loose, airy texture. By the time Bettina rang the doorbell, Pamela was standing in her entry wearing a jacket over the sweater and with knitting bag in hand.

"What did Richard say?" Bettina asked as soon as Pamela opened the door.

"He thinks it's going to rain," Pamela said.

"That was all?" Bettina's face resembled that of a marionette whose puppet master had tugged strings to signal astonishment: brows aloft, eyelids wide, and mouth agape. "I could see the way he was looking at you, even from all the way across the street. He still cares for you and he's only going out with that other woman because he's given up all hope that you'll ever care for him."

As Bettina spoke, Pamela had felt herself frowning. Now she spoke. "We're not going to talk about him anymore. Okay?"

"I can't believe you turned down his invitation to that banquet—"

Without responding, Pamela frowned more deeply and stepped over the threshold. Looking chastened, Bettina edged out of the way and Pamela pulled the door closed behind her. Bettina waited until they were halfway down the walk to say, "April showers bring May flowers. I have an umbrella in my car in case we need it."

Pamela and Bettina were the last to arrive. When Holly ushered them into her artfully decorated living room, with its walls the color of graphite, Nell and Karen were already settled on the streamlined ochre sofa, knitting projects at the ready. But the current focus of their attention was Karen's smart phone.

"What a sweet little face," Nell was cooing, staring at the small screen.

"And she's started to smile." Karen smiled too, and flicked a finger over the screen. "Here's a good one. And here's another."

"No teeth yet," Nell said.

"No. No teeth."

Bettina swooped across the room and joined them, dislodging a cat whose ginger coat almost blended with the sofa. It leapt nimbly to the floor and padded off toward the dining room.

"Is this baby Lily?" Bettina exclaimed, leaning toward the little screen. She watched as Karen's finger continued to move and after a few moments murmured, "Too, too adorable."

Not to be left out, Pamela deposited her knitting bag near the other large piece of furniture in the room, a loveseat upholstered in bright orange and chartreuse fabric with an abstract design that hinted at flowers. Then she circled behind the sofa to gaze over Karen's shoulder at the images of four-month-old Lily, Karen and Dave Dowling's first child. Smart phones hadn't existed yet when her daughter Penny was a baby, but Pamela and her husband had documented Penny's early years just as thoroughly. She felt a little tug at her heart to remember that time and to realize it didn't seem all that long ago, and now Penny was in college.

Holly, who being Karen's neighbor and best friend had presumably seen not only the photos but the baby herself on many occasions, waited off to the side. After several minutes and many more enthusiastic exclamations, the smart phone was stowed away. Pamela returned to the loveseat, made herself comfortable, and lifted one of the lilac tunic's sleeves from her knitting bag. Tonight's task would be stitching the long seams that made the sleeves whole. And surely at some point responding to congratulations that the project was nearing completion.

"Only five of us tonight," Holly observed as she took a seat on one of the angular chairs that flanked the coffee table across from the sofa. The streak in her hair was a spring-like shade of green. "Thank you for passing the word on about Roland not coming, Bettina, though I really wouldn't have expected him anyway. Poor man! Does anyone know how he's doing?"

"I called and spoke to Melanie a few days ago," Nell said. Concern banished the age-minimizing delight that the photos of Lily had evoked, and she looked her full eighty-plus years. "We know Roland isn't a murderer. This nightmare has got to end soon."

"He's interviewing lawyers," Bettina said, "and knitting." She described the visit she and Pamela had paid that morning. "He and Melanie aren't eating much," she added. "So if anyone wants to deliver food—things to tempt their appetites—I'm sure they'll be grateful."

"Healthful things though," Nell said. "Healthful things will be best."

"I guess the police think their job is all done now," Holly said. "The *Register* hasn't had anything about the case since they reported that Roland had been arrested and was out on bail."

"Nothing new from Clayborn for the *Advocate* either." Bettina looked up from the knitting pattern she was studying. "And I know there are lots of people in town following the story."

"There's plenty of other news in the *Advocate*," Nell said. "It doesn't have to pander to people's interest in the sensational."

"I agree." Karen spoke up in her meek voice. A blush reddened her fair cheeks as all eyes turned to her. "I enjoy those profiles of local artists, and the reports on the town meetings, and what's happening at the library . . ."

"Some people don't even read it." Holly's tone suggested amazement. "How could anybody who lives in Arborville not want to keep up with what's going on in this awesome town?" She had reached the end of a row and transferred the needle that held her swath of knitting to her left hand, taking up the now-empty needle in her right hand. "My neighbor, for example, right over there." She nodded toward the side of her living room closest to the house uphill of hers. "He just lets copies of the *Advocate* pile up in his driveway. Even though they're in those plastic bags, water seeps in when it rains and they get all soggy. Then he runs over them with his car. What a mess!"

"One of my neighbors does that too," Nell said.

Pamela stole a glance at Bettina. Thankfully she seemed too engrossed in figuring out the next step in her knitting project to be paying attention to this sad testimony that not everyone found the *Advocate* indispensable.

Holly laughed, displaying her perfect teeth and activating the dimple that accompanied her frequent smiles. "*My* neighbor got a scare though." In response to the startled faces that greeted the statement, she amended it. "Just a little scare. Actually, it was more funny than anything else. Somebody left a note in his mailbox, a handwritten note. He showed it to Desmond when Desmond was on his way to the Co-Op the other day, and he asked if we'd ever gotten such a thing."

"Did it say the *Advocates* were an eyesore?" Pamela

asked, remembering the note that someone had dropped off at Cassie Griswold's tag sale.

"Why yes," Holly said. "That's exactly what it said. Desmond remembered 'eyesore' particularly. 'Your soggy *Advocates* are an eyesore and you had better clean them up.'"

"Did you ever get a note like that?" Karen asked, looking alarmed.

"Of course not." A smile activated Holly's dimple again. "We bring the *Advocate* in every week on the day it comes and we read every word of it."

They knit in silence for a bit then. Nell had embarked on another infant cap in the same soft yellow yarn she'd been using the previous week. Karen's project was another tiny piece for a lacy pink garment undoubtedly destined for Lily. Holly was making another square, dramatic orange this time, for her color-block afghan. And Bettina, after her extended consultation of her knitting pattern, was back at work on the Nordic-style sweater for Wilfred.

"It's gotten late," Nell murmured after a time. She was staring at the eye-catching sunburst clock that decorated one wall of Holly's living room. "Past time for our break." She lowered her knitting into her lap.

Holly jumped to her feet, exclaiming, "Roland always reminds us!" She hurried toward her dining room and the kitchen beyond. Bettina followed her, turning to observe, "Too many cooks spoil the broth, as Wilfred would say. You all just stay here and I'll give Holly a hand."

Nell was flexing her fingers and seemed happy to relax for a bit. Karen's fingers were still busy with her slender needles and delicate pink yarn, but she and Nell began to chat about Dave Dowling's growing expertise in diaper-changing and lullaby-singing.

Across the room on the loveseat, Pamela had put her work aside. She'd already sewn up the two sleeve seams that had been her task for the evening. Only a tiny bit remained to do before the tunic was complete and ready to be presented to Penny when she arrived home. It was time to think of a new project. But maybe she'd spend a few weeks paging through knitting magazines until inspiration struck. In the meantime . . .

"Nell?" she heard herself say. Nell turned from Karen to gaze across the room at Pamela. "I'll make some caps," Pamela went on, "if you'll show me how."

"Extra hands are always welcome," Nell said. "And you can use odds and ends of leftover yarn, as long as it's soft and not itchy. A cap doesn't take much." Nell slid her knitting bag onto her lap and began to root around in it, coming up with a partial skein of yarn in a pale shade of peach. "I'll get you started with this tonight."

The tantalizing aroma of brewing coffee had been growing stronger as Nell spoke. Now Bettina stepped into the opening between Holly's living room and her dining room. Looking past Bettina, Pamela could see Holly's elegant chrome coffee pot and a squat pottery teapot sitting side by side on the mid-century modern dining room table.

"There's coffee for the coffee-drinkers and tea for the tea-drinkers," Bettina announced. "And wait until you see what Holly has created for tonight's nibble."

Pamela rose, but she let Nell and Karen lead the way to the refreshments. Holly and her creation were still in the kitchen. But in addition to the coffee and tea (and cream and sugar), cups and saucers and dessert plates waited on the table's pale wood surface, along with sleek flatware and fancy paper napkins.

"Melmac," Nell murmured, picking up a heavy plastic cup and saucer set in an arresting shade of pink. "I can't believe these fashionable young people like all these things I remember from the fifties."

"The fifties were awesome," came a cheerful voice from the kitchen doorway. "You were so lucky to be alive then."

"Oh, my dear!" Nell's smile was tinged with pity. "People had the same worries and fears then— even more, in some ways, but—" She had turned and was gazing at the platter Holly carried. The pity vanished from her smile and it became wider. "I used to make that every Easter," she said, "when my children were little." It occurred then to Pamela that Nell's crusade against sugar had not been lifelong.

Holly carried the platter to the table and set it down near the stack of dessert plates. She acknowledged the chorus of ohs and ahs with a dimply smile. "I found the most amazing recipe blog," she said. "It's called 'Grandma's Kitchen.' "

Centered on the platter as if squatting in a field of exceptionally green grass was a bunny—a cake bunny with a pink jelly bean nose, chocolate drop eyes, and white icing fur made more convincing by the addition of shredded coconut.

"How did you do the ears?" Bettina asked, leaning close.

"I bought ladyfingers," Holly explained, "and I spread lots of the white icing on them and rolled them in coconut. The grass is coconut too, dyed with food coloring." She surveyed her handiwork fondly and then picked up a knife.

"Ohhh!" Bettina raised her fingers to her face, hiding her brightly lipsticked mouth but displaying her matching nail polish, bright pink. "How *can* you? It would be like . . . it would be like eating . . ." The ginger cat had wandered in from the kitchen.

"I'll pour the coffee," Pamela said, stepping up to the table.

As Pamela tipped the chrome coffee pot over the Melmac cups, Holly began to serve slices of the bunny cake, starting at the back. The first serving included the coconut-covered tail, and she offered it to Karen.

"I can't eat that much." Karen waved a delicate hand at the plate. The slice had revealed that beneath the icing and coconut fur, the cake itself was yellow.

"Just the tail is fine for me," Nell said.

Meanwhile, Pamela had moved on to pouring out tea for Karen and Nell. Bettina had stepped up to the table again. She had sugared her coffee and was adding cream to achieve exactly the pale mocha shade that she preferred.

"I hope your husband got to see your creation,"

Pamela said as she accepted a Melmac plate with a reasonably sized portion of cake.

"He did," Holly said. "I made it last night. He's at the salon—we have clients who come in after work—but he'll have cake when he gets home."

Holly began to cut a slice of cake for herself. Bettina was still standing at the edge of the table, sipping her coffee and watching. Holly transferred the slice of cake to a plate and glanced around. Karen and Nell had already returned to the living room with their tea and cake, having divided Karen's original portion of cake into two.

"Is that it then?" Holly inquired, her eyes shifting from Bettina to Pamela then back to Bettina again.

"*Well* . . ." Bettina raised her brows and tilted her head, casting a sideways glance at the slice of cake on Pamela's plate. "When a piece is on the plate, it doesn't look so much like a bunny, so maybe I could . . ."

Holly laughed and handed Bettina the serving she had just cut for herself. "Go on into the living room," she said. "I'll be with you in a minute."

Pamela took a seat in the other angular chair that flanked the coffee table, which was a long slab of granite on spindly legs. There was plenty of room on the table for five dessert plates and five cups and saucers. Holly joined them, and the five women sat cozily facing one another, Pamela and Holly in the angular chairs, and Nell, Karen, and Bettina on the sofa.

Knitting was forgotten for a time. Perhaps it was that Roland wasn't there to keep them focused on the task. Or perhaps, with no man present, topics arose that wouldn't have seemed suitable for general discussion. In any event, when Pamela finally checked the sunburst clock, only fifteen minutes remained until Knit and Nibble's customary quitting time.

There was just time for Nell to get Pamela started on an infant cap, lending her needles of an appropriate gauge for the pale peach yarn and guiding her as she cast on the requisite number of stitches and embarked on the knit two, purl two ribbing that would form the cap's edge.

Chapter 16

Pamela awoke, not to the morning sun brightening her bedroom's white eyelet curtains, but to the steady tattoo of raindrops. She stirred slightly and felt a soft motion at her side. Something was on the move, or rather two somethings, creeping over her belly and chest. A small hump appeared under the folded-back edge of her sheet, then a head appeared. Amber eyes peered at her from a heart-shaped face covered in black fur. In a moment another head appeared, ginger this time, with eyes the color of jade.

The clock on her bedside table said that it was past eight. A gloomy morning made for a lazy rising, but it was time to be up. And if Pamela herself didn't awake thinking immediately of food, her bedmates certainly did. Catrina was kneading her chest in an importunate way and Ginger had already leapt from the bed and was standing at the bedroom door.

Downstairs, her house was dark and chilly. The view through the oval window in the front door was of a yard with colors dimmed by the glowering storm, and of the dark, rain-slicked street beyond. Once she'd switched the kitchen light on though, that room was cheery enough, with its yellow walls and a vintage cloth in a colorful print covering the table. The clicking sounds coming from the baseboard radiators said that the house was warming to the thermostat's daytime setting.

Pamela gave the cats their breakfast and refreshed their water dish, then she took her umbrella from the closet, traded her slippers for boots, and hurried out to collect the *Register.* She left the wet boots and umbrella on the porch by the side of the door and gratefully reentered a house that felt cozy in contrast to the dank outside, tugging her fleecy robe more closely around her.

Inhaling the smell of fresh ground coffee beans and the deeper, richer smell of brewing coffee, as water dripped from the filter cone into the carafe below, made Pamela feel quite ready for whatever the day had to offer. She sat at her table nibbling the last few bites of whole-grain toast and letting the coffee, in its wedding china cup, warm first her fingers then her whole being.

She folded the *Register*'s first section, put it aside, and contemplated the front page of Local. The lead article was about the upcoming Easter egg roll at the county park. As she was turning the page to find the rest of the article, she heard feet on her front porch.

Thinking it was Bettina, who was known to pay unannounced calls when she had something important to communicate, Pamela headed for the entry. But no figure was visible beyond the lace that curtained the oval window. Perhaps, then, the mail had arrived, though nine a.m. was very early for the mail—especially on a day when one would expect the rain to slow the delivery process.

Pamela opened the front door and peeked out. There was no sign of anyone, though the mail carrier had been known to move quite fast with his short cuts from yard to yard. She lifted her mail box's hinged cover and reached inside. *Something* had been delivered, though it didn't exactly feel like an envelope or a catalogue. A flyer, maybe. Some industrious soul offering lawn service now that spring was approaching.

But the words she read when she unfolded the somewhat damp sheet of paper had nothing to do with lawn service—though one might say they had to do, in a sense, with home improvement. "Recycling is not to be put at the curb until 6:00 p.m.," she read. "Yours was out too early last night. Recycling bins are an EYESORE and they degrade the esthetic effect of the neighborhood. Moreover, the longer the bins are out, the more chance there is for paper or containers to escape and create even more of an EYESORE. Do not let this happen again! P.S. I KNOW WHERE YOU LIVE."

Pamela stood on her threshold for a moment. She stared toward Bettina's house, checking to see whether the person who had delivered the note she held in her hand was possibly tucking a similar note into Bettina's mailbox at this very moment, since Bettina's recycling had gone out at the same time Pamela's had. Bettina's porch was empty, however, and glances up and down Orchard Street revealed no one braving the rain for any errand whatsoever.

So Pamela returned to the remains of her coffee and toast, first setting the damp note on the counter to dry. It would have to be shown to Bettina. In the meantime, AccessArborville might well be buzzing with discussion of the note-writing Arborville resident who objected to tag-sale posters, uncollected copies of the *Advocate*, and recycling bins that appeared at the curb before six p.m.

When the coffee carafe was empty and only a few crumbs marked the spot where toast had lain on a small wedding china plate, Pamela rinsed her breakfast dishes and climbed the stairs to her bedroom. Ten minutes later, dressed for the day in jeans, a sweater, and loafers, she lowered herself into her desk chair, poked her computer's ON button, and watched as her monitor's screen came alive with icons.

Pamela had mixed feelings about AccessArborville. On the one hand, it served a useful purpose. People could share news about town events, give away objects they no longer needed, locate babysitters and housecleaners, and exchange information about local contractors. On the other hand, it allowed people to express ideas that they might not express, at least in such blunt language, if they were communicating face to face with the same people who were reading their posts.

A lively discussion of the "nutty neat freak," as he (or she) had been dubbed, was indeed underway. Many people posting had received notes delineating their infractions against public tidiness. And many posters—perhaps those who had not received notes but only heard about them—thought that the neat freak had a point. One poster even proposed a seasonal event, perhaps called Arborville Cleans, to address some of the issues that concerned the neat freak. Another pro-neat freak poster brought up the fact that political candidates didn't bother to collect their campaign materials after elections were over, the late Bill Diefenbach, may he rest in peace, being the worst offender.

Other posters, those who called him (or her) the nutty neat freak—and worse things—felt that campaign materials left to deteriorate in public places were perhaps worthy of criticism, but that people had a right to be as messy as they wanted on their own property. Anyone who didn't like it just didn't have to look.

Before visiting the AccessArborville site, Pamela had checked her email. Her boss had already been busy, and the article about the indigo trade was now back in Pamela's inbox with instructions to edit it, along with the article on women's weaving collectives in Peru. "We'll run them both this summer," her boss's email read. "The August issue is shaping up to have a strong social consciousness slant." Pamela set to work and had soon lost herself in the task of making the article on the indigo trade at least a bit more accessible to the average reader. She was grateful when the doorbell's chime rescued her from the task of untangling a half-page-long sentence.

Pamela nearly tripped over Ginger as she crossed her entry. Catrina had pounced on the ball of yarn that Ginger had clearly been chasing, and after dodging Pamela's foot, Ginger began tussling with her mother for the prize. Bettina's pumpkin-colored coat was visible through the lace that curtained the oval window, and her bright yellow umbrella. In a moment, she had left the umbrella by the side of the door, wiped her yellow rubber booties on the doormat, and stepped inside. She was carrying a white cardboard bakery box.

"What would you say to lunch?" she asked.

Pamela looked at the box. "I wouldn't say no," she said. "But it's barely ten."

"Lunch at Hyler's I mean." Bettina laughed. "With Brandon MacDonald." She held the box out. "This is for now—if you can take a break."

"I certainly can," Pamela said, thinking of the syntactical chaos waiting upstairs. "I just have to save my document and I'll be right back down."

When she entered the kitchen, Bettina had removed her coat, revealing a jersey wrap dress in a swirling yellow and chartreuse print. The burner under the kettle had been lit and the bakery box placed on the table, along with two cups and saucers and two small plates. Bettina was holding the note Pamela had found in her mailbox.

"We got one too," Bettina said, flourishing the

still rather limp sheet of paper from Pamela's counter. "Wilfred found it when he collected the mail. He just laughed, but I thought it was sad. Orchard Street has always been a live-and-let-live kind of street. Most people keep their property up nicely, but if somebody gets a little behind on grass-mowing in the summer, or puts an old washing machine out a few days before the proper collection date, people understand."

Pamela turned. "The note-writer"—she resisted the urge to use the term *neat freak*—"might not live on Orchard Street. Marjorie got a note about the tag-sale signs, and last night Holly said her neighbor got one about letting . . . newspapers . . . pile up in his driveway. And according to AccessArborville, lots and lots of people are getting them, for all sorts of things." She described some of the posts she'd read that morning.

"I suppose Richard Larkin got one." Bettina set the note down. Pamela tipped a few measures of coffee beans into her coffee grinder, and for a few moments conversation was replaced by the crunch and whirr of the beans being ground.

Pamela arranged a paper filter in the plastic cone that fit atop her carafe and poured in the fragrant ground beans. By now the water in the kettle was boiling. She tilted the kettle over the carafe, and soon the slow drip of the boiling water was amplifying the coffee beans' fragrance as the carafe filled with fresh-brewed coffee.

Meanwhile, at the table Bettina had untied the string that fastened the bakery box and revealed the contents: two cheese Danish reposing on squares of waxy paper. "I think they'd be better with forks," Bettina said as she transferred them to the plates. "They're quite sticky." The cheese Danishes were smooth rounds of golden pastry, palm-sized, and glistening with a sugary glaze. In the center of each was a smaller round, paler gold, of soft, sweet cheese.

Pamela added forks, and napkins, and the cut-glass sugar bowl with its matching cream pitcher to the table setting. Bettina fetched the carton of heavy cream from the refrigerator and dribbled a bit into the cream pitcher, then she returned the carton to the refrigerator and plucked a spoon from Pamela's silverware drawer.

"The lunch with MacDonald was my editor's idea," Bettina said after coffee had been poured and they had taken their accustomed places on either side of the table. "I used to interview him all the time when he was mayor. It was my idea to invite you—because we might learn something useful that will help Roland. But here's why my editor at the *Advocate* is interested in MacDonald. Arborville's town government is in turmoil now. Arborville has never had a lieutenant mayor or a vice-mayor—so according to the bylaws, if the mayor is out of the picture, governing is left up to the town council, with the senior council member in charge. But most of the people on the council are MacDonald supporters." Bettina paused to dig her fork into the edge of her cheese Danish. Since Pamela had already sampled hers, she took up the idea Bettina had launched.

"I suppose the Diefenbach supporters are aghast

that their leader's agenda is to be abandoned," she said.

Bettina was chewing, but she nodded vigorously, the scarlet tendrils of her hair bobbing in time with the motion. "And the MacDonald supporters—and maybe MacDonald himself—are thinking that it's only fair to let the council run things, since according to the Wendelstaff College poll, MacDonald was supposed to win anyway."

"The Diefenbach supporters want to hold a new election." Bettina put her fork down and set to work sugaring her coffee and adding cream. "They want to run another 'The Future Is Now' candidate, a woman named Martha Cosgrove." She stirred her coffee, now a pale mocha hue. "So I'm to lunch with MacDonald and get his take on all of this. I imagine AccessArborville is buzzing with the topic."

"At the moment," Pamela said, "at least as of this morning, people were more interested in the scolding note-writer."

"An article in the *Advocate* will be good then. People need to be informed about what's going on politically in their town." Bettina sampled her coffee, smiled, and returned to her Danish.

Pamela was enjoying her own Danish. The pastry's flaky crust was crisp around the edges, yielding to a chewy interior like sweet yeast bread. Bites closer to the center melded that effect with the creamy richness of soft, sweet cheese. The coffee, bitter and black the way she liked it, was the perfect complement.

"So," Bettina said, "we're to meet MacDonald at Hyler's for lunch. Twelve thirty sharp."

"I hope I'll be hungry by then." Pamela regarded the half Danish waiting on her plate. "Speaking of the *Advocate,* you said you were seeing Detective Clayborn Friday?"

"You're thinking about the basket of eggs, aren't you? Whether the police found them when they responded after Diefenbach was murdered." Pamela nodded. "This week's *Advocate* will already be out, but that's the only time he could only fit me in." Bettina gave a disgusted laugh. "I don't know what he's doing that keeps him so busy. He's already pinned Diefenbach's murder on poor Roland."

Pamela picked up her fork and teased off another bite of the Danish. But before she could lift it to her mouth, she let the fork clatter back onto her plate. Bettina's eyes widened in surprise. "What is it?" she asked.

"MacDonald could lead us to the person who left the basket of eggs on Diefenbach's porch," Pamela said as an extra-loud thump of her heart acknowledged how exciting was this realization.

"He could?" A slight frown replaced the surprised expression.

"One of the complaints the Diefenbach supporters had about MacDonald was that he refused to crack down on the person in town who has the rooster. So he must know the person who has the rooster—a pal of his even. And why would a person have a rooster if he, or she, didn't also have hens? Hens that lay eggs?"

"Yes!" Bettina slapped the table with both hands. The forks jingled against the china plates. "I'll ask him about the rooster. I'll work it in—the question makes perfect sense, for my article."

"It does." Pamela nodded. "And the answer could be just the lead we're looking for. We won't be able to follow up any further with Haven until Saturday, but meanwhile . . ."

She returned to her Danish with new enthusiasm. Lunchtime was still a few hours away.

Chapter 17

"**B**ettina!" A rumpled looking man rose from a table near the big window that allowed patrons of Hyler's to keep tabs on the passing scene as they ate. It was Brandon MacDonald, in jeans and a fleece pullover zipped part-way up, with a T-shirt showing in the open V. The bit of logo that was visible suggested that the shirt alluded to a brand of beer.

Brandon MacDonald reached out a welcoming arm and guided Bettina toward a chair. "I've missed our chats," he said, "and seeing my name and picture in the *Advocate* every week." His gaze shifted from Bettina to Pamela. "You've brought a friend."

Bettina was still standing. She turned, drew Pamela closer, and said, "My friend and neighbor, Pamela Paterson."

"I didn't quite catch the name." MacDonald

leaned toward Bettina and cupped a hand around the ear that faced her.

"Pamela Paterson," Bettina repeated, raising her voice above the lunchtime din.

MacDonald lowered his hand from his ear and smiled at Pamela. "You look familiar, Pam. Don't tell me"—he snapped his fingers a few times—"the reception. You were at the reception for our dearly departed Diefenbach!"

"That's right." Pamela mustered her social smile.

"I'm glad you could join us. Shall we sit down?" Brandon MacDonald accompanied the suggestion with an expansive gesture that included pulling out a chair for Bettina and then one for Pamela. He waited until they were both settled before lowering himself back into his own chair.

Pamela had stopped at the Co-Op on her way to Hyler's, and she carried a canvas shopping bag containing two pounds of ground beef, half a dozen potatoes, and a pint of milk. She took the seat across from MacDonald and tucked the bag and her umbrella under her chair.

Despite the fact that they'd arrived when the restaurant was at its busiest, a server appeared the instant they had taken their seats, the middle-aged woman who had worked at Hyler's forever. Mac-Donald had held court at Hyler's throughout his many terms as mayor, and apparently the fact that he was no longer mayor hadn't diminished the staff's attentiveness.

"How're you doing, Bran?" the server asked. "Finding ways to keep busy?" She held three of the oversize menus that were a feature of Hyler's.

"Busy as I want to be," MacDonald responded. "Not as busy as you, I bet." He reached out a hand and in a moment they were each studying a menu.

"I'm thinking tuna melt." Bettina's eyes appeared over the top edge of her menu. "And a vanilla shake." Pamela agreed that a tuna melt sounded like an appealing choice, but MacDonald was still studying his menu when the server returned. With a genial laugh, he stabbed a finger at the menu murmuring "Eeny meeny miny moe" and announced that he would have a tuna melt too.

"So," he said as the server retreated, "the *Advocate* is wondering what I think about the current state of things political in our fair town?"

"I'm sure our readership would like to know your views." Bettina accompanied the statement with a flirtatious wink.

"Am I glad Diefenbach is out of the way?" MacDonald rested his elbows on the table and knit his fingers together. He frowned as if formulating an answer to a question he had never considered before. Then he pounded the table with both fists, causing a couple at a neighboring table to aim startled glances his way. "Yes!" he said at last. "I was born in Arborville and I've lived here all my life and I don't want to see it become another River Ridge."

River Ridge was a nearby town, right on the edge of the Hudson, where high rises had begun to sprout, snarling traffic and turning a once-charming community into a bedroom for Manhattan commuters.

"I actually hated the guy," he went on. Then he

looked around in a jokingly furtive way. "Is it too soon after the funeral to admit that?"

"What do you think of Martha Cosgrove's chances?" Bettina asked. "If there's a special election, that is."

"There won't be a special election." MacDonald folded his arms across his ample chest. "The town council would have to agree and they won't. The rabble rousers can raise all the rabble they want but they're just going to have to wait four years."

The milkshakes arrived then, in tall glasses dewy with condensation and crowned with bubbly froth. The server lingered at the table after she set them down. "Are people pestering you?" she asked MacDonald.

"What's that again?" MacDonald swiveled his head to look up at the server.

"Are people pestering you?" She repeated it louder. "Nosy people? Being that you live right next door to where Diefenbach lived?"

"Not so much." MacDonald shrugged.

"But the police must have had a lot of questions. Were you one of the neighbors who said they heard shouting? Before"—she paused and shuddered—"it happened?"

"I didn't hear a thing," MacDonald said with a decisive headshake. "Not a thing."

"Lucky, I guess," the server commented as she turned to go. "I'd have nightmares. Tuna melts coming right up."

"Were you at home after all?" Pamela blurted. "Not out with your friends?" Then she grimaced as she realized she had only thought MacDonald wasn't at home at nine p.m. because of something Wilfred

had said—that MacDonald usually joined other
members of the historical society for a few beers
after the Monday night meetings.

Bettina took a long sip from her straw, leaving a
smudge of her bright lipstick behind. She looked
up from her milkshake and mirrored Pamela's grimace.

But MacDonald didn't seem to notice that the
question implied more knowledge of his doings
than a woman he had just met could realistically
have. "I thought I was getting a cold," he said.
"Change in the weather, I guess." He laughed.
"Too bad too. Could have stayed out till the cows
came home. My wife's been at her sister's the past
couple weeks."

The server had returned, managing to deliver
all three platters in one trip. She settled each onto
its paper placemat and went on her way again with
a cheery "Enjoy it!"

As MacDonald contemplated his lunch, Bettina
stole a questioning glance at Pamela. In response
to Pamela's answering nod, Bettina mouthed, "*No
alibi after all.*" Then she quickly added, in a voice
designed to carry to MacDonald's ears, "This looks
delicious!"

It did indeed. The bread, glowing with a buttery
sheen, had been grilled to a perfect shade of
golden brown. Tuna salad, creamy with mayonnaise and streaked with melted cheese, spilled
from the gap between the upper and lower slices.
Tucked alongside each sandwich was a pickle
spear, pale greenish yellow with a dark green strip
of peel.

They addressed their meal in silence for a few

minutes, tackling the sandwiches with forks and sipping their milkshakes.

"You said you could have stayed out till the cows came home," Bettina observed after a bit.

"What's that again?" MacDonald looked at Bettina, fork in hand.

"You said you could have stayed out till the cows came home. I guess you know that in some circles you're referred to as 'Old MacDonald.'" Bettina added a smile flirtatious enough to imply that she herself couldn't imagine anyone applying the word "old" to the man sitting next to her.

But the flattery wasn't needed. MacDonald let out a boisterous laugh and brayed "E-I-E-I-O," provoking another round of startled glances from the couple at the neighboring table. "That's me," he said cheerfully, "Old MacDonald and proud of it. Like I said, I don't want Arborville to turn into River Ridge, at least not in my lifetime."

"There's a rooster . . ." Bettina let the sentence trail off.

"Indeed there is." MacDonald pounded the table, with just one fist this time, since the other hand was occupied holding a fork. "And a very fine rooster it is. I was proud to be that rooster's mayor."

"The owner is a friend then . . ." Bettina again let the sentence trail off.

"Darn right! My good pal Jack Delaney. Jack of all trades, master of none." MacDonald returned to his sandwich then. He carved off a huge bite with the edge of his fork and conveyed it to his mouth oblivious of the fact that the forkful trailed a long string of melted cheese and a gobbet of tuna salad. The tuna salad remained behind on his chin, and as he chewed he lifted his napkin from his lap and dabbed it away.

He continued to work on the sandwich until nothing was left, interspersing forkfuls of tuna melt with bites from the pickle. Pamela and Bettina had returned to their sandwiches as well. Pamela was just savoring the last toasty morsel of hers, enjoying the contrast between the sharp cheese and the mild creaminess of the tuna salad, when MacDonald deposited the stem-end of his pickle on his platter, pushed the platter away, and spoke again.

"Yeah, Jack of all trades, master of none," he repeated, as if he'd been ruminating on this theme as he finished his meal. "He gets by okay though— I'll say that for him. Never had a real job in his life as far as I know, but he does handyman work here and there, and lives off the land."

"Where does he live?" Bettina asked, in tone that suggested she was just making conversation.

"Up by the community gardens," MacDonald said. "At the end of that road that kind of trails off where the gardens start. It's an old house, just a bungalow really. Inherited it from his parents. He's a lifelong Arborvillian too."

The server approached then. Pamela slurped the last sweet sips of her milkshake and relinquished the glass as the server began to clear away. MacDonald leaned back in his chair with a contented sigh. "My treat, ladies," he said with a genial smile. "It's been a pleasure."

* * *

"You'll take a ride home, I hope." Bettina and Pamela had just parted from MacDonald and were lingering on the sidewalk outside Hyler's. "I can't believe you came out on foot like that in the rain. Walking everywhere in good weather is one thing, but—"

"It wasn't raining when I came out," Pamela said. "In fact it was already starting to clear up. And now look." She tilted her head and gazed toward the east, over the shop fronts ranged along the opposite side of Arborville Avenue.

The roofline was silhouetted against a strip of blue sky. Overhead the blue was streaked with filmy wisps of gray that trailed the storm's retreat. To the west a pale, chilly sun blazed through a break where lingering clouds still massed.

Pamela gave her friend a fond smile. "I will take a ride though. We have a lot to talk about."

Bettina led the way through the narrow passageway that connected Arborville Avenue with the parking lot shared by the municipal complex, library included, and the town park. She stepped smartly around the few lingering puddles in her yellow rubber booties, Pamela following, and soon they were both settled in the front seat of Bettina's faithful Toyota.

"He doesn't have an alibi after all," Bettina said, jingling her keys.

"And he does have a motive," Pamela added. "But we knew that."

"He's such a nice man though." Bettina pursed her lips.

"He did seem nice," Pamela agreed. She thought for a minute. Bettina's car faced the park. A rambunctious dog was frisking on the wet grass. "And if he really did it, why would he be so open about the fact that he was home, right next door to Diefenbach, around the time that the murder happened?"

"He must have told the police that too," Bettina said. "And they must have believed him, even though his wife was away so there's nobody to vouch that he didn't leave his own house."

"He said he didn't hear anything. That was weird. But then, he doesn't seem to hear too well in general."

"Hyler's at lunchtime is very noisy," Bettina pointed out. She slipped her key into the ignition and with a twist of her fingers the car chugged to life. But Pamela was still thinking.

"If he felt like he had to prove his innocence, wouldn't he say he *did* hear something—even build it up?" she said. "Maybe say he heard the other voice too, maybe even say it was a *woman's* voice?"

Bettina backed out of the parking space and aimed the Toyota toward the exit that ran along the side of the library.

"Jack Delaney's probably at home now," Pamela said.

Bettina lifted a hand from the steering wheel to consult her pretty gold watch. "Drat!" she exclaimed. "I promised to watch the Arborville grandchildren this afternoon and I have to be there at two."

"First thing tomorrow?"

"Ten a.m." Bettina nodded. "I'll pick you up." She turned left and then right and in a few moments they were speeding south on Arborville Avenue.

"He and MacDonald could be in on it together," Pamela commented as Bettina slowed to make another turn. They had reached the stately brick apartment building that marked the corner of Orchard Street. "Linked by a vision of preserving the old Arborville."

"With a rooster," Bettina added. "And probably hens. We'll find out tomorrow."

They had reached Pamela's driveway. "I'm making two meatloaves tonight," Pamela said as she lifted her canvas grocery bag and umbrella from the floor. "And lots of scalloped potatoes. I'll divide them between two casseroles. And we'll drop a meatloaf and some scalloped potatoes off for Melanie and Roland on our way to see Jack Delaney."

Chapter 18

It wasn't ten a.m. In fact it was barely eight. Catrina and Ginger were still crouched companionably over their breakfast, tails switching back and forth with pleasure, when the doorbell and then frantic knocking summoned Pamela to the door.

Bettina stood on the porch, her pumpkin-colored coat pulled over a flowered nightgown that trailed to her ankles. Her face, still marked by signs of sleep, was bare of makeup and her hair was uncombed.

"He's giving LeCorbusier away," she moaned. LeCorbusier was the name Richard Larkin had given to the cat he adopted from Catrina's litter.

"How do you know?" Pamela stepped aside to let Bettina enter.

"Wilfred saw him, two minutes ago, when he went out to get the paper. Richard was putting a cat-carrier into the back of his Jeep Cherokee."

"Maybe it was empty," Pamela suggested. "Maybe he's loaning it to someone."

"He was talking to it." Bettina's hazel eyes were tragic. "Or rather to the cat that was in it. He was saying not to be nervous. Wilfred could hear him from across the street."

"Maybe he was just taking LeCorbusier to the vet," Pamela said.

Bettina shook her head, stirring the disordered tendrils of her scarlet hair. "He was saying that LeCorbusier would be happy in his new home."

"Oh, dear." Pamela sighed. "What can be going on? He was so enthusiastic about the adoption."

"I don't know." Bettina shook her head again. "I don't know. Maybe Wilfred can find something out. He and Richard often have little chats."

"I haven't even started coffee yet," Pamela said. "So why don't I make extra, and we can—"

Bettina grabbed Pamela's hands. "I'd love to stay, but I've got to get dressed and hurry over to the *Advocate* office. Then we have our errands at ten." She gave Pamela's hands a squeeze, released them, and turned toward the door. "But I just don't know how I can concentrate on anything," she moaned, "when this tragic thing has happened."

Pamela's own cats had vanished by the time she returned to the kitchen. But as soon as the sun was high enough to brighten the worn thrift-store rug in the entry, Catrina would seek out her favorite sunny spot, Pamela knew. And LeCorbusier would be fine. She was sure of that. Richard Larkin was a kind man, and he'd been a responsible cat owner. What could have happened, though, to make him decide he could no longer give a home to LeCorbusier?

She set the kettle boiling on the stove, fetched the *Register* from her front walk, and slipped a slice of whole-grain bread into the toaster.

A short time later, fortified by her morning toast and coffee and dressed in her cool-weather uniform of jeans and a sweater, she removed Ginger from her computer's keyboard and sat down to work. When she checked her email, the article on Hmong story cloths reappeared, with instructions from her boss to edit it and return it by the next morning.

Before embarking on that task though, she dallied a bit by scrolling through the photographs that had charmed her so much on first reading the article. The author had included images of story cloths that ranged from panoramic views of riverside villages to intimate scenes of women at work. Rivers, plied by watercraft large and small, teemed with fish. Farm yards boasted fruit-laden trees, well-fed poultry, and jovial pigs. Women squatted over fires, tending steaming cauldrons, while children frolicked nearby.

Such a human impulse, she reflected, to express oneself with whatever art materials were at hand. And women, whose world was so much narrower in some cultures, had found in crafts like needlework or weaving or quilting or *knitting* vehicles for their artistry. She immersed herself in the article itself then, untangling a sentence here and there, correcting a bit of spelling, and making sure the punctuation and capitalization conformed to the *Fiber Craft* style manual. As ten a.m. neared, she saved her work and stepped into the bathroom to neaten her hair. By the time Bettina rang the doorbell, she was standing in the entry staring into the closet where she kept her outdoor wear.

"You won't need your winter jacket," Bettina said as she stepped over the threshold. "It's starting to feel like spring again."

Bettina's homage to the change in the weather involved replacing her pumpkin-colored down coat with her bright yellow trench coat and her rain booties with her chartreuse pumps. A bit of chartreuse framed in the V of her coat collar suggested the dress beneath the trench coat matched the shoes, and dangling earrings set with chartreuse stones carried out the chartreuse theme.

"Wilfred is going to talk to Richard tonight," she added. "He wants to ask him for advice on the castle he's building for the Arborville grandchildren, but he'll find a way to inquire about LeCorbusier." She smiled down at Catrina, who had claimed her sunny spot and was dozing on the entry rug.

Pamela slipped into a favorite old tan jacket, parka style in cotton twill, with a zipper front.

"The *Advocate* got a letter to the editor from that nutty note-writing person," Bettina said as Pamela collected her keys and reached for the doorknob. "He—or she—wanted to remind people that it's officially been spring for more than three weeks and it's time for spring yard cleanup. But they shouldn't put yard waste out on any night other

than Sunday, and then not before six p.m. because
it's an—"

"Eyesore?" Pamela suggested.

"Eyesore." Bettina nodded.

"Well, he's nothing if not consistent," Pamela
commented.

"Or she," Bettina said. "We don't know for sure."

The meatloaf and scalloped potatoes had been
delivered, with instructions to microwave portions
as needed, and gratefully accepted. Now Bettina
was navigating her way up a curious winding road
at the upper edge of The Farm where the slope
that led to the cliffs overlooking the Hudson
began.

She left the last well-groomed block of The Farm
behind and made a sharp turn onto a narrow road.
The road ran through a bit of hilly woods that still
remained from the days before anyone except the
Lenni Lenape inhabited the land that was now
Arborville. When the road emerged from the
woods, it trailed off into a gravel surface that was
little more than a wide path. Ahead were the community gardens, fallow now, and a gravel-covered
lot where people parked when they came to work
on their gardens. And tucked off to the left, on the
edge of the woods, was a little one-story house that
looked like something out of a fairy tale.

Its shingled siding had weathered to a shade of
gray-brown that blended with the woods, but the
window frames, shutters, and front door looked

freshly painted, and in a pleasing shade of dark
green that complemented the color of the house.
A tidy brick path led from the road to the door,
and the yard seemed carefully planned. There was
no lawn, not even a brown stubble waiting for
more rain and sun to come alive, but rather trees
just beginning to bud, and shrubs, and beds of
dark earth where crocus and daffodils had already
appeared and green nubbins suggested that tulips
and more were in the offing. Near the porch was a
neatly arranged pile of split logs. A wheelbarrow
filled with mulch was parked near an open gate
that gave a glimpse into the backyard. A smaller
brick path branching off from the main one led to
the gate and continued beyond.

Bettina continued on for a bit and steered the
Toyota into the lot for the community gardens.
Then crunching over the gravel, Pamela and Bettina made their way back to Jack Delaney's house.
As they reached the brick path, the door of the
house opened and onto the front porch stepped a
man wearing faded blue jeans and a fringed suede
jacket. His luxuriant moustache was a grayish
blond color, as was the hair that flowed over the
collar of the jacket. Jack Delaney, Pamela realized,
was the man who had been so extremely vocal
about his dislike of Diefenbach at the memorial reception. Had she known that he was the person
they were coming in search of, she might have
given more thought to a strategic approach.

Bettina hesitated at the end of the path and
Pamela hesitated with her. But Jack Delaney had

caught sight of them. "Hey!" he called in a gravel-voiced but genial enough manner. "I won't bite!"

Pamela ventured forward, Bettina following. But as they got closer, his manner changed.

"You two were at that confab for the fans of Daffy-brain, weren't you?" he said scowling. "What do you want with me?"

Pamela mustered her social smile, though Jack Delaney didn't seem like the type who responded to conventional social signals. Bettina, meanwhile, stepped out from behind Pamela. "We're from the *Advocate*," she said cheerily, sticking out a hand. "I'm Bettina Fraser. Perhaps you recognize my by-line." She accompanied the words with a bright smile.

"Can't say I pay any attention to that thing," Jack Delaney said.

"Community journalism serves a valuable purpose." Bettina's smile was undimmed. "Most people are more affected by what happens locally than what happens nationally."

"Umph!" It was hard to read Jack Delaney's expression because his moustache hid his mouth, but his eyes looked slightly kinder. "I don't want to talk about politics, and I know that's what's on everybody's mind right now."

"Oh, no!" Bettina made a pretty gesture with her hands, as if pushing away the very idea of politics. Her nails, lavender today, glittered. "I drove up here with my associate Pamela Paterson"—she thrust an arm around Pamela's waist—"to report on the state of the community gardens. But I don't think I'll find anything there to compare with your yard." Bettina left the brick path and stepped delicately over a bare patch of earth in her chartreuse pumps. She paused when she reached a stand of daffodils that softened the geometry of Jack Delaney's porch railing. The daffodils were the exact bright yellow of her trench coat. "I love daffodils," she said, "and I see you've got crocus coming up, and"—she pointed toward a bed where green nubbins were pushing up—"tulips?"

"Imported from Holland." Jack Delaney crossed his arms over his chest and nodded. "I order new ones every year. Hybrids don't come back the same, you know." He uncrossed his arms and waved toward the stand of daffodils, setting the fringe on his jacket sleeve in motion. "Daffodils, on the other hand—plant bulbs once and you'll have them for the rest of your life, more and more every year." He edged toward the large tree that anchored one side of his yard. "She's been with me forever too," he said, patting its trunk fondly. "She'll be getting her blossoms soon, and she gives me a good crop of apricots every year."

"Do you grow other food?" Bettina asked.

We already know he does, said a voice in Pamela's head. Brandon MacDonald told us that. But she stilled the voice and remained where she was, lingering at the end of the brick path. Bettina had ways of getting people to reveal things, and Jack Delaney was definitely warming up to her.

"Most of what I eat." The moustache made it hard to tell if he was smiling, but crinkles had appeared at the corners of his eyes.

"You must have a *very* extensive vegetable gar-

den then." Bettina met his gaze with a wide-eyed
expression that suggested amazement and respect.
She glanced toward the open gate. "I don't suppose . . ."

"Awww." Jack Delaney really did seem pleased
now, if looking at the ground in embarrassment was
a sign. "There's not much to see yet, though I do
have some tomatoes starting in a cold-frame . . ."

"I always wondered how people did that," Bettina said as she took a few steps toward the open
gate.

Jack Delaney strode ahead and moved the
wheelbarrow out of the way. He stood aside as Bettina passed through the gate and waited as Pamela
hurried along the brick path to join them.

The garden was dormant, but its layout was
clear—a rectangle that took up half the back yard,
marked by long parallel ridges where crops would
be sown in neat rows and valleys where irrigation
water would flow. Here and there a desiccated
stalk, a bit of stubble, or a brittle tangle of vines remained from the previous year's harvest. At one
end was a line of long stakes planted in clusters of
three and joined at the top teepee-style. They were
similar to constructions Pamela had seen in Nell's
garden—frameworks for runner beans to climb on
Nell had said.

Behind the garden was a mini-replica of Jack
Delaney's house, complete with faded shingle siding and dark green paint accenting the two small
windows and the open doorway centered between
them. A chicken-wire fence marked out an expan-

sive yard surrounding the little house. As they watched, a rooster appeared in the doorway, a magnificent creature with glossy feathers that shaded from fiery orange on his neck and chest to the iridescent blue-black plumes that formed his exuberant tail. He strutted forth, turning his head this way and that as if to display the proud serrations of his bright red comb and his quivering wattles.

With a delighted squeal, Bettina reached for Jack Delaney's leather-clad arm. "Oh, my goodness!" she said. "So this is where the Arborville rooster lives!" She gazed awe-struck at the rooster then, without altering her expression, tilted her head to gaze at Jack Delaney. "That rooster certainly has plenty to crow about." Jack Delaney gazed back at Bettina and fingered his moustache.

Pamela was quite impressed by the rooster too, as she was by Bettina's success in breaking through Jack Delaney's defenses, though she hoped Bettina's flirtation was no more than an act.

"Does he live there all by himself?" Bettina had let go of Jack Delaney's arm but was still gazing at him with wide eyes.

"What do you think?" Jack Delaney asked in a teasing tone. "Could an impressive fellow like that be content to live alone?" The gravel in his voice lent the question a seductive quality.

Bettina answered the teasing tone with a teasing smile and murmured, "That would be a waste . . ."

"The house is actually a henhouse." Jack Delaney nodded. "Heated, comfortable as can be.

I've got a few Araucanas and a Faverolle and a
Barnevelder—she's a pretty little thing. My rooster
has a whole harem. And I've got eggs for breakfast
every day."

He was silent for a bit then, watching as the
rooster scratched around in the dirt.

"The cold-frames," Bettina said. "You were going
to show us the cold-frames."

"Over here." Jack Delaney set off toward the
back of his house. "Around the side here, the
south side." He led them to an area where what
looked like salvaged windows had been set atop
shallow wooden boxes built to fit them. Hinges fastened the windows to one long side of the boxes.

Pamela was interested in tomatoes. She enjoyed
growing her own in the summer, though she had
never been so ambitious as to start them from
seeds. So she should have been paying attention as
Jack Delaney described to Bettina the ins and outs
of cold-frames. But as he talked, she was reflecting
that one of the questions she and Bettina had
come with had been answered. Yes, Jack Delaney
had hens, hens that laid eggs. But then there was
the other question: What had Jack Delaney been
doing the night Diefenbach was killed?

"You must have more eggs than you can use,"
she heard herself say. "With so many hens."

"Umph?" He had been stooping over the cold-
frame, pointing out the tiny seedlings getting a
head start on their growing season. Now he stood
up and looked at Pamela. "Angling for a sample,
are you?" he asked with a frown.

Pamela took a step backwards, startled. "No . . . I . . . it just seemed . . ."

"I guarantee eggs from free-range chickens don't taste like grocery store eggs," Jack Delaney said. "Lots of people don't like them."

"Did Bill Diefenbach?" Pamela asked, ignoring the vision of Bettina, peeking out from behind Jack Delaney with a horrified expression on her face.

"Bill Diefenbach? What does he have to do with anything?" The brusque manner that had been on display at the memorial reception returned. Jack Delaney lowered his head like a bull about to charge and clenched his fists. Pamela took another step backwards. He whirled around to glare at Bettina. "What's all this about? Buttering me up so you can . . . because you think you're—what?— an investigative journalist?" Scorn compacted the gravel in his voice and it rose in pitch. "For the *Arborville Advocate?* The lamest newspaper on earth?"

He stepped back so Pamela and Bettina were between him and the gate that they'd entered earlier. "Interview's over, ladies." He flung his arms wide and gestured in a herding motion, causing the fringe on his jacket sleeves to flap wildly. "It's been nice knowing you."

Pamela and Bettina headed obediently toward the open gate and retreated along the brick path that led to the road. But before they reached the road, Bettina stopped and turned. "I'm sorry my associate upset you," she called to Jack Delaney, who was standing near his wheelbarrow watching them leave. "Thank you for showing us your rooster and the cold-frames."

Pamela wasn't sure exactly what she was seeing at that distance, but it almost seemed that Jack Delaney winked. "I am the walrus," he called.

Chapter 19

Bettina was silent until they reached the Toyota, stalking ahead of Pamela and crunching recklessly over the gravel of the parking lot despite the delicacy of her chartreuse pumps. Then, before even extracting her car key from her purse, she spoke. Glaring across the hood of the car at Pamela, who was standing near the passenger-side door, she said, "Why on earth did you ask him that? You ruined everything."

"I didn't see that things were moving in the direction we wanted." Pamela tried to keep her voice neutral.

"You didn't trust me?" Bettina ended the question with her brows raised and her bright lips parted.

"You seemed so interested in the tomato seedlings . . ."

"Of course I seemed interested in the tomato seedlings. Jack was interested in them and he

wanted to show them off, and he was really warming up to me." Bettina's brows rose higher and she
spoke in the dry tone of someone clarifying the
obvious.

"I could see *that*." The statement popped out
before Pamela had a chance to censor it. She tried
to recover by adding, "But the tomato seedlings
didn't seem to have much to do with Diefenbach
and . . ."

"I was going to ask Jack if he had a girlfriend."

"Bettina!" Pamela flopped a hand down onto
the hood of the car and the hood responded with
a metallic thump. "You're a married woman."

"I liked his moustache." Bettina's lips shaped a
mysterious smile.

"And so what if he has a girlfriend? What does
that have to do with Diefenbach?"

Bettina burst out laughing, setting her earrings
in motion. "Wilfred had one of those walrus moustaches when I met him," she said after a bit, her
face pink from the hilarity that had convulsed it.
"I've always liked moustaches. But as to my interest
in Jack Delaney, a girlfriend could provide useful
information about his comings and goings—such
as where he might have been the Monday before
last at nine p.m. But now that door has closed."

Pamela felt her shoulders sag. "I'm sorry," she
said in a small voice. "I should have realized you
had a plan."

Bettina shrugged. "Water over the bridge, as
Wilfred would say. At least we know he has eggs."

"And fancy chickens."

"And fancy chickens," Bettina echoed as she unlocked her car. She slipped behind the steering

wheel and reached over to unlock the passenger-side door.

"He said he was a walrus," Pamela commented as she climbed in.

The refrigerator door was open and Wilfred was bent over peering into its interior when Pamela and Bettina entered the Frasers' kitchen. Pamela was carrying a foil-wrapped parcel. Woofus had been curled up in his favorite corner, his nose nearly touching the tip of his shaggy tail, but he raised his head in greeting.

Wilfred straightened up and turned toward the new arrivals. "The larder is bare, dear wife," he announced. "Except for the Easter ham, of course. I have been derelict in my duty."

Pamela held up the foil-wrapped parcel. "Left-over meatloaf," she said. "If you have bread . . . and mayonnaise . . ."

"Meatloaf sandwiches!" A smile creased Wilfred's ruddy face and he rubbed his hands together briskly. "You have made my day, Pamela!" He turned back to the refrigerator and bent back down. "Mayonnaise," he murmured, lifting it from a shelf. Bettina sprang forward, took it from his hand, and placed it on the high counter that divided the cooking area of the kitchen from the eating area. "And pickles." He stood up, holding a portly jar in which dim greenish oblongs floated, and eased the refrigerator door closed.

Pamela had already unwrapped the meatloaf and taken six slices from the half-loaf of Co-Op sourdough bread she found in the bread drawer.

She placed the meatloaf on a cutting board and set to work on it with one of Wilfred's sharpest knives, carving off two slices for each sandwich.

Bettina fetched three of her sage-green plates from the cupboard and arranged them in a row along the high counter, then she began spreading a generous layer of mayonnaise on each slice of sourdough. Meanwhile Wilfred had joined Pamela at the lower counter and on a cutting board of his own was slicing a large pickle into careful slices so thin that they were almost translucent.

When the bread was ready, Wilfred began to assemble the sandwiches, two slices of meatloaf for each, sprinkled with salt and a generous grinding of pepper, and garnished with two slices of pickle. Meanwhile Bettina was bustling between the cooking area and the eating area of her spacious kitchen, laying out placemats, napkins, and flatware on the scrubbed pine table.

She looked up from her task. "What shall we drink?" she inquired. "What goes with meatloaf sandwiches?"

"How about root beer?" Wilfred spoke as he completed the final sandwich by lowering the top slice of bread into place. "I think we still have a few bottles of that root beer Wilfred Jr.'s friend makes." He cut each sandwich in half.

Pamela delivered the sandwiches to the table, arranging the sage-green plates on Bettina's colorful rust, cream, and maroon placemats, as Wilfred set off to the basement in quest of the root beer. Soon the three friends were settled companionably around the pine table, with bubbling glasses of root beer at hand to complement the hearty meatloaf sandwiches.

The Frasers' spacious kitchen was not original to their house, a Dutch Colonial that was the oldest house on Orchard Street. The kitchen, which they added when they bought the house early in their marriage, featured sliding glass doors that looked out onto the backyard. The view today was of a broad lawn in the early stages of turning green, shrubs that didn't shed their leaves in the winter but looked woebegone nonetheless, and a splendid maple tree whose branches were dusted with the faint green haze of new foliage.

"Did you ladies succeed in tracking down Jack Delaney?" Wilfred asked after the first few bites of his sandwich.

"Indeed we did." Pamela gave Bettina a look that was part teasing, part disapproving.

"Pamela thought I was flirting with him," Bettina said with a laugh.

"You can catch more flies with a spoonful of honey than with a barrel of vinegar," Wilfred remarked sagely.

"He *is* the person who has the rooster that people complain about," Pamela said. She had sampled her sandwich too, enjoying the interplay between the comforting taste of her none-too-adventurous meatloaf and the piquant vinegar-dill of the pickle slices. "Somebody left a basket of eggs on Diefenbach's porch the night he was killed, eggs dyed like Easter eggs. Roland saw them, and we were thinking it might have been Jack Delaney—which could be a good clue about who killed Diefenbach."

"And we found out that Jack Delaney has hens too, besides the rooster," Bettina added. "Rare breeds, he said. He's quite proud of them. Funny names, like a . . . raucana, or something. And he eats their eggs for breakfast. But then Pamela came right out and asked him if Diefenbach liked his eggs and he got mad and we had to leave." She picked up the second half of her sandwich. "He said some insulting things about the *Advocate* too." She took a bite and chewed it thoughtfully.

"I'm sure he didn't mean them." Wilfred reached over and rubbed Bettina's shoulder. "Everyone in Arborville appreciates the *Advocate.*"

"Delicious," Bettina murmured after she had swallowed. "You make the best sandwiches, Wilfred."

"Credit where credit is due, sweet wife," Wilfred said. "Pamela made the meatloaf." He looked pleased nonetheless.

"Jack Delaney has one of those moustaches, like you had when we met." Bettina gazed at Wilfred as adoringly as if more than thirty years hadn't elapsed since their courtship and marriage.

"He seemed quite proud of his moustache too," Pamela said. "He kept fingering it. And as we were leaving he said he was a walrus."

"Tell me more about these hens." Wilfred had finished his sandwich. He reached for the remains of his root beer. "Rare breeds?"

"With funny names." Bettina nodded.

"Araucana?" Wilfred asked.

Bettina nodded again. "And 'barn'-something. And one of them sounded like 'favorite' but not quite."

"Favor roll," Pamela said. "That's what it sounded like to me."

"The historical society had a speaker a while ago." Wilfred leaned back in his chair. "She teaches animal husbandry at Rutgers, and she talked about the breeds of chickens that the Dutch and English farmers in Revolutionary-Era New Jersey would have known." In his bib overalls and plaid flannel shirt, Wilfred himself resembled a farmer, though perhaps not from the Revolutionary Era. He paused and looked first at Pamela and then at Bettina as if to signal that a dramatic revelation was at hand. "Some breeds of chicken lay colored eggs."

"Oh, my goodness!" Bettina jumped up from her chair and darted toward the living room. Soon she was back, flourishing her smart phone. She lowered herself into her chair and began fingering the device, whispering "Araucana . . . araucana." A few minutes passed, then she looked up with a delighted smile. "Turquoise eggs," she sang out. "The hens lay turquoise eggs. Wilfred, you are a genius!"

Wilfred beamed.

"And there's a whole chart here," Bettina went on. " 'Favor rolls'—that's a breed called Faverolle. The eggs in the picture here look almost pink. And there's a kind that lays ones that are kind of olive green, and some yellowish ones . . ."

"Well!" Pamela leaned back in her chair. "We don't know for sure, but it's certainly tempting to think he's the person who left that basket of eggs on Diefenbach's porch. So that could put him right on the spot around the time Diefenbach was killed. And maybe Diefenbach comes out and says,

'What do you think you're doing? I don't want your stupid eggs.' "

Bettina took up the story. "They start arguing—we know that Diefenbach was a guy who lost his temper easily, and Delaney isn't the calmest person either—"

Suddenly Wilfred leaned forward, resting his hands on the edge of the table. "Jack Delaney *did* deliver those eggs to Diefenbach!" he announced.

Pamela and Bettina stared at him.

"He said he was the walrus," Wilfred explained. "That means he's also . . . the egg man."

"The Beatles!" Pamela slapped the side of her head. "Why didn't I think of that?"

Wilfred gazed toward the sliding glass doors and the yard beyond. His lips curved into a secret smile. "The *Magical Mystery Tour*." His tone was reverent. "The music of my youth."

"I'm seeing Clayborn in the morning," Bettina said. "I'm definitely going to ask him about the basket of eggs. If they were still there, the crime scene people should have taken them as evidence. And if they can be traced back to Delaney . . . even if the police have already questioned him once—and we don't even know that—the eggs should be grounds to question him again."

Catrina and Ginger crept in warily. Pamela kept the door to Penny's bedroom closed when her daughter was away, but it was Friday morning. Penny was due home this afternoon and Pamela had flung the door open wide. The cats tiptoed here and there, peering around corners, sniffing and probing, and Pamela stood in the doorway, surveying her daughter's room with the same satisfied pleasure she'd felt when she and her husband put the finishing touches on it so long ago.

They'd splurged on the luxury of wallpaper, pale blue wallpaper with tight little pink rosebuds, and put it up themselves. Though Pamela wasn't a seamstress, she'd managed the simple white eyelet curtains, practicing first on the set that still hung at the windows in the master bedroom. The dresser had been a thrift-store find that Michael Paterson had freshened up with a coat of glossy white paint. Later a small desk and chair had been added, painted glossy white to match the dresser. Gradually the room's décor had come to include examples of Penny's own handiwork: oil paintings, sketches, and watercolors—produced in art classes, on rambles around town, or during impromptu sessions with friends and relatives as models. A portrait of Pamela depicted her as looking rather forbidding, though the need to sit absolutely still for what had seemed an endless amount of time might have inhibited a more mobile expression.

But there was work to be done. Furniture and window sills would need to be dusted, dust bunnies routed from under the bed, and rag rugs shaken. The bed would need to be made up with fresh sheets, and the down comforter and patchwork quilt smoothed back into place.

Pamela folded the two rag rugs and set them in the hall, to be taken outside for a good shaking. Then she set to work with her dust cloth. Once the dust-cloth dusting was done, she tackled the floor with her dust mop. This activity sent Catrina scurrying from the room. Ginger, however, had managed to bound up onto the bed. Now she was stretched out atop the hump formed by the pillow like an elegant fur piece, watching Pamela's industry with particular absorption.

Perhaps, Pamela reflected, as Ginger explored she'd come to recognize the room, and the bed, by means of smells too subtle for a human nose. During Penny's Christmas visit home, Ginger had discovered she could have a bed and a human of her own, leaving Catrina full claim to a share of Pamela's bed.

When the floor had been adequately dusted, Pamela fetched sheets from the linen closet in the hall. A sachet of lavender buds hung on the inside of the door, and everything that came from the closet carried with it the dusky sweet aroma of lavender. She lifted Ginger gently from the pillow and set her on the floor, receiving an annoyed stare in the process. But the bed had to be changed.

She folded the quilt as gently as she'd handled Ginger. It was an heirloom that her own grandmother had made for her when Pamela was a child. On a white background, squares cut from ancient tiny prints faded to pastel formed interlocking circles to create the quilt pattern known as Double Wedding Ring. She laid the quilt on the desk, piled the down comforter on top, and stripped the sheets from the bed. They, along with the pillow case, joined the folded rugs in the hall.

Then she smoothed the fresh lavender-smelling sheets onto the bed, added the comforter, slipped the pillow into a fresh pillow case, and nestled it into place at the base of the headboard. She gently replaced the quilt and paused to see if Ginger wanted to reoccupy her comfortable lounging spot. But the cat was nowhere to be seen.

The final touch was to fetch the lilac tunic and arrange it on the bed. Pamela studied her handiwork with satisfaction. The separate pieces of the tunic had come together nicely—unlike the puzzle pieces that still refused to coalesce in a solution to the murder of Bill Diefenbach.

Chapter 20

"Cassie Griswold was murdered!"

The white bakery box in Bettina's hands suggested she'd come prepared to chat, but the message she'd blurted out as soon as Pamela opened the door shifted Pamela's focus from the box to Bettina's face. Bettina's eyes were moist and the buoyant cheer that plumped and rosied her cheeks had fled, leaving her wan and pale despite her careful makeup.

"How on earth—?" Pamela stepped back and motioned Bettina over the threshold. "You've been with Detective Clayborn," she said once Bettina was inside.

Bettina nodded. "The autopsy results . . ." she managed to say before her voice thinned and then went silent.

"Come into the kitchen and have some water." Pamela took charge of the bakery box and helped

Bettina off with the bright yellow trenchcoat. Then, carrying the box by the string with one hand, Pamela used the other hand to shepherd Bettina toward the doorway that led into the kitchen.

"I hardly knew her," Bettina murmured after she found her voice again, "but it was just such a shock to hear."

Pamela settled Bettina in a chair and furnished her with a glass of water. More water went into the kettle and the kettle went onto the stove with a burner alight beneath it. Pamela busied herself grinding coffee and arranging a paper filter in her carafe's plastic filter cone. She glanced at Bettina from time to time, hoping that the comforting sights, sounds, and smells of coffee being brewed would restore her friend's equilibrium.

When the kettle began to hoot, Pamela poured the boiling water into the filter cone. She stole another glance at Bettina and was heartened to see that Bettina had untied the string on the bakery box and lifted the lid. Apparently sensing Pamela's eyes on her, Bettina looked up.

"Some people eat them with their fingers," she said, "but they're very sticky so I think we'll want plates and forks." Pamela peeked inside the box. Nestled side by side on a small sheet of waxed paper were four crullers, long twists of pale golden pastry.

As the seductive coffee aroma infused the small kitchen, Pamela set out cups, saucers, and small plates from her wedding china, and added forks and napkins. She fetched the cut-glass sugar bowl and cream pitcher from the counter and filled the pitcher with the heavy cream that Bettina favored. Bettina meanwhile transferred the crullers to the plates, two on each.

Pamela poured the coffee and took her seat. Of course she was longing to know the full story behind Bettina's startling announcement, but she waited as Bettina sugared her coffee and then dribbled in cream, stirring all the while. When the coffee had reached the perfect tint and Bettina had sampled it, Pamela spoke.

"Had Detective Clayborn told you earlier there was to be an autopsy?" she asked.

"No," Bettina said. "But Cassie had that lingering illness, and no one was able to figure out what it was. So apparently her doctor suggested that an autopsy could be valuable—if only to help in future diagnoses."

"But the autopsy showed she didn't die of the illness . . . ?" Pamela had neither sipped her coffee or tasted a cruller yet.

Bettina had picked up her fork but now she put it down. "The illness was that she was being slowly poisoned!" Pamela stared at Bettina. Time seemed to stop, like when a streaming video suddenly freezes on the screen.

"With what?" she managed to ask after a bit.

"They don't know for sure." Bettina shuddered. "There was damage to her heart and her lungs and her kidneys and all over—but slow doses of lots of things can do that." She picked up her fork again, carved off the rounded end of a cruller, and lifted the glazed knob of pastry to her mouth.

Bettina seemed to have recovered from the grim import of the news she had delivered. But Pamela's brain was racing. She had gotten up that morning filled with anticipation, expecting the arrival of her daughter—and maybe some news from Bettina about whether the eggs from Diefenbach's porch had been taken into police custody. But she'd hardly anticipated learning that a second resident of Arborville had been murdered—and that the second murder had actually happened *before* the first murder.

The methods had been very different, but both of the victims had lived on the same street. Did that mean anything? And what were the implications for Roland? Would Detective Clayborn see a connection between the two murders?

Her mind was racing and her coffee was getting cold—and now Bettina had finished her first cruller and was talking again—something about jam and . . .

Pamela blinked a few times and shook her head, trying to settle the commotion in her brain. "What?" she asked, gaping at Bettina.

"Lab reports," Bettina said, enunciating the words patiently, as if for an inattentive spouse. "You were a million miles away. What I said was, besides the autopsy, lab reports came back on the broken jar of jam from Diefenbach's kitchen floor. It turns out the jam was poisoned—with cyanide."

For the second time that morning, Pamela felt time stop. There were so many questions to ask, she didn't know where to start.

"Yes," Bettina said, and she began to answer at least a few of the unspoken questions. "The damage to Cassie's body revealed by the autopsy could have been caused by cyanide. And it has occurred to Clayborn that there could be a link between Diefenbach's murder and Cassie's."

"Roland?" Pamela asked.

Bettina shrugged. "I asked him about Roland but he wouldn't answer."

"Why didn't the killer just wait till Diefenbach ate enough of the jam to get sick and die too? Or maybe Diefenbach realized what was going on when the first jar of jam was delivered, so he smashed the jar?"

Bettina shrugged again.

"And then the murderer picked up the nearest heavy object and went after him?" Pamela said.

"It *could* have happened that way—if Diefenbach somehow realized the jam was a plot to kill him." Bettina leaned over to peer inside her coffee cup. "Is there more coffee?"

"Of course. It needs to be warmed up though." Pamela jumped from her chair and reached for her own cup. "I didn't even taste mine yet," she said, "so I'll just pour it back in the carafe and warm it up too."

Once a gentle flame was going under the carafe, Pamela turned from the stove. "If the same person murdered Cassie as murdered Diefenbach, and if Haven murdered Diefenbach, you know what that means, don't you?"

"Haven murdered her own mother." Bettina's lips stretched into a close-mouthed grimace.

"From what Nell said, the Griswolds sounded like the model family, very proud of their over-achieving daughter and her lofty prospects." Pamela swiveled back around to check on the coffee. A few tiny bubbles had formed around the edges of the dark liquid in the carafe.

"But things didn't work out so well, at least as far as her marriage to Axel Crenshaw was concerned." Bettina picked up her fork and aimed it at her remaining cruller, but then she set the fork down again. "I'm waiting for my coffee," she said. "And I don't want to finish both my crullers before you even taste one."

Pamela inspected the carafe again. Violent boiling wasn't called for, lest the coffee become bitter, but the bubbles around the edges had become larger and, touching the side of the carafe briefly, Pamela judged that the coffee was exactly the right temperature to serve. She refilled the cups, using an oven mitt to transport the carafe, and once the carafe had been returned to the stove, took her seat across from Bettina again.

"Maybe Haven didn't appreciate being the focus of such high expectations," Pamela said after she had, at last, taken a sip of her coffee. "And we haven't been able to find any evidence, on the internet at least, that she's launched a brilliant writing career, or a brilliant career of any kind."

Pamela carved off a piece of cruller and sampled it, enjoying the way the brittle glaze, with its startling sweetness, yielded to the chewy and not too sweet pastry. "You knew Cassie—a bit at least.

Did she seem like the kind of mother who would remind her daughter whenever she could that she hadn't turned out the way she was supposed to?"

"That would be a very sad thing." Bettina's expression took on a mournful cast. "Haven came around to visit her mother though. She could have just stayed away."

"We'll know more about Haven soon," Pamela said. "After we follow her home tomorrow." She tackled her cruller again and Bettina launched her own fork at the one remaining on her own plate.

"What about the eggs?" Pamela asked after a bit. "We got so caught up in this startling news about Cassie—but you were going to ask Detective Clayborn whether the crime scene people found that basket of eggs on the porch."

"Whoa! Yes!" Bettina mumbled around a mouthful of cruller. She gestured toward her mouth, continued chewing, and nodded vigorously, setting her earrings to swaying. "Lots to report there," she said at last, after swallowing. "The eggs were taken as evidence, and eggshells can retain fingerprints, but the fingerprints didn't match any in the database. Get this though—the eggs were naturally those colors, not dyed!"

"Jack Delaney's hens." Pamela felt her lips curve into a smile. "He really is the egg man then."

"Clayborn had never heard of hens that laid colored eggs," Bettina said with a smile of her own, but quite smug. "I told him everyone knows there are hens like that. Special breeds like Araucanas."

"And you told him that Jack Delaney has a flock of hens that lay colored eggs?"

Bettina nodded, setting her earrings in motion again. "I did, but he said the police can't arrest a person and take fingerprints without serious evidence."

"Jack Delaney is known to have hated Diefenbach," Pamela said. "Did you tell him that?"

"Of course, but he said the police can't arrest a person for hating someone. Otherwise the jails would be full. He did say, though, that the police interviewed MacDonald—*and* some of MacDonald's supporters." Bettina tipped a spoonful of sugar into her coffee, and then then another. She stirred the coffee and then added cream.

"Jack Delaney certainly fits into that category."

Bettina had raised the coffee cup to her lips, but before taking a sip she paused to answer. "I asked him whether Delaney was one of the people the police interviewed, and he said he couldn't divulge that information. But something about the way he said that made me think the answer was yes, so I suggested he explore whether Jack Delaney has an alibi for the night Diefenbach was killed and I recommended he ask Jack Delaney if he has a girlfriend."

Bettina gave Pamela a look that might accompany the deployment of a particularly valuable letter in a game of Scrabble.

Pamela didn't try to hide her smile. "What did he say?" she asked.

Bettina sighed and bowed her head. "He told

me that the residents of Arborville pay taxes so that they don't have to solve crimes themselves." She studied the nubbin of cruller that remained on her plate and then speared it with her fork.

Pamela had finished one cruller, enjoying every last pastry crumb and flake of sugary glaze. "I think I'll save the other," she said. "They're delicious, but one was plenty."

"That's why you're thin and I'm not." Bettina laughed. "And the black coffee too. What's that about?"

"Habit, I guess." Pamela shrugged. "I like those European coffee and milk things though." As if reminded that she'd barely tasted her coffee, she reached for the rose-garlanded cup and took a sip. With all the talking, it was no longer the steaming brew that she'd poured from the carafe, but instead of warming it up she made do with it in its lukewarm state.

Bettina consulted her pretty gold watch. "I've got to get going," she said. "Wilfred is doing the shopping for the Easter feast, but we still need to confer about the menu—and I've got to get out my table linens and make sure I have clean napkins from the set I want to use." She stood up. "Of course, there's to be ham, and we all decided on asparagus when we were talking about it the other day, and I think we'll do potatoes—maybe mashed. Then instead of salad, we'll have one of those vegetable trays with carrots and celery . . ."

"Sounds delicious!" Pamela stood up too. "And I'll bring my lemon-yogurt cake."

"And little Penny's coming home this afternoon." Bettina clapped her hands. "What a nice time we'll have! It will be just the four of us though. The Arborville children and grandchildren are coming in the morning for Wilfred's special bunny pancakes, and then they're going to Maxie's parents for Easter dinner."

In the entry, Catrina was dozing in her favorite sunny spot and Ginger was playing with one of the toys that the cats had received at Christmas, a weighted ball sporting a feathery topknot. As she batted the ball, it rocked to and fro, but came to rest with the feathers sticking straight up.

Bettina slipped into her bright yellow trench coat, Pamela reached for the doorknob, and in a moment Bettina was hurrying across the porch. She stopped before she got to the steps, however, and whirled around. "There was something else I was going to tell you," she exclaimed. "I remembered just now, looking over at Richard Larkin's house."

Pamela smiled uncertainly. What could be coming? Her uncertainty was heightened when Bettina backtracked across the porch and grasped Pamela's hands, squeezing them tightly.

"Wilfred talked to Richard." Bettina's tone was portentous. "And he found out what happened . . . with LeCorbusier."

"What?" Pamela felt her heart thump, but she was alarmed more by Bettina's manner than by the content of her message.

"*Jocelyn.*" Bettina nodded toward Richard Larkin's house as she uttered the name.

"The . . . the woman we saw him with?" Pamela asked, trying to sound interested but unconcerned.

"Jocelyn felt that a black cat was a bad omen for their budding relationship."

"Where . . . where did he take LeCorbusier?" Pamela asked. She blinked as Bettina studied her closely.

"That part of the story at least has a happy ending." Bettina let go of Pamela's hands and stepped back. "One of his colleagues at work had been looking to adopt a cat and was thrilled."

Pamela nodded.

"You're okay then?"

"Of course I'm okay." She *was* okay, really. Richard Larkin had a right to find himself a companion, now that she'd . . . *she'd what?* There had never really been anything between them. Never anything at all.

"Tomorrow then?" Bettina was cheerful again.

"Tomorrow."

"I know it's just a few blocks, but . . ."

"I'll drive," Pamela added quickly. "We'll need a car if we're going to follow Haven. The sale lasts until five, so we'll head up there at about four-thirty."

"I can hardly wait," Bettina said. "What on earth has she been doing since she stopped being the queen of the neighborhood and the wife of Axel Crenshaw?"

Pamela watched as Bettina made her way down the walk and across the street, her bright yellow coat more vivid than anything else in sight. Then she stepped back into her own house. "Maybe Haven really is the killer," she said half to herself as she closed her front door. "Jack Delaney had a reason to kill Diefenbach, but why would he want to kill Cassie?"

Chapter 21

After a quick lunch of a fried egg sandwich with mayonnaise on toasted whole-grain bread, Pamela fetched one of the free notepads that turned up so regularly in her mail and set about making a shopping list.

First of all, she'd need ingredients for the lemon-yogurt cake. Her larder contained plenty of flour, sugar, and eggs, but she'd have to replenish her butter supply, and the recipe required yogurt and a lemon, of course. For the icing, she added cream cheese and powdered sugar to the list.

Then there was the question of what to cook for Penny. Sunday would be the splendid Easter meal at the Frasers', with Wilfred's ham. And Saturday Penny would probably go out with friends. But for a welcome-home dinner that evening, Pamela thought chicken and dumplings would be perfect. Penny had always loved the dish, and the weather was still cool enough that a fragrant pot of chicken stewed with onion, carrots, and celery and garnished with parsley dumplings would accent the coziness of the home Penny was returning to. So Pamela checked to make sure she had an onion and at least one carrot and a few stalks of celery, and added "a whole chicken" to the shopping list.

Five minutes later, she was strolling up Orchard Street with two canvas grocery bags in hand and her purse slung over her shoulder. When she reached the corner, she paused and stared east, at the stretch of Orchard Street that continued above Arborville Avenue. She and Bettina had driven that route barely twenty-four hours ago, on their way home from their visit to Jack Delany. But something was different, quite different.

In the intervening time, perhaps during the night, trees that had previously displayed their bare barks to the world had acquired knitted garments. Not whole sweaters, though, but barely more than narrow bands just wide enough to cover the red X's that very likely lurked beneath them.

Pamela crossed Arborville Avenue and inspected the band on the first tree she came to. The knitting had definitely been done in haste, as if the knitter was frantic to rescue the trees from the axe. Looking farther up the block, she could see that each band was a solid color, rather than the fanciful patchwork effect of the large tree-sweaters. On the band that she was inspecting, which had been knit from bright purple yarn, lumps and holes showed where stitches had been bungled or dropped. Instead of the buttons and buttonholes that characterized most of the tree-sweaters Pamela and Bettina had seen, this band, and presumably the others, had been simply wrapped around the trunk it adorned and the edges stitched carelessly together. The person doing the stitching hadn't even bothered to match the yarn to the purple of the band. The stitching had been done in a clashing shade of olive green.

Pamela continued farther up Orchard Street and examined a few more of the rudimentary bands, an exercise that confirmed her impression that these latest additions to the Arborville tree-garment mystery had been done in great haste. Then she retraced her steps to the corner and proceeded on her way to the Co-Op. This development would need to be discussed with Bettina, but meanwhile there were groceries to buy.

The new issue of the *Advocate* had appeared at the end of Pamela's driveway while she was away. The canvas grocery bags, laden with ingredients for that evening's dinner and Sunday's dessert—as well as a fresh loaf of whole-grain bread, a pound of Vermont cheddar, and a basket of mini-tomatoes— were heavy. So Pamela hurried to the porch to set them down before retrieving the newspaper.

In the kitchen, she stowed the groceries in the refrigerator and cupboards and added the glossy lemon, whose seductive aroma was a citrusy preview of the cake in which it would figure, to the wooden fruit bowl on the counter. Then she returned the canvas bags to the entry closet and sat at the kitchen table to page through the *Advocate*.

The lead article focused on a contentious meeting of the town council at which the Diefenbach supporters, though few in number, fought off a proposal to give property tax breaks to people who grew their own food. Then there was Bettina's coverage of the memorial reception for Bill Diefenbach—complete with a photo of the memorial sheet cake—and also Bettina's interview with Brandon MacDonald. Other articles focused, more cheerfully, on the bingo tournament at the senior center and the spring fashion show organized by the St. Willibrod's women's club.

On an inner page, along with an editorial reminding readers of the *Advocate* to support the scouts' spring "Feed the Hungry" food drive, Pamela came across the letter to the editor Bettina had described—urging Arborvillians to clean up their yards now that spring had arrived but admonishing them to put green waste out only on Sunday night after six p.m.

As Pamela was folding the *Advocate* back up, she heard a click as the knob on the front door turned. She stepped into the entry to see Catrina and Ginger staring at the door, their bodies tense with expectation, their tails twitching back and forth, and their ears at attention. The door swung inwards and revealed Penny standing on the threshold.

Pamela had seen her daughter as recently as January, when Penny returned to her college in Massachusetts after Christmas break. But she studied Penny intently, just to make sure that nothing had happened in the few intervening months to diminish Penny's customary cheer. Content that Penny's face, beneath her tousle of dark curls, still glowed with health, and her blue eyes were still bright, Pamela relaxed and let herself smile.

Meanwhile, Penny had advanced beyond the threshold. She stooped toward Ginger and the cat hopped lightly into the crook of her arm. As Penny rose, Ginger scaled her chest to rest her forepaws on Penny's shoulder and nuzzle her neck.

"Kyle doesn't want to stop in for minute?" Pamela asked. Penny rode back and forth from college with a fellow student who also lived in New Jersey.

"He has a girlfriend down here now," Penny said. "He can't wait to see her."

"Well, come on in then, and welcome home." With that, Pamela hugged her daughter, cat and all. The top of Penny's head, bouncy curls included, reached only to Pamela's chin. Penny took after her father's side of the family, rather than Pamela's, and Pamela had had to constantly remind herself, as Penny was growing into a young woman, that height wasn't the only indicator of maturity.

"My suitcase is still on the porch." Penny transferred Ginger to Pamela's arms and wheeled her suitcase into the entry. "It's full of dirty laundry," she added, "so I'll just park it here for now."

"Are you hungry?" Pamela scrutinized her daughter's face again.

"We stopped for something on the way down." Penny slipped out of her jacket, revealing one of Pamela's creations, a pullover knit from yarn in a glowing shade of golden yellow.

At that moment, the doorbell chimed. "I know Bettina's anxious to see you," Pamela said. She glanced toward the oval window in the front door that, though curtained by lace, offered a clue to a visitor's identity. But in fact there were two visitors, and neither sported Bettina's vivid scarlet hair.

"Probably Laine and Sybil. We texted this morning." Penny turned, twisted the knob, and tugged.

A chorus of *"Hi"*s overlapped as Laine and Sybil bounced through the door. They were Richard Larkin's daughters, back in the suburbs from their dorm at NYU for the Easter weekend. Penny had bonded with them shortly after their father, divorced from their mother, bought the house next to Pamela's.

Laine and Sybil were both tall, like their rangy father, and Penny seemed all the smaller now (and suddenly younger, to her mother), dwarfed by the three much larger beings now sharing the entry with her. Both Laine and Sybil were devotees of vintage clothing, and had introduced Penny to the joys of thrift-shop treasure-hunting. Laine assembled her finds to create an effect of urban sophistication, while Sybil's look veered toward bohemian chic.

Pamela could catch up with her daughter over dinner, she knew, so she smiled and waved as Penny and her friends headed for the stairs and Penny's room beyond. Then she set Ginger back down and wheeled Penny's suitcase through the kitchen and down the hall into the laundry room.

As she was passing back through the kitchen she heard feet on the stairs, and Penny greeted her when she reached the entry. Penny was holding the lilac tunic, her arms stretched out before her and a hand grasping each of the tunic's shoulders.

"It's just beautiful, Mom," Penny said, her pretty lips parting in a wide smile.

"Merry Christmas." Pamela smiled back. "I'm anxious to see it on you."

"I'll wear it when we go to Bettina and Wilfred's on Sunday." Penny turned and started for the stairs, but then swiveled back around to add, "Laine and Sybil think it's *amazing*."

When Penny was gone, Pamela hesitated in the entry. It was too early to start dinner, and no new assignments from *Fiber Craft* had appeared in her inbox since she returned the edited article on Hmong story cloths. What useful thing could she do?

After a bit more thought, she settled down on the sofa, near where her knitting bag reposed on the carpet. Catrina approached curiously, as if puzzled at this variation in her mistress's routine. With rare exceptions, Pamela was normally on her feet, cooking or doing household chores, or she was sitting at the kitchen table or at her desk in her office upstairs. The sofa was for relaxing after dinner. But when Pamela reached into her knitting bag and extracted the beginnings of the infant cap she had begun under Nell's tutelage the previous Tuesday, Catrina scaled the heights of the sofa with a graceful bound and sprawled out along Pamela's thigh.

An hour later Pamela was standing at her kitchen counter chopping an onion. Two carrots and two stalks of celery waited their turn nearby, and the free-range chicken from the Co-Op had already been cut up into serving pieces. She was so absorbed in her task, and the prospect of the crisp onion dice with their pungent odor soon transforming to pliant sweetness as they sautéed, that she was startled when an equally startled voice spoke up behind her.

"*Mo-om!* You're not cooking!" Pamela turned to see Penny, looking contrite, with Laine and Sybil hovering behind her, their faces puckered with distress as well.

"I thought I might." Pamela turned from the onions. "It's your first night home, and you always loved stewed chicken with parsley dumplings."

"You didn't have to, Mom." Contrition twisted Penny's lips. "We were just going to get pizza."

"We came out to spend the weekend with our dad," Sybil explained, and Laine added, "but he has a date tonight."

Pamela wished she hadn't turned, and was still facing the counter and gazing at the small pile of chopped onions. "Oh," she said, focusing instead on one particular floor tile. "So you're sort of at loose ends."

Though she didn't notice their nod because her head was still bent toward the floor, she looked up and made her suggestion anyway. "Let's all eat here then. There will be plenty of chicken."

Chapter 22

So many elements of the scene were familiar. In the dining room, a long table was piled with yarn in every color and weight. In the kitchen, cluttered counters held a lifetime's worth of pots, pans, and cooking utensils. In the living room, tables offered china, crystal, knick-knacks, and travel souvenirs to buyers eagerly elbowing each other out of the way. There was even an attractive young woman in attendance, wearing a striking, obviously hand-knit, sweater.

But the young woman wasn't Haven. The young woman was Penny. And she was knitting, something like a long—*very* long—sack. Its festive patchwork of colors suggested that it was being fashioned from the yarn leftovers piled on the table.

Somehow, though in a part of her mind Pamela knew the young woman was Penny, she approached the young woman as if she were a stranger and mustered her social smile.

"That's an interesting project," she said in a pleasant I'd-like-to-make-your-acquaintance sort of voice.

"She just died. I've been knitting non-stop," the young woman replied, not lifting her eyes from her busily clicking needles. Pamela felt her head jerk back slightly and she blinked.

Condolences were certainly in order. As Pamela was searching for the appropriate words, the young woman spoke again. "I keep remembering things about her," she said mournfully. "Just silly little things—like how she always used to pick up coins if she was walking and found one on the sidewalk."

Someone else had joined them, as if from nowhere. Pamela felt a sense of foreboding, though the newcomer—an elderly woman wearing a belt with a zippered pouch—seemed kind.

"Her mother died yesterday," the woman whispered to Pamela. "Penny is knitting her shroud."

Pamela raised a hand to push back whatever was tickling her cheek. It was soft, like a drift of yarn, but the shroud couldn't be enfolding her so soon. Penny was still working on it, and from the looks of the project, several inches of knitting remained if it was to accommodate Pamela's five-foot eight-inch body.

She opened her eyes and another familiar sight greeted her, a welcome sight: her own bedroom ceiling. And looming in the foreground was a furry, heart-shaped face, lustrous black with glowing amber eyes. Catrina was stroking Pamela's cheek with one of her paws. The dream, for that was what it had been, evaporated, the last image to vanish being a glimpse of the festive shroud.

The white eyelet curtains at Pamela's bedroom windows were bright with spring morning sun. She rolled onto her side to consult the clock on her bedside table. It was after nine o'clock! No wonder Catrina had gotten impatient enough to climb up from her comfy spot cuddled along Pamela's thigh and notify her mistress that the time to be lazing in bed was long past.

Laughter rippled up the stairs as Pamela, slippers on her feet and a fleecy robe over her pajamas, stepped out into the hall. Then from downstairs she heard a voice, Penny's voice. Was Penny talking to herself? Or to Ginger?

Catrina had bounded ahead and now stood on the landing. She glanced back at Pamela and then continued on her way. Downstairs, a cheery voice that wasn't Penny's chimed in. Pamela hurried after Catrina, negotiating the stairs and darting through the entry to reach the kitchen door.

Bettina looked over from her seat at the kitchen table. "I'm not here to see you," she said, winking at Pamela. "I came by to catch up with your fashionable daughter."

At the moment Penny didn't look like the fashionista she was gradually becoming under the influence of Bettina, Laine, and Sybil. She was still in her robe and pajamas, and her hair showed a more recent acquaintance with a pillow than with a comb.

Bettina, on the other hand, was already dressed for the day, in an ensemble the same tender green as the leaves just unfolding from their tight buds on the trees outside. A double-breasted jacket with a wide notched collar topped sharply tailored pants. The linen fabric suggested that the forecast called for warm weather.

Catrina scurried across the tile floor to the corner where the cats were accustomed to receive their meals and applied herself to the large scoop of cat food already set out in the food bowl. Penny had evidently taken care of that early-morning chore, and Ginger had already eaten and gone on her way. The half-finished cups of coffee before Penny and Bettina, and the fragments of toast, testified that the human breakfast had been managed as well.

Penny jumped up from the table and in a moment had slipped two more slices of whole-grain bread into the toaster.

"I can do my toast," Pamela said, joining Penny at the counter. "And I'll get my own coffee. Go ahead and sit back down."

"Have some of the jam," Penny said before returning to her chair. "It's that jam Wilfred and Bettina brought us from Vermont—wild blackberry. Bettina found it in the cupboard. You hadn't even opened it."

There was no need to wonder how two chairs would accommodate three people because, with a last long swallow of coffee, Bettina stood up. "I'm off to cover the Easter egg roll at the county park," she announced, dusting a few toast crumbs from the front of her jacket. With a toss of her head that set her Faberge egg earrings swaying, she gave Pamela another wink. "See you at about four-thirty?" she whispered.

Pamela saw Bettina to the door and returned to the kitchen to find Penny regarding her with a mixture of suspicion and concern. Her usually smooth forehead was furrowed and her lips shaped a grim half-smile.

"I heard that," she said, "and I saw the wink. And Bettina told me about Roland."

"Yes." Pamela strove to adopt a conversational tone. "It's been quite hard for Roland and Melanie, but I'm sure the police will untangle things and figure out who's really guilty."

"You and Bettina aren't up to some kind of secret sleuthing?" Penny's expression hadn't changed.

"Not at all," Pamela said gaily, crossing her fingers behind her back. "Not at all."

"What's happening at four-thirty then?" Penny crossed her arms over her chest and the furrows in her forehead deepened. Pamela had not considered herself a fearsome authority figure as a mother, but she reflected that Penny must be modeling this inquisition on some episode remembered from childhood.

"A tag sale," she answered. "Just up the hill. It's the last day, so there are bound to be bargains—especially right at the end."

Pamela wasn't sure if Penny was satisfied but, after a last swallow of coffee, Penny announced that she was heading upstairs to get dressed for a mall outing with her friend Lorie Hopkins.

"Will you be seeing Aaron while you're here?" Pamela didn't like to pry into her daughter's romantic life, but when Penny was home at Christmas she'd seemed quite smitten with an attractive Wendelstaff College student she'd met.

"He's cooking dinner for me at his house tonight," Penny said, trying unsuccessfully to hide a smile.

After Penny was gone, Pamela transferred the carafe with the remaining coffee to the stove to reheat. The extra toast Penny had launched had long since popped up and grown cold, but Pamela buttered a piece anyway. She considered adding a layer of wild blackberry jam, but breakfast habits were breakfast habits, and Pamela had always eaten her toast with butter alone.

She left the jar of jam in a prominent spot on the counter, however, to encourage Penny to help herself to Wilfred and Bettina's gift while she was home. The *Register*, no doubt retrieved by Bettina, waited on the table, still in its plastic sleeve, and soon Pamela was crunching toast and sipping coffee as she leafed through its pages.

An hour later, Pamela was standing at the kitchen counter again, showered, dressed, and with email checked, hard at work. She had set her oven to 325 degrees and greased and floured two round cake pans. Her favorite mixing bowl, heavy caramel-colored pottery with three white stripes circling the rim, stood ready, along with measuring cups and spoons and her old, slightly rusty, flour sifter.

The first order of business, however, was the lemon. It reposed on the counter before her, recalling a small oval sun in its yellow brightness.

Lemon-yogurt cake called for half a lemon's worth of grated rind and juice, so Pamela cut the lemon in half. Industrious as she was, she had no patience for grating that much lemon rind. She used a potato peeler to shave fragrant strips of the bright rind from the lemon half, strips so thin they were nearly translucent and bore none of the bitter white part that lurked beneath.

She set the peeled lemon half, no longer gleaming yellow, aside to yield up its juice later. The next step was to lay the strips out on a cutting board and mince them with a chef's knife, going over them again and again and again, until they resembled a small pile of very fine sand, bright yellow and glazed with lemony oil.

Now the sifter and the caramel-colored bowl came into play. Pamela often made a loaf-shaped version of lemon-yogurt cake, like a quick bread. She had served it to the knitters at meetings of Knit and Nibble, and she and Bettina had had many morning or afternoon chats over coffee and slices of lemon-yogurt cake. The creation she envisioned for the Frasers' Easter dinner, however, would be worthy of a festive holiday meal. She planned to bake the cake in two round cake tins and then complement its deliciousness with cream cheese icing.

For the cake, she sifted flour, salt, baking soda, and baking powder into the bowl and stirred in sugar, using a large wooden spoon. She cracked two eggs into a smaller bowl, beat them lightly with a whisk, added a cup and a third of plain yogurt, and whisked the yogurt with the eggs until the result was smooth, creamy, and pale yellow. She used her thrift-store juicer, a shallow glass round with a ribbed dome rising from the center, to juice the peeled half-lemon, and whisked the juice into the egg-yogurt mixture, along with the minced rind.

Melted butter, seven tablespoons' worth, was the last ingredient for the cake. Pamela took a stick of butter from the refrigerator, sliced at the mark on the wrapper that indicated she was removing one tablespoon from the stick, unwrapped the larger portion, and set it to melt in a small saucepan with her stove's simmer burner turned to the very lowest flame.

While the butter melted, she added the moist ingredients to the dry ingredients in the large caramel-colored bowl and stirred the batter smooth with the large wooden spoon. Finally, she mixed in the melted butter, divided the batter between the greased and floured cake pans, and slid them into the oven. She set the timer for 35 minutes.

Bettina rang Pamela's doorbell at four-thirty sharp. Pamela was sitting in the chair in her entry, wearing her tan twill jacket and holding her car keys. Penny had returned from the mall, but she had her date with Aaron that evening, so Pamela didn't need to worry about how long the adventure she and Bettina planned would take.

When she heard the bell, she jumped up to greet Bettina and they headed for Pamela's car. As Pamela steered up Orchard Street, she said, "More of those knitted things have appeared on some of the trees above Arborville Avenue. I noticed them yesterday when I walked to the Co-Op and I forgot to say anything this morning."

Bettina leaned forward in her seat and stared through the windshield. "Tiny though," she commented. "Like the trees are just wearing little bras."

"Wide enough to cover red X's though." Pamela braked for the stop sign at the corner and waited until Arborville Avenue was clear to cross. Once through the intersection, she drove slowly along the few blocks before the turn for Cassie's street, passing several trees that sported the colorful knitted bands. "Whoever's doing this seems really in a hurry now."

A few cars at the curb directly in front of Cassie's house indicated that even in its waning hours the sale still had patrons, and the sign that had announced the sale the previous week was in place on the door: "TAG SALE TODAY. COME IN." But Pamela drove past the house, nearly to the end of the block. She made a U-turn and parked facing Cassie's house, so she and Bettina could watch for Haven to come out.

"So," Pamela said, as they headed back toward Cassie's house, "we're going to make sure Haven is here, and we're going to look around a bit to make it seem we just came for last-minute bargains. Then we're going to go back to the car and wait for Haven to leave. If we can figure out where she actually lives and/or what she actually does, maybe we can make some progress with the question of whether or not she has an alibi for the night Diefenbach was killed."

"What about Cassie's death?" Bettina squeezed

the words out between pants. Anticipation was
making Pamela's normally long strides even longer,
and Bettina was struggling to keep up.

Without slowing, Pamela answered. "If Haven
has an alibi for the night Diefenbach was killed,
that probably means she isn't the person who poisoned Cassie."

As she and Bettina stepped inside the house,
Pamela felt a shiver as details of her dream, in
which she had so accurately recalled the house's
layout, came back to her. To the left was the living
room, with tables now holding only odds and ends
that hadn't succeeded in catching anyone's eye.

Where was Marjorie? she wondered. The woman
had been such an enthusiastic hostess on the busy
sale days the previous weekend, stationed in the
entry with her zippered pouch at her waist. Pamela
ventured into the living room, not sure whether
she wanted to encounter Marjorie or not, given
Marjorie's role in the unsettling dream.

A few women were browsing along the tables,
and a bearded man was examining a brass candle-
holder that he'd picked up from the mantel,
where its mate waited. The sofa and matching
armchairs now had SOLD tags taped to them, as
did the small hooked rug before the fireplace.
Pamela shivered again when she glanced toward
the dining room.

A slender dark-haired woman wearing an interesting hand-knit sweater was sitting at the table.
She was intent on a knitting project, so intent she
didn't notice Pamela regarding her. The woman

was Haven, not Penny, the sweater was the same bright color-block sweater Haven had been wearing the previous weekend, and the project wasn't the long, sleeping bag-like object that in Pamela's dream Marjorie had identified as a shroud—*a shroud for Pamela herself.* But Pamela's shiver intensified nonetheless.

Haven was knitting frantically on a swath of knitting about a foot wide and three feet long, drawing from a fat ball of fuzzy gray yarn perched among the odds and ends of yarn still littering the table. She was muttering to herself, "One more almost done . . . just a few more rows then time to cast off . . . hurry hurry hurry."

Pamela and Bettina looked at each other and, without further consultation, backed as silently as they could away from the wide arch between the dining room and the living room. Pamela checked her watch and tipped the watch face toward Bettina. Both nodded, and in a few moments they were on their way back to Pamela's car.

Chapter 23

Five p.m. came and went. At about ten minutes after the hour a few people straggled out, but none was wearing a bright color-block sweater. Pamela started her engine and eased slowly down the block until she had a view of Cassie's front door.

The TAG SALE TODAY sign had been removed. After ten more minutes, the door opened and Haven stepped out, accompanied by Marjorie. Marjorie turned and locked the door, giving the doorknob a little shake to make sure all was secure. The two women descended the steps, strolled to the end of Cassie's front walk, and parted ways at its end, Haven heading toward Orchard Street and Marjorie heading toward where Pamela and Bettina were parked. As Marjorie approached, Pamela bent toward the steering wheel as if napping and Bettina slid down in her seat until her eyes were level with the dashboard.

After a few minutes, Pamela raised her head. Marjorie had passed, and Haven, wearing a light jacket over her color-block sweater and carrying a large tote bag, had just turned the corner at Orchard Street and was walking in the direction of Arborville Avenue. Pamela waited a few more minutes and then started her engine. She followed Haven, creeping slowly down the hill, thankful that the residential streets of Arborville were lightly traveled, especially on weekends.

A person intending to catch a bus into Manhattan would at this point cross Arborville Avenue. Busses headed south through Arborville and then Meadowside, veered west onto the Turnpike and reached the city via the Lincoln Tunnel. That had been Penny's commute the previous summer when she worked at an upscale home furnishings store in Manhattan. But Haven didn't cross Arborville Avenue. Instead, she turned again, to the right.

Pamela *did* cross Arborville Avenue, after pausing at the stop sign and making sure the way was clear. Then she used the parking lot behind the stately brick apartment building at the corner to turn around. She pulled out onto Orchard Street again and coasted in along the curb facing the intersection. From there, she and Bettina had a view of the bench and small Plexiglas shelter that marked the bus stop for people wanting to travel north. Haven was sitting on the bench, her tote bag at her side. A strand of yarn emerged from the tote bag and Haven was knitting. It was a new project, cobalt blue this time rather than gray like the other. But though it was only an inch long at this point, it was the same width as the gray creation

Pamela had been sure was intended to rescue yet another tree from the depredations of the Arborists.

By the time the bus came, Haven's project had grown by an inch. Bus service to and from Arborville was not too frequent on Saturday evenings. As the bus, with a sigh and a huff of exhaust, pulled away, Pamela made her turn and eased in behind it.

The bus headed north on Arborville Avenue, past the grammar school and the Co-Op and through the intersection where a cross street led down to the library and the police station. It huffed past the bank on the far corner of the intersection, and the row of shops that filled out that block, and it stopped again, with a sighing wheeze, at the bench in front of another bank at the end of the block.

As the bus neared St. Willibrod's, it picked up speed. It cruised through the residential northern end of Arborville, past well-tended yards coming alive with trees in delicate blossom or weighed down by the pink exuberance of unfurling magnolias. It made a few more stops there, then it cut to the west on a well-traveled street that marked the border with Timberley.

Soon the bus, with Pamela and Bettina in pursuit, was making its way along the street where most of Timberley's commercial enterprises were located. Pamela drove past the yarn shop, the florist, the cheese shop, and the bakery. And when the bus stopped to discharge a passenger, they found themselves halted temporarily in front of a store window that featured child-size mannequins in charming pastel dresses and black patent-leather shoes.

"It wasn't Haven that got off," Bettina reported, ducking her head back into the car and raising her window. "She must be heading further north."

"I certainly wouldn't have thought of her living up here," Pamela said. "Timberley and the towns beyond just don't seem like her kind of places."

Indeed, the further north one went in the county occupied by Arborville, the richer people became. And with that increase in wealth came an increase in conservative tendencies.

Leaving Timberley's commercial district behind, the bus veered west to pick up County Road. Unlike the busy stretch of County Road that served the towns to the south, up here County Road meandered, curving past estates hidden from view by walls and evergreen hedges, a park with gently sloping lawns, a pond with a stone bridge and ducks.

Half an hour after leaving Arborville, they reached the upscale community of Kringlekamack. A finely wrought wooden sign at the edge of the road announced in elegant gilt script that Kringlekamack dated from 1698. No houses, large or small, were in sight, nor parks, nor duck ponds. The road cut through thick woods, a mix of evergreens and other trees just coming into leaf.

A wheezing sound suggested the bus was slowing. Pamela slowed too, curious about who would be disembarking with no evident destination in sight. The bus stopped then, just before the spot where a break in the woods marked an inconspicuous road leading off to the right. Idling behind the bus, Pamela waited as Bettina—who had a bet-

ter view from the passenger seat—lowered her
window and stuck her head out.

"It's her," Bettina reported, though not too
loudly, lest even at a bus length's distance Haven
might hear her and recognize them.

As the bus pulled away, Pamela once more hid
her face by bending toward the steering wheel,
and Bettina slid down as low as she could in the
passenger seat. "We'll wait until she's a good bit
ahead of us before we follow," Pamela said. "I don't
think we'll lose her because there's not much of any-
where she can go except straight ahead or down
that side road."

When Pamela lifted her head from the steering
wheel, there was no sign up ahead of a tall woman
in a light jacket carrying a large tote bag. Bettina
swiveled backwards to check in the direction they
had come, but there was no sign of Haven behind
them either.

Stepping on the gas, Pamela eased toward the
break in the trees where the side road cut off. As
she turned onto that road, Bettina exclaimed, "Yes,
yes! There she is!" Then she added, "Wow, look at
this!"

This portion of Kringlekamack was not as unin-
habited as they had assumed. They had entered a
development of grand, grand houses, built on lots
large enough to accommodate their magnificence,
with space left over for sumptuous landscaping.
Drifts of azaleas and rhododendron were merely
sculpted greenery at the moment, but Pamela
could imagine the palette of yellows, pinks, reds,
and purples that early May would bring. Each
house seemed set on a small rise that emphasized

its owner's stature, and driveways that curved past splendid entries offered a chance to display a luxury vehicle or two.

Haven strode forward, past a house built from smooth rose-colored stone and one in a more modern vein, all jutting angles sheathed in pale stucco. No other cars were on the road, and Pamela suspected that if they had been, her serviceable compact would have been conspicuous anyway, for its ordinariness. So she crawled along well behind Haven.

After they'd tracked her for what seemed like at least half a mile, Haven stopped in front of an impressive brick construction to their left. This house was more traditional than its neighbors, with shutters at the windows and grand white pillars flanking its double doors. The house was no smaller than its neighbors however. Symmetrical wings on either side of a massive central structure suggested the house contained more rooms than anyone could possibly need.

Haven started up the curving driveway and Pamela increased her speed, putting the house behind her. "I'll turn around," she advised Bettina, "and you watch for the address when we pass the house again. We can do some research online and try to figure out what goes on here."

But in fact they didn't have to consult the internet to learn the truth about Haven's secret life.

As Pamela approached the house from the other direction, she saw that Haven had now reversed course and was running down the driveway toward the street. When she reached the end of the driveway, Haven sped up instead of stopping, veered to the left so she was heading right toward Pamela, and lunged in front of Pamela's car.

Bettina shrieked. The sound was nearly as startling as Haven's lunge, and Pamela felt a prickle of sweat at her brow as she thrust down on the brake. Haven stood square in front of Pamela's car, the tote bag discarded on the asphalt and her arms outstretched like one of Arborville's crossing guards facing an uncooperative driver.

Before Pamela's car had even come to a complete stop, Bettina had flung her door open and leapt from the car. Now Bettina was poised a few feet from Haven, the distraught expression on Bettina's face at odds with the serene cheer projected by the spring-green ensemble in which she had started the day. "You could have been run over! What on earth do you think you're doing?" she screamed at Haven in a ragged voice Pamela had never heard her use before.

"I could ask you the same thing!" Haven, looking more irritated than distraught, responded in a voice that was nonetheless equally ragged. "And you too," she added, shifting her gaze to glare at Pamela, who was now standing beside her car. "How did you find me?" she asked and paused, as if waiting for an answer. Her voice modulated from irritation to curiosity. "And why did you even want to?"

Pamela and Bettina looked at each other. They hadn't planned what to do or say if Haven realized she was being followed.

"Was it to tell me my mom was poisoned?" Haven sounded almost gentle, as if in acknowledgment of this imagined kindness, but she went on, adding, "You needn't have bothered. Claymore, or whatever his name is, tracked me down. He got my cell from Marjorie."

As if something in their expressions told her that this was not the reason for their presence, Haven's irritation returned. "That's not it, is it?" She slapped the hood of Pamela's car. "This is all about that Diefenbaugh thing and putting sweaters on trees and you think they're related and that I had something to do with them even though my mom was murdered now too. Well, they're not related and I didn't."

Pamela was about to ask how a person who didn't have anything to do with those two things would know they weren't related, and she was going to bring in the fact that Haven was very definitely responsible for at least some of the little tree-bras that had started showing up. And she was also going to tell Haven that she had been sorry to hear the news about her mother. But she was distracted by a new arrival.

A woman who resembled a dark-haired Melanie DeCamp was making her way down the final few yards of the curving driveway that served the impressive brick house with the pillars. Like Melanie, she was slim and elegant, and carefully groomed in a way that didn't advertise the effort behind it.

"Haven, dear," she said as she got closer. "Whatever is happening?"

"Nothing," Haven said, her tone changing to polite deference. "Nothing at all. I'll be right in. I know Olive and Wellesley are expecting their dinner." She stooped to retrieve her tote. "These are"—she waved a vague hand in the direction of

Pamela and then Bettina—"acquaintances. They just happened to be passing by."

The Melanie-like woman nodded graciously. "I'm Samantha Tassle," she said, and paused as if waiting for Pamela and Bettina to supply their names. But Haven was already walking toward the driveway. "They're not that kind of acquaintances," she called over her shoulder. Samantha Tassle shrugged, smiled apologetically, and started to follow Haven.

Bettina found her voice. "I'm Bettina Fraser," she blurted suddenly, "and before you leave, where was Haven on the night of the Monday before last?"

Samantha Tassle's head twitched and she blinked a few times. Haven had paused a few yards from the end of the driveway and was glaring at Bettina with her lips tightened into a firm line.

"Why . . . where she always is." Samantha Tassle laughed slightly, like a delicate hiccup. "Here, with me and my husband and the children. She's a jewel. We don't know what we'd do without her. The agency was right . . . really one in a million." She nodded again. "If you'll excuse me now . . . the children will be wondering where I've gotten to."

Pamela opened her car door and started to climb in, but she noticed Haven conferring quietly on the driveway with the woman she now realized was Haven's employer. Samantha Tassle then proceeded toward the house's grand, white-pillared entrance. Haven, however, was heading back toward the street. Pamela joined Bettina on the side of the car closest to the house.

Haven waited until she was a few feet away before she spoke.

"Okay"—for some reason she was whispering—"so now you know. Things didn't work out with Axel Crenshaw, and I couldn't survive on my own in the city with just the income from the writing, which wasn't going all that well anyway. This isn't bad, really. I have my own room, and a big, fancy bathroom of my own." She gestured toward the house, though it was clear without her pointing it out that there was no lack of space within. "I like the kids. And Samantha's cool. Actually very down to earth." Haven closed her eyes and grimaced. When she resumed speaking, with eyes still closed, her manner suggested someone unaccustomed to asking for mercy.

"You won't tell anyone in Arborville, will you? How I turned out?"

"Kind of sad," Bettina commented as they turned back onto County Road. They had both been silent as they again passed the grand houses that marked the route they had followed in pursuit of Haven.

"She's made a life for herself," Pamela said. "She could still be writing. I hope she is. If she hadn't grown up being treated like the queen of the neighborhood, she'd have no reason to be embarrassed about what she's doing now."

"Do you think Cassie knew?" Bettina asked. Pamela shrugged and they were both silent for a time.

It wasn't until they were driving past the duck pond with the stone bridge that Pamela said, "We found out for sure that, tree-sweaters or not, she didn't kill Bill Diefenbach."

"So she didn't kill Cassie either . . . her own mother." Bettina shuddered. "Did we ever actually think she could have?"

"People do," Pamela said with her eyes on the road. They were navigating the meandering stretch of County Road now.

"Oh, Pamela!" Bettina gripped Pamela's arm and the car swerved. "If Haven had money, she could quit the nanny job and move back to the city and write full-time. Cassie's estate is probably quite sizeable, with that nice house and all . . ."

Pamela concentrated on her driving for a long minute. Then she spoke slowly, as if trying the idea out.

"So Haven didn't kill Bill Diefenbach"—she paused and thought for a bit—"but in the case of her mother she decided she just couldn't wait the decade or so until Cassie died of natural causes . . ."

"I hope not," Bettina said, her voice quavering. "I really hope not."

"We'll look for you and Penny at about six tomorrow," Bettina said as Pamela's car came to a stop in her own driveway.

Penny was at Aaron's, but Pamela was welcomed enthusiastically by Catrina and Ginger. They greeted her in the entry and, as she proceeded, interwove their sleek bodies around her feet in a way that threatened to trip her up. Without even taking off her jacket, she hurried as best she could to the kitchen, where she scooped cat food in the "chicken" flavor into a fresh bowl and refreshed their water.

While her own chicken dinner—leftover chicken and dumplings from the night before—heated on the stove, Pamela studied the recipe for the icing that would make the lemon-yogurt cake she'd baked that morning special enough to grace an Easter feast.

The recipe was simple—just cream cheese, butter, and powdered sugar. The cream cheese and butter would be more manageable if they weren't cold. So as her dinner continued to warm, its savory aroma reminding her that it had been quite a while since she'd eaten, she set the caramel bowl with three white stripes on the counter and took the package of cream cheese and two sticks of butter from the refrigerator.

She unwrapped the sticks of butter and, holding each over the bowl, carved off slices of half an inch or so. The cream cheese would sit nearby in its foil wrap, and by the time she had eaten and checked her email, both butter and cream cheese would be soft enough to blend easily with each other and with the powdered sugar.

By the time Penny returned, Pamela was dozing on the sofa with one cat in her lap and the other nestled against her thigh. On the screen in front of her, pandas munched on bamboo while a narrator with a cultured voice described their mating habits.

"How was it?" she asked, coming awake as Penny greeted her.

"He's nice, Mom," Penny said. "He might not be *the one*, but he's fun to hang out with when I'm in Arborville."

On the kitchen counter, the completed cake waited to be carried across the street at the appointed time the next day. The round layers had slipped easily from their pans. One layer had been centered on a plate of Pamela's wedding china and a liberal amount of cream-cheese icing smoothed over its golden top. The other layer had been gently lowered into place and the remainder of the icing spread over its top and down the sides of what was now a two-layer cake. The cake glowed with a soft radiance, as if from the golden yellow layers beneath the translucent icing.

Chapter 24

"You're the perfect model for your mother's handiwork!" Bettina exclaimed as Penny stepped into the Frasers' kitchen. Pamela, following close behind, nodded in agreement. The air was infused with the rich, unctuous aroma of roasting ham, and Woofus was stretched out along the wall near the sliding glass doors that looked out on the Frasers' patio.

Penny was wearing the lacy lilac tunic. She had paired the tunic with skinny jeans in a deep indigo shade and ankle boots in the same dark blue. Bold turquoise ceramic beads filled in the slightly scooped neckline of the tunic and shiny silver hoop earrings peeked from Penny's dark curls.

Bettina herself was wearing one of the jersey wrap dresses she favored, the fabric a lovely swirl of colors that evoked an impressionistic flower garden. In deference to the occasion, Pamela had searched her sweater collection for the light pullover she'd knit a few years ago from a cotton and linen blend in a pale amber shade. The color was more autumnal than spring-like but the sweater's weight was appropriate to this bright spring day.

"Watch for eggs," Bettina warned, after she'd relieved Pamela of the cake she carried and set it on the high counter that divided the cooking area of the kitchen from the eating area. She hugged Penny and then Pamela. From his post near the stove, Wilfred beamed.

"We hid some eggs for the grandchildren to find," Bettina explained. "And Wilfred got out his special griddle for the bunny pancakes."

With a mock grunt, Wilfred hefted the griddle, impressive in its cast-iron solidity, from the stove.

"But we did the hunt indoors," Bettina continued, "and two eggs are still missing."

Four wine glasses waited on the high counter, ranged next to a basket of simple round crackers and a small oval bowl containing a pouf of creamy orange cheese flecked with red. A small cheese paddle sat nearby.

"Have a glass of rosé," Wilfred called from his station near the stove, "and there's pimento cheese and crackers to munch on."

"Rosé? Sure," Pamela said, and after a glance at her mother Penny echoed the assent. Bettina had already advanced to the refrigerator, and in a moment she was twisting the cork from a graceful bottle and pouring a few inches of the rosy-pink liquid into each glass.

"Thank you, dear wife," Wilfred said as Bettina

delivered a glass of wine. He was at work on a bundle of asparagus, trimming the very bottom from each spear and then standing the spears upright in his gleaming stainless steel asparagus steamer. The lid of a saucepan already on the stove jiggled, advertising that its contents had reached a full boil.

Pamela, Bettina, and Penny sipped their wine as Bettina further described that morning's festivities with the Arborville children and grandchildren. But conversation ceased when Wilfred opened the oven door and stooped to remove the ham, all tawny crackled rind and succulent pink flesh. He hoisted the roasting pan to the center of the stove top and tented a long piece of foil over the ham.

"Now it must rest, dear ladies," he announced, "but no rest for the wicked."

"Woofus and Punkin had their dinners before you came," Bettina said. "Otherwise Woofus would be underfoot—and he knows he'll get a tiny ham treat later."

Wilfred lifted the lid from the eagerly boiling pot and probed inside with a fork. Nodding with satisfaction, he drained the pot into a large Pyrex measuring cup, plucked a potato masher from a drawer, and began to mash the contents of the pot. From time to time he added a generous pat of butter or a splash of the reserved water from the Pyrex cup.

"I don't know about you two," Bettina announced suddenly, turning away from the entertaining sight of Wilfred's skillful cookery, "but I'm going to eat some of this pimento cheese be-

fore we've all sat down to dinner and it's too late
for hors d'oeuvres."

"About ten minutes," Wilfred called.

Bettina picked up a cracker and used the cheese
paddle to top it with a scoop of pimento cheese,
sculpting the cheese with the paddle. At the stove,
Wilfred lit the burner under the asparagus steamer.
Pamela and Penny joined Bettina in sampling the
pimento cheese, which combined the rich tang of
cheddar with piquant bits of chopped pimento and
a hint of cayenne—the whole smoothed out by mayonnaise and complemented by the crisp crackers.

Wilfred was back at work on the contents of the
pot now. He'd set the potato masher aside in favor
of a large wooden spoon, and with the spoon he
was easing a small mound of something from a
saucer into the pot.

"Crushed garlic," he explained, noticing the curious looks on the faces of his audience, as he
stirred vigorously with the wooden spoon. "Getting very close," he advised, "and I can't forget to
heat up my Hollandaise sauce." He nodded toward a small pot on another burner.

Bettina hastily prepared and ate another pimento cheese cracker, then she hurried to the refrigerator, swung the door back, and bent to the
refrigerator's interior. She emerged holding a
shallow wooden bowl that held carrot and celery
sticks, cucumber spears, black olives, and cherry
tomatoes, neatly arranged in parallel rows.

"My handiwork," she said with a pleased smile.
"And Pamela," she added, "there's another bottle
of rosé in here. Can you do the honors?"

Bettina started toward the door that led to the dining room, and just as she reached it, a brightly colored egg skittered through in the opposite direction, careening toward the scrubbed pine table. Bettina hopped to the side with a little shriek, thankfully not losing her grip on the crudités. After the egg came Punkin, in delighted pursuit. Punkin dove under the chair where the egg had come rest and sent it spinning away again in the direction of Woofus, who leapt to his feet with a startled "Arf."

"That accounts for one of the missing eggs!" Bettina laughed, but shakily. Penny had joined her near the doorway and taken the platter of crudités from her hands.

Bettina's handiwork was also evident in the dining room. The table was spread with a cloth from her collection, a rustic weave in shades of peach, tan, and gold. Four places were set with her sage-green dinner plates and stainless steel flatware, whose style echoed the sleek Scandinavian lines of her candleholders. Peach napkins and a bouquet of golden tulips echoed the colors of the tablecloth.

Pamela drew the cork from the bottle of rosé and lowered the bottle into the waiting wine coaster. Wine glasses from the hand-blown set with the faint purple tint and the elaborately twisted stem awaited the fresh bottle of wine. Penny set the tray of crudités at the end of the table farthest from Wilfred's accustomed seat. She knew he would be carving and serving the ham.

And then the ham arrived, on Bettina's largest

sage-green platter, its tawny rind glistening with melted fat. Wilfred set it down with a triumphant sigh and turned back toward the kitchen.

"Can I carry something?" Pamela asked, but Penny hurried after him without inquiring.

When they returned, Wilfred was carrying a bowl of steaming mashed potatoes in one hand and an oval dish of asparagus spears garnished with Hollandaise sauce in the other. Penny was carrying a small bowl of mustard and a huge carving knife with matching fork.

In a pleasant bustle, plates were passed to the head of the table to receive generous slices of ham, each rimmed along one curving edge with a strip of rind cushioned by a layer of pale, nearly transparent fat. Pamela served scoops of mashed potatoes, buttery and with a hint of garlic. At the foot of the table, Bettina used tongs to add asparagus spears to the plates, and a spoon to top each with a dribble of Hollandaise sauce. Once the plates had circled back around to their owners, Penny set the crudités in motion by handing them to Wilfred.

After Wilfred's genial "Bon appetit!" no one spoke for several long minutes—unless inarticulate expressions of pleasure count as speech. The meal was simple but perfect. The ham was moist and flavorful, with a hint of the smokehouse and a hint of brine. The mashed potatoes, despite the suggestion of garlic, tamed the assertive ham, as did the tender earthiness of the fresh green asparagus.

When speech resumed again, Wilfred acknowledged the many compliments that came his way. Then conversation turned to Penny's plans for the summer, which would be here before they knew it, everyone agreed. Penny explained that she'd probably return to the upscale home furnishings store in Manhattan where she'd worked the previous summer—though there was also the possibility of an internship with an interior design firm.

"And how about your future plans?" Bettina asked, switching her attention to Pamela. "For your next knitting project," she hastily added, seeing Pamela's confusion, "though how you could top this exquisite tunic I can't imagine."

"I haven't decided," Pamela said, "and meanwhile I've joined Nell on the infant cap project." Pamela's and Bettina's voices overlapped as they described the infant cap project to Penny, then Bettina detailed her slow progress on the Nordic-style sweater she had undertaken for Wilfred.

"I may have bitten off more than I can chew," Bettina said, then laughed as alarmed looks suggested her listeners had taken her words literally. "The knitting, I mean," she added. "The pattern is quite challenging."

"I'll wear the sweater with pride, dear wife," Wilfred said loyally.

"What do you think will happen with poor Roland?" Penny asked.

As Bettina opened her mouth to speak, Pamela tapped Bettina's foot gently with her own. She caught Bettina's eye, tightened her lips, and twitched her head in the slightest of warning head-shakes.

(She'd so far succeeded in keeping from Penny the fact that she and Bettina were sleuthing again.)

"I'm sure the police will untangle things and figure out who's really guilty," Pamela said, trying to sound serene.

"That's exactly what you said the other day when I caught Bettina winking at you." Penny focused her bright blue eyes on her mother, but her attempt to look grim didn't detract from her rosy prettiness. "Word for word. I didn't believe you then and I don't believe you now," she added. She shifted her gaze to Bettina. "Either of you. You're both up to something."

Pamela didn't answer. Instead, she studied her plate and poked at a spear of asparagus.

"Now, now, now," came Wilfred's genial voice from the head of the table. "I'm sure the police know what they're doing, Penny. And Roland will be cleared and Bettina and Pamela and the rest of the Knit and Nibblers can go back to knitting and nibbling just like always. Who's for more ham?" He brandished the carving knife in a theatrical gesture.

But Penny wasn't looking convinced and she didn't seem interested in more ham. In raising Penny, Pamela had always stressed the importance of critical thinking, and she had to admit that Wilfred's statement, though it sounded comforting, had not actually dismissed out of hand the notion that Bettina and Pamela were dabbling in matters better left to the police.

"No one wants more ham?" Wilfred surveyed his fellow diners.

"I'll take more," Bettina said quickly, routing her plate to Wilfred by way of Penny, "and potatoes and asparagus too. And plenty of Hollandaise sauce."

"I'll have more too," Pamela chimed in. "More of everything." She was actually quite full, but the mechanics of replenishing the plates looked to be an effective distraction from Penny's interest in Pamela and Bettina's doings.

Then everyone was eating again, even Penny, and the conversation had meandered onto the benign topic of where the last missing Easter egg could possibly have gotten to.

When the newly filled plates were empty again, Penny and Pamela cleared away while Bettina set about preparing coffee. Soon boiling water was seeping through the grounds in the filter cone of Bettina's carafe, and the aroma of brewing coffee was edging out that of baking ham. At the high counter, Pamela cut four slices from her lemon-yogurt cake and slipped them onto Bettina's sage-green dessert plates, whose duskiness set off the golden yellow and the translucent creaminess of the cake and icing.

"Absolutely perfect!" Bettina pronounced when the plates had been delivered to the table and she had sampled her first bite.

Pamela tasted her slice to make sure Bettina was telling the truth. Bettina was right. It *was* good, very good. Though the cake was agreeably sweet, the lemon zest gave it a nice bite, and the cream cheese made the icing richer and more complex than a simple buttercream.

Wilfred contributed "Delicious," and Penny's reaction was "Yum!"

Bettina set her empty coffee cup down with a contented sigh. "Another culinary triumph!" she proclaimed, beaming down the length of the table at Wilfred and tilting her head toward Pamela. "The people who didn't cook do the cleanup," she added, pushing back her chair and rising to her feet.

Pamela started to stand but Bettina motioned for her to stay put. "You cooked," she said. "You baked that delicious cake."

Penny jumped up, exclaiming, "I definitely didn't cook."

"No, no, no!" Pamela was on her feet now. "You're on vacation. Please stay right where you are and talk to Wilfred. Finish your coffee, both of you."

Pamela waited until the whoosh and gurgle of the dishwasher could be counted on to mask the sound of her voice before she raised the question that had preoccupied her since she woke up that morning.

"Do we actually have any suspects for Diefenbach's murder left?" she asked from the sink, where she was scrubbing the mashed potato pot.

Bettina was bent over, returning the asparagus steamer to its home in a cupboard beneath the counter. She straightened up. "We know for sure that Haven was in Kringlekamack taking care of Olive and Wellesley," she said.

"And MacDonald admitted he was home alone at the time Diefenbach was killed"—a rush of water interrupted the thought as Pamela turned on the faucet to rinse the now-scrubbed pot—"but we decided he wouldn't have told us that if he had something to hide." She went on, "Eloisa volunteered where she was Monday night before she had any idea we might be probing for an alibi. She thought she was just chatting with a couple of women who were interested in bargain designer clothes. Besides, why would either of them have wanted to kill Cassie?"

Bettina nodded.

"There's still Jack Delaney," Bettina said. Was there a slight taunt in her voice, implying that they might have probed a bit more for an alibi if Pamela hadn't been so impatient?

Pamela acknowledged the taunt by closing her eyes and bowing her head. Then she said, "It would have been interesting to get him talking about that Monday night, or find out if he had a girlfriend we could track down—but that was before we knew Cassie was a murder victim too." She handed the pot to Bettina, who had picked up a dish towel again, and then she lowered the unwieldy ham-roasting pan, with its dark film of baked-on grease, into the sink. "As far as Jack Delaney is concerned now, it's the same as with MacDonald and Eloisa. Kill Diefenbach? Yes, they had reasons. Kill Cassie? Why?" She turned from the sink frowning. " Of course, it *is* possible the two murders aren't connected at all . . ."

"That means Haven didn't kill Diefenbach but could have killed her mother—" Bettina left off, looking stricken, as if the thought was too unbearable to contemplate.

"The poisoned jam sort of connects the two murders though." Pamela frowned harder and turned back to the sink. "But how?" She squirted liquid detergent into the greasy pan and twisted the faucet handle to send a splash of steaming water after it.

"Is it too late for these cups to go in the dishwasher?" came a voice from somewhere near the scrubbed pine table.

They both looked over to see Wilfred. He had set a pair of coffee cups and their matching saucers on the table and was stooping to retrieve something from the floor.

"It's that egg"—he held up a bright pink egg—"the one Punkin was chasing. No point in leaving it around for someone to step on."

He advanced, with a cup and saucer in each hand and the egg in a cup. As he deposited the cups near the sink, he said, "Actually, I've got an idea about Diefenbach's murder that I'll bet Clayborn hasn't thought of."

"You do?" Pamela turned toward Wilfred, happy to abandon the greasy pan for a moment. And she was also curious. Wilfred had sometimes been a useful partner when she and Bettina engaged in sleuthing.

"The Arborville neatfreak." Wilfred surveyed them with a pleased smile. "The person who wrote that letter to the editor of the *Advocate* about spring cleanup—and who's been dropping off the threatening notes. We got one, and Bettina said you did too."

"I did." She'd thought it was quite silly, but she was glad Penny wasn't hearing this.

"Those bedraggled Diefenbach signs left from last fall," Wilfred explained. "They're all over town and they really are an eyesore. So maybe the neatfreak showed up at Diefenbach's to deliver one of his notes. They argued. The argument became violent, and that was the end of Diefenbach."

The evening had come to a close. Pamela, Penny, Wilfred, and Bettina had stepped out onto the Frasers' front porch, enjoying the mild evening air with its promise of warm weather to come. Pamela was carrying a plastic bowl containing eleven hard-boiled eggs dyed in bright colors.

"Your deviled eggs are so good," Bettina had said, "and what else is there to do with an over-abundance of Easter eggs?"

As they all stood there, prolonging their good-nights in a reluctance to see the end of such a pleasant evening, headlights appeared at the top of the block. The vehicle the headlights belonged to drew closer and closer, at last turning into Richard Larkin's driveway, where the light from the streetlamp revealed it to be Richard Larkin's Jeep Cherokee.

The driver's side door opened and Richard Larkin climbed out. But he didn't head immediately for his front door. Instead, he circled around the back of the car to open the passenger-side door. He extended a hand and, clutching the hand, a woman emerged. Details were difficult to make out with only the streetlamp for illumination, but her dark hair seemed to be arranged in a fashionable side braid.

Addressing no one in particular, Penny observed that Laine and Sybil had returned to their dorm in the city that afternoon.

Chapter 25

On Monday morning Bettina arrived with more eggs, this time presented in a charming basket.

"What will I do with them?" Pamela exclaimed. "I'm already going to be busy with the eleven from your Easter egg hunt."

"Twelve of those now," Bettina said. "We found number twelve after you left last night." She fingered a vivid orange egg perched atop the others, whose shells were muted shades of turquoise, green, and pink. "It was on the sofa, nestled against an orange throw pillow. Wilfred sat on it but luckily it didn't break."

"Where did these others come from then?"

They were standing in Pamela's entry, which was bright with April morning sun. Pamela was still in her robe and pajamas, but Bettina was dressed for the day in a fetching yellow and white checked shirtdress paired with her red sneakers. She'd added a red cardigan to ward off the slight morning chill.

"Jack Delaney brought them over first thing. He was on the porch when Wilfred went out to get the *Register*, so Wilfred invited him in. He was going to just leave them with a "Happy Easter" note—like he said he did with Diefenbach—but Wilfred offered him coffee and he became quite chatty."

The mention of coffee reminded Pamela that she'd been just about to fill a rose-garlanded cup with her first coffee of the day when the doorbell's chime had summoned her.

"Come on in here," she said, taking the basket of eggs from Bettina's hand and leading her through the kitchen door. Penny was sitting at the table drinking coffee and finishing up a piece of toast and jam.

Bettina started to fetch an extra chair from the dining room, but Penny jumped up and drained her coffee cup in one long swallow. "I'm just leaving," she said, giving Bettina a hug.

As Penny's feet echoed on the stairs, Pamela poured two cups of coffee. "Catching up with her school friends on her smart phone, no doubt," she commented, "but now you can tell me all about Jack Delaney without Penny getting curious." She served Bettina her coffee. Penny, being relatively new to coffee-drinking, didn't share her mother's taste for black coffee, so Pamela's cut-glass cream and sugar set was already on the table. Bettina added cream and sugar to her cup and Pamela returned to the counter.

"Are you making toast?" Bettina asked hopefully.

"Of course." Pamela laughed and slipped two pieces of whole-grain bread into the toaster.

"Jack liked my interview with MacDonald," Bettina said. "He thought it was very fair. He liked it so much that he said he forgave me for sending Clayborn after him."

"So Detective Clayborn *did* follow up." Still on her feet, Pamela sipped at her coffee. It was quite hot.

"Of course." Bettina raised her chin. Her brightly painted lips—red today—formed a smug smile. "Clayborn values my advice."

With a *kerchunk*, the toast popped up. Pamela delivered a buttered slice to Bettina on a small plate of wedding china, prepared one for herself, and joined Bettina at the table.

"Do I see jam?" The wild blackberry jam from the previous day sat on the table near the cream and sugar set.

"Help yourself." Pamela nudged the jam closer to Bettina and got up to fetch her a knife.

"Jack *does* have a girlfriend," Bettina said, "and he *was* with her the night Diefenbach was killed, and she vouched for him, and if you had let me continue in the direction I was going that day we talked to him . . ." She gave Pamela a meaningful look and opened the jar of jam.

"I'm sorry," Pamela said. "But I guess we can cross him off our list of suspects for sure now."

Bettina was concentrating on the jam, spreading it liberally on her slice of toast, but she glanced up. "And that leaves?" she inquired.

Pamela shrugged. "The neat freak? But why would he have poisoned Cassie?"

It was Bettina's turn to shrug.

"There have to have been two killers," Pamela said. "Despite the jam connection. Somebody poisoned Cassie and somebody clunked Diefenbach on the head with a heavy object. And they weren't the same person. But the one who killed Diefenbach definitely isn't Jack Delaney or Cassie, and probably isn't MacDonald or Eloisa."

Bettina nodded.

They ate their toast and drank their coffee then, chatting about their respective plans for the day. Bettina had an event to cover at the middle school, and Pamela's early morning check of her email had revealed five articles waiting to be evaluated for *Fiber Craft.*

At nine-thirty Bettina lifted her wrist to consult the pretty face of her gold bracelet watch. "I must be off," she commented, and rose. But as Pamela escorted her toward the kitchen door, she turned back toward the table with a quick intake of breath.

"I just thought of it," she said. "All that apricot jam in Cassie's kitchen cupboard is likely full of cyanide, and Marjorie probably doesn't realize it. Luckily, she had a NOT FOR SALE sign on the shelf, but I guess that means she's saving it for herself. Somebody should tell her not to eat it."

"If Detective Clayborn conferred with her to find out how to track Haven down, he must have mentioned the poisoned jam," Pamela said.

After seeing Bettina to the door, Pamela returned to her kitchen. She stared at the jar of jam on the table. It was blackberry jam, not apricot like the jam on the shelves in Cassie's kitchen, but thoughts involving apricot jam invaded her mind.

When they visited Eloisa in her shop, she said Cassie had given Diefenbach a jar of jam. It must have been the poisoned jam. Haven said the jam was homemade, a gift, and there was more of it than Cassie wanted or could use. But Cassie didn't know the jam contained poison. If she had, she wouldn't have eaten it—that was clearly what had killed her. And she wouldn't have given a jar to Diefenbach.

Who *would* know the jam contained poison?

Pamela didn't pause to rinse the coffee cups before running up the stairs and dressing. She detoured past the bathroom to call to Penny, who was in the shower, that she was going out on a quick errand, then she was on her way. Was the errand she contemplated a life-saving errand, or something else? She wasn't sure, but she tucked her cell phone in her pocket just in case.

True to her word, Marjorie was on duty at Cassie's house, still engaged in the challenging task of emptying it out so it could be sold. When Marjorie opened the door, Pamela could see an assortment of cardboard boxes ranged behind her.

At first Marjorie looked surprised, her raised brows and half-open mouth animating her aged face. Then she said, not unpleasantly, "The sale's over. There's nothing left that anyone would pay money for."

Pamela smiled a smile that she intended to be disarming. "Could I persuade you to change your mind about selling that apricot jam?" she asked.

"It's always been my favorite kind, and homemade makes it all the better."

"The jam is not for sale," Marjorie said, her voice still pleasant.

"I think I know why."

"Oh?" Marjorie cocked her head and completed the syllable with a close-lipped smile.

"It's the rest of the poisoned jam that killed Cassie." Pamela stepped closer to the door. From there she had a clearer view of the cardboard boxes. Curiously, Marjorie seemed to have been emptying them rather than filling them.

"Oh my heavens! What terrible news!" Marjorie raised one of her large, well-shaped hands to her cheek. She retreated from the doorway, as if in shock. Pamela reflected that Bettina's acting, overdone as it seemed at times, was infinitely more convincing.

"You knew the jam was poisoned because you made it." Pamela's voice was calm. "You even told me how much you enjoyed preserving food. The apricot flavor provided a cover for the taste of cyanide and maybe you even got the cyanide from the pits."

Marjorie's manner suddenly changed. "I *did* make the jam," she said, "and it's not poisoned." She retreated farther and swung the door all the way open. "Come in! Come right in, and you can buy all you want."

Marjorie was tall, and she looked strong for her age. But Pamela was tall and strong. She wasn't exactly sure why Marjorie wanted her to come in, but she was curious about the boxes in the entry. She patted the back pocket of her jeans where she had tucked her cell phone and stepped over the threshold into the house that so resembled her own.

The puzzle pieces of the mystery's solution were coming together, in the same way that the pieces Pamela had knit for the lilac tunic had come together to form the pretty gift for her daughter. But a major piece of the puzzle was still missing, as if the tunic had turned out to be, let's say, backless.

As Pamela surveyed the room she had just entered, however, she recognized the missing puzzle piece. The contents of the cardboard boxes Marjorie had been emptying proved to be stacks of yellowing papers, bulging file folders, and bundles of clippings from newspapers and magazines.

"The Arborville town archives." Pamela pointed toward the boxes.

Marjorie nodded.

On the Sunday that Pamela and Bettina had visited the tag sale together, Pamela had overheard Haven complaining that Marjorie was spending too much time dealing with the boxes of archives when there were more pressing tasks.

"Why do the contents have to be sorted? Can't the boxes just be passed on to whoever takes over the archivist job?" Pamela asked, though she knew why Marjorie's answer would be no.

One of the file folders lay open and a few clippings, brittle and discolored with age, had been set aside.

"You must be looking for something in particular," Pamela said.

"No." Marjorie shrugged. "I just always loved history."

"American Dream, American Nightmare," Pamela observed, then she stooped and quickly snatched up the clippings that had been set aside. The headline on the top one read, "Triple Murder Shakes Arborville: Mistress Kills Man, Wife, Self." In smaller letters below were the words, "Infant Spared."

"You were that infant, weren't you?" Pamela said. "And you couldn't bear the thought of your family tragedy being exposed in that macabre library exhibit."

Marjorie had begun to weep. "I didn't mean to kill anyone," she said. "I was only trying to make Cassie sick—so I could step in, help gather material for the exhibit, and destroy anything I found about my own family."

"And you didn't mean to kill Diefenbach either?"

"I didn't. I really didn't." With her apparent resignation to the fact of aging—the gray pony tail and the sensible shoes—Marjorie hadn't seemed the type to care about her appearance. But as she sobbed and gulped, she raised her large hands to hide her face. "I was trying to save him. And myself. I didn't want him to discover the jam was poisoned." Her voice emerged from behind her hands in a tight wail. "I was horrified that Cassie had given it to him. I was trying to get it back—but it fell and broke. And then he exploded. He had such a temper. I was just trying to keep him from hitting me."

Marjorie removed her hands from her face, which was smeared with tears and had turned a splotchy red color. She looked around. Despite her preoccupation with the archives, she had apparently made some progress organizing the odds and ends left from the sale. Just beyond the arch between the entry and the living room, more boxes were staged, boxes full of objects wrapped in newspaper. And kitchenware was arranged in piles, pots with pots, pans with pans, cookie sheets with cookie sheets. In one pile, cast-iron skillets and griddles were stacked atop one another.

Pamela recalled Wilfred's pride in the cast-iron griddle he'd used for his Easter bunny pancakes, his comic grunt as he'd lifted it to show its heft.

"You sold the murder weapon!" Pamela exclaimed. "To that tall young man in the leather jacket at the tag sale. That's why the police never found it. Diefenbach was killed in his kitchen. What more handy weapon to find in a kitchen, for defense *or* offense, than a solid cast-iron griddle?"

Marjorie had been standing in the middle of the entry. Suddenly she darted past Pamela and grabbed up a formidable cast-iron griddle from atop the skillet and griddle pile.

"Lucky I didn't sell all the ones that were Cassie's," she proclaimed, her voice still strained with grief.

She lunged for Pamela, aiming the griddle at her head. Pamela ducked and the griddle missed, but the threat jolted Pamela almost as much as if the griddle had made contact with her skull. Marjorie raised the griddle again and adjusted her aim.

The kitchen was straight ahead, Pamela knew, just like in her own house, though here one turned left instead of right for the living room and dining room. She bolted through the kitchen doorway, slammed the door, and leaned against it to hold it closed.

Through the door, she could hear Marjorie cursing, and heavy feet drawing near.

She pulled her cell phone from her jeans pocket and keyed in 911.

Chapter 26

Nell was hosting that evening's Knit and Nibble, and Pamela and Bettina were en route in Bettina's car, climbing the long hill that led to the section of Arborville known as the Palisades. In her kitting bag Pamela carried two completed infant caps and half a skein of soft white yarn she'd found in one of the plastic bins where she stored her knitting supplies. She'd spent part of the day on Easter leafing through knitting magazines, but she still hadn't decided what her next project would be. Meanwhile, knitting infant caps would keep her hands from being idle.

Midway up the hill, they passed a vacant lot, one of the few remaining in Arborville. It was half a double lot bought long ago. The original purchaser had built a house on one lot but let the other lie fallow—except for weeds, wild vines, and volunteer maple saplings that were on their way to becoming full-fledged trees. Neighbors complained about the untended lot, in the same way that neighbors complained about Jack Delaney's rooster. Besides the weeds and saplings, the lot attracted litter—and political signage. Since the previous fall, a row of Diefenbach's campaign posters had valiantly trumpeted "The Future Is Now" despite their increasingly woebegone condition.

At the moment, however, someone seemed to be addressing the lot's unsightliness.

"Nell?" Bettina murmured as she braked to slow the car.

Standing at the edge of the lot, among a tangle of faded vegetation not yet revived by the advent of spring, was a tall, lean woman with a cloud of white hair. She was facing away from the street, but her bearing and clothes—loose jeans and a utilitarian jacket—were so Nell-like that Bettina swung toward the curb and parked.

As they watched, the woman tugged up the stake attached to one of the Diefenbach posters and hurled both stake and poster into the street. It landed near a partly filled plastic garbage bag, suggesting that removing the Diefenbach posters was part of a more extensive clean-up.

"It's not Nell," Pamela said. In the act of hurling stake and poster, the woman had turned and offered a glimpse of her face. She had also caught sight of Pamela and Bettina.

"Don't just sit there gaping," she barked in very un-Nell-like tones. "Give me a hand with this—or do you enjoy living in a town that's full of eyesores everywhere a person turns? Honestly, I cannot understand how people can be so sloppy and careless!"

Pamela and Bettina looked at each other. "*Eye-*

sore!" Bettina mouthed. And Pamela responded with *"Neat freak."*

The woman had stepped over the curb and was standing, hands on her hips and an expectant expression on her face, as if waiting for them to leap from the car and join her.

Bettina rolled her window down. "We can't . . . right now," she called. "We're on our way to a meeting." The woman scowled. She had strong, handsome features and the effect was quite formidable. "But," Bettina went on, "we agree with you. Both of us. We both try to be very neat. And we'll never put our recycling out before six p.m. again."

Holly and Karen were seated side by side on a loveseat that faced its mate across Nell's coffee table. The loveseats, upholstered in faded chintz, flanked Nell's grand fireplace, which like her house itself was built of natural stone. Logs waited on brass andirons within the fireplace, lest spring still had a few chilly evenings in store, but in the summer the fireplace held a huge arrangement of dried flowers. A wide hearth provided extra seating, and travel souvenirs decorated the mantel, including an African mask, Indonesian puppets, and a statue of an Egyptian god carved from dark stone.

Nell herself, the real Nell, had greeted Pamela and Bettina at the door. She had led them into her gracious living room, with its high, beamed ceiling, and urged them to make themselves comfortable on the other loveseat. Bettina's recounting of their adventure with the neatfreak postponed by a bit the comments and questions that Pamela had known would be inevitable. But her encounter with Marjorie had happened in plenty of time for the story to feature prominently in the *Register*, along with the welcome news that Roland had been cleared of charges.

She acknowledged Nell's gentle reminder that what she had done was very foolhardy, while at the same time accepting, gracefully, Holly's applause and Karen's murmured, "You were very brave."

"I see that the heroine of Arborville has arrived!" came a booming voice from the hallway that led to the kitchen. Harold Bascomb advanced to the edge of the living room. Like his wife, he was in his eighties but enviably vigorous, with an unruly forelock of thick white hair.

"Don't encourage her, Harold!" The tone in which Nell offered this reprimand wasn't as gentle as the tone in which she had addressed Pamela, but Harold simply grinned in response.

Nell seemed about to elaborate, but Pamela jumped in with, "Have you heard from Roland?"

No sooner had she asked the question than the doorbell chimed. Harold was closest to the door, and in a moment he had ushered into the living room not one but two DeCamps.

Roland had come accompanied by his wife. Melanie was her soigne self once again, with perfect hair and makeup and wearing slim camel-colored slacks and a matching belted jacket over a cream turtleneck. Roland was dressed in one of his pinstripe suits, with his shirt collar and cuffs as flawless as ever. But in place of his usual briefcase he carried a very large shopping bag from the fanciest store at the mall. Melanie, on her part, carried a white cardboard bakery box.

"Thank you so much, Nell," she said, "for letting us contribute tonight's nibble."

She advanced to Nell's coffee table and folded the top and sides of the box back to reveal a cake, nearly as tall as it was wide, iced in satiny pink fondant and decorated with a cascade of fondant posies. The words "Thank You Knit & Nibble" were inscribed across the top in a shade of green that matched the posies' foliage.

"It's from the bakery in Timberley," Melanie added. "They do such charming work." She leaned toward the loveseat, grasped Pamela's hand, and said, "Thank you so much!" Her voice thinned, as if she was fighting tears, but she carried on, grasping Bettina's hand and repeating her thanks.

Then she straightened up and looked around. "And all of you, for the food, and the phone calls, and just . . . just . . . knowing . . . that Roland was innocent." With a mighty sniffle, she stopped, blinking furiously. Roland pulled a faultlessly laundered handkerchief from his pocket and offered it to his wife.

"Melanie has spoken for me," he said, his lean face serious. "You"—he surveyed the group, his gaze lingering when it reached Pamela—"didn't have to do anything. But you did." He looked around again. "All of you."

"We are all each other's responsibility," Nell said, "and this cake looks very sugary!" She sup-

pressed a smile when she caught sight of Harold
shaking a finger in a way that mocked her ten-
dency to scold. "But we do have something to cele-
brate tonight, and a little sugar won't be
amiss—though, Pamela—*and* Bettina—you know I
disapprove of these dangerous things you get up
to."

Melanie took her leave then, after repeating her
thanks. Harold retreated, bearing the cake off to
the kitchen. Nell took a seat on the long sofa that
faced the fireplace and motioned Roland to join
her.

As people dipped into their knitting bags for
yarn, needles, and works in progress, Pamela retrieved the two completed infant caps from her
own bag. She rose from the loveseat and edged
past the coffee table to deliver them to Nell.

"More to come," she promised, as Nell fingered
the two little pale peach offerings.

Next to Nell, Roland had begun to extract his
work in progress from the large shopping bag that
had taken the place of his usual briefcase. Cries of
amazement from Holly and Karen greeted it as it
emerged—a seemingly endless swath of angora
the color of pistachio ice cream.

"Have you joined the Yarnvaders?" Holly inquired. The entire work in progress now occupied
the sofa cushion between Nell and Roland in a
giant fuzzy heap. One end of it still hung from a
knitting needle and was tethered to a partial skein
of angora yarn. "That looks like it could dress one
of those . . . one of those . . ."

"Baobab trees," Nell supplied. "The nature

channel had a program on them the other night. Their trunks are so big someone built a pub inside one."

"If he was in the Yarnvaders, he wouldn't be able to tell us," Bettina said. "The members are sworn to secrecy. There have to be at least a few Yarnvaders around here though. Pamela and I talked to one person who's been involved in knitting those tree-sweaters—though she didn't come right out and say she was a Yarnvader. But it seems that someone else, or lots of someones, must come around at night to put them on."

Karen looked up from her knitting. "Lots of people must be knitting the tree-sweaters too. They're everywhere."

Roland looked up too, though he wasn't knitting. He'd just been staring at the fuzzy results of his industry. "Did they actually do any good?" he asked, his forehead creasing. "Save any trees?"

"They might have," Bettina said. "A senior member of the town council called the *Advocate* today. The council is going to consider a resolution that would let property owners hire tree surgeons to trim branches away from the power wires and deduct part of the cost from their property taxes."

Roland, surprisingly, had no response.

Pamela returned to her place on the loveseat. She took up the partial skein of soft white yarn she'd brought and began to cast on for another infant cap. Next to her Bettina was studying the instructions for the sleeve of the Nordic-style sweater. Across the coffee table, Holly was casting off on a vibrant green rectangle for her color-block afghan. Karen was at work on a tiny pink sleeve in a lacy pattern.

Nell's voice broke the silence. "This yarn would make a lot of infant caps," she said, fingering a bit of the pistachio angora that had encroached onto her lap.

Roland looked startled, as if he'd been summoned back from somewhere far away. "I . . . I'm not sure . . . do you think . . . ?"

Pamela fielded more questions. Yes, the police had responded quickly to her 911 call. No, Marjorie hadn't put up a struggle. She had in fact been quite docile as she was carried off, despite her menacing behavior with the griddle. Pamela hadn't gone around to Cassie's house knowing exactly that she was about to solve Diefenbach's murder. But sitting in her own kitchen after Bettina left, she had gradually become sure that Marjorie was behind Cassie's death by poisoning.

"But why didn't Marjorie just dispose of those jars of jam?" Holly asked. "Since she was responsible for them and knew what was in them?" The article in the *Register* had gone into quite a bit of detail about the reason Pamela showed up at Cassie's house.

"Good question," Roland murmured. He was no longer contemplating the fuzzy heap but had switched his attention to Nell's busy fingers as she shaped an infant cap, baby blue this time.

"Haven, I suppose," Pamela said. "Better to let Haven assume she just wanted to put the jam aside so she could eat it herself than to raise suspicion by making a big deal about having to get rid of it."

Roland spoke again, but not to follow up on the topic of the jam. He addressed only Nell, and his voice was quiet, confiding almost. "I'm not sure I could make one," he said, his eyes on the bit of cap taking shape on Nell's needles. "There's no pattern? You just do it out of your head?"

"It's not very hard." Nell turned toward Roland with a kindly smile. "It starts with ribbing, and you know how to do that. Then it's just plain knitting for a while." She pulled one of Pamela's caps from her knitting bag and handed it to Roland. "It only gets tricky when you get near the end." She pointed to the top of the cap, where strategic decreasing shaped the round. "And I can show you how to do that when the time comes."

Roland nodded and slipped the giant swath of knitting off the needle from which it hung. "I won't unravel the whole thing now," he said. "I'll just—"

Nell handed him scissors and he snipped the strand that bound it to the skein of pistachio angora. In a few minutes he was casting on a new project as Nell bent toward him, quietly counting one, two, three . . .

He applied himself industriously to his new project, silent as conversation surged around him. But suddenly he stopped, as if responding to some inner signal. He rested his knitting on the arm of the sofa, and pushed back his faultlessly starched shirt cuff to reveal his impressive watch.

"It's eight p.m.," he announced. "Time for our break."

Pamela suppressed a smile as Holly applauded.

*   *   *

In the kitchen, as the pleasant gurgle of her percolator signaled that coffee was in progress and as steam rose from the spout of her tea kettle, Nell sliced the pink fondant cake from the Timberley bakery. Everyone got an extra-large piece.

KNIT

Cozy Pillow

This project is a knitted cover for a throw pillow. For added visual interest and to make it easy to put on and take off, it has a flap that folds over and buttons. Ready-made pillow forms in various sizes can be found at most hobby shops or ordered online. These directions will make a cover for a pillow that is 18" square. Use yarn identified on the label as "Bulky" and/or #5, and use #10 needles.

If you've never knitted anything at all, it's easier to learn the basics by watching than by reading. The internet abounds with tutorials that show the process clearly, including casting on and off. Just search on "How to knit." You need only learn the basic knitting stitch. Don't worry about "purl." That's used in alternating rows to create the stockinette stitch, the stitch you see, for example, in a typical sweater. If you use "knit" on every row, you will end up with the stitch called the garter stitch. That's a fine stitch for this project. The project requires about 330 yards of yarn, three typical-sized skeins—but check the label to make sure of the yardage in the skeins of yarn you plan to use. You might need more skeins, or fewer.

The project requires a lot of unrelieved knitting, so it's fun to choose an ombre yarn with colors that change every few feet. You'll enjoy seeing the patterns that form naturally as you knit, and you'll end up with a very colorful pillow cover.

Cast on 40 stitches, using the simple slip-knot cast-on process or the more complicated "long tail" process. Now knit until your piece of knitting is 36" long. After about 15" you will need to start a new skein of yarn, and again when you reach 30"or so. Just tie the beginning of the new skein to the end of the old one, leaving tails of about two inches. The tails will be hidden on the inside of your pillow cover when you join the sides—just make sure that when you join your third skein the tails are on the same side as when you joined your second skein.

If you're using ombre yarn, you might want to pull yarn from the new skein until you get to a color that matches where you left off on the old skein—that way the patterns forming as you progress through the changing colors will remain symmetrical. Just cut off the extra yarn from the beginning of the new skein and set it aside.

At the 36" mark, it's time to start forming your flap. You do this by decreasing one stitch at the beginning and end of each row. To decrease, instead of sticking your right-hand needle through one of the stitches looped around the left-hand needle, stick it through two. Then knit the stitch as usual. Each row will thus be shorter than the previous row by two stitches and you will gradually create something that looks like an envelope flap.

When you get to the stage where there are 12 stitches remaining on your needle, it's time to form your buttonhole. This buttonhole will fit a button that's 1¼" across or slightly larger. Start the row by decreasing one stitch as you did for the other rows. Then knit 3 stitches. Cast off two stitches and continue knitting, decreasing one stitch at the end of the row. You will now have eight stitches on your needle with a 2-stitch gap in the middle. For the next row, decrease one stitch at the beginning, knit two stitches, cast on two stitches, and continue knitting, decreasing one stitch at the end of the row. You will now have eight stitches on your needle again, but with no gap.

Continue knitting as you were doing before you made the buttonhole, decreasing a stitch at the beginning and end of each row. After three more rows, you will have only two stitches left. Knit them together, cut your yarn off leaving a tail of a few inches, slip the last stitch off the needle, feed the tail through it, and pull tight.

Fold the bottom of your piece of knitting up so you have a pocket 12" deep. Make sure the tails left from when you added new skeins are on the inside. Thread a yarn needle—a large needle with a large eye and a blunt end—with leftover yarn and sew up the sides, using an overcast stitch and trying to catch only the outer loops. Start at the bottom corners and leave tails of several inches when you reach the top of the folded section.

Now fold the top of your piece of knitting—the part with the flap—down, so that the edges right before where the flap starts meet the top edges of the pocket you sewed. The triangular flap should be lying over part of the pocket, and the pillow cover should be about 36" square. Rethread the yarn needle with the long tails you left and continue sewing up the sides. When you reach the top corners, loop the remaining tail to make a tight knot.

To hide the tails left from casting on and from sewing up the sides, use the yarn needle to feed them inside the pillow cover, then cut them to a few inches. Hide the tail left at the tip of the flap by threading the yarn needle with it and stitching in and out along the edge of the flap in an inconspicuous way for about an inch. Cut off the remains of the tail.

Lay the pillow cover flat and smooth the flap so it lies flat. Position your button under the buttonhole. If your button has big enough holes, use the yarn needle to fasten it to the pillow with yarn. If the holes are too small, use a regular needle and sewing thread.

For a picture of a finished Cozy Pillow, visit the Knit & Nibble Mysteries page at PeggyEhrhart.com. Click on the cover for *A Fatal Yarn* and then scroll down on the page that opens.

NIBBLE

Lemon Yogurt Easter Cake with Cream Cheese Icing

Since Easter comes in the spring, sometimes quite early, local seasonal fruit is usually not available. Now we can buy almost any fruit at almost any time, thanks to efficient transport systems. But in earlier times, people based their cooking on what was close at hand. For this reason, traditional Easter desserts don't usually rely on fresh fruit. Often instead they are based on cheese.

In acknowledgment of that culinary tradition, this recipe for an Easter dessert uses yogurt and cream cheese, with lemon as flavoring. The cake will not be light and airy. Instead the texture will be rather like pound cake.

Ingredients for the cake:
  2 cups flour
  1 cup sugar
  ¾ tsp. salt
  ¾ tsp. baking soda
  Scant ½ tsp. baking powder
  2 eggs
  1⅓ cup plain yogurt
  7 tbsp. melted butter
  Juice and minced or grated rind of ½ lemon
      (about 2 tbsp. juice)

If you find grating lemon rind tedious—not to mention that most of it ends up stuck in those little holes in the grater—you can use a potato peeler to carve strips of the yellow part of the rind away from the bitter white part and then use a chef's knife to mince the strips *very* finely.

Ingredients for the icing:

6 oz. cream cheese
1 cup butter, softened
2½ cups powdered sugar
Set the butter and cream cheese out a few
    hours ahead of time to soften.

To make the cake:

Sift the flour, salt, baking soda, and baking powder into a large bowl. Mix in the sugar using a large spoon. Crack the eggs into a smaller bowl and beat them lightly with a fork or whisk. Add the yogurt, lemon juice, and minced or grated lemon rind to the smaller bowl and use the fork or whisk to blend them thoroughly with the egg. Add the moist ingredients to the dry ingredients and blend them together with the big spoon. Blend in the melted butter.

Divide the batter between two greased and floured 9" cake pans and bake at 325 degrees for about 35 minutes. Test for doneness with a toothpick. If the toothpick comes out clean, remove the cake pans from the oven and let them cool.

To make the icing:

Using a mixer, cream the cream cheese and butter until soft and blended. Add the sugar and continue to cream until fluffy.

Remove the cake layers from their pans. Place one on your serving plate and spread about one-quarter of the icing on it. Top with the other layer and ice the top and sides of the assembled cake with the remaining icing.

For a picture of Lemon-Yogurt Easter Cake with Cream Cheese Icing, visit the Knit & Nibble Mysteries page at PeggyEhrhart.com. Click on the cover for *A Fatal Yarn* and then scroll down on the page that opens.

Connect with Us

Visit us online at
KensingtonBooks.com
to read more from your favorite authors, see books
by series, view reading group guides, and more.

Join us on social media

for sneak peeks, chances to win books and prize packs,
and to share your thoughts with other readers.

facebook.com/kensingtonpublishing
twitter.com/kensingtonbooks

Tell us what you think!

To share your thoughts, submit a review,
or sign up for our eNewsletters, please visit:
KensingtonBooks.com/TellUs.

Nail-Biting Romantic Suspense
from Your Favorite Authors

Grab These Cozy Mysteries
from
Kensington Books